OTHERWORLDS

Short Fiction Anthology

Editors

Sonya Bramwell & Guy Worthey

OTHERWORLDS
Short Fiction Anthology

ISBN: 1-949827-40-2
ISBN-13: 978-1-949827-40-8

CONTENTS

ACKNOWLEDGMENTS

Many thanks to the talented authors of the region. This anthology is by them, but also for them. Certainly, it could not have happened without them. The editors gratefully acknowledge the inventors, farmers, shippers, roasters, and sellers of coffee.

An alien surely exhibits otherness. But aliens can be created in a human society, too. First comes a dehumanizing label or two. Next comes fear and willful ignorance. Next, social exclusion. Finally, ostracism. In this compassionate adventure, James C. Glass juxtaposes both sorts of aliens.

GEORGI

James C. Glass

A North Dakota winter storm was charging in from the southwest. The sky was white as milk, and snow was already swirling in the back alleys of Fargo as Otis Boswick frantically searched for the basics of life: food, warm clothing or rags for feet, hands and head, a pot or utensil, and anything that would burn. Moms had made her rounds in the morning, had returned with a shopping basket piled high with old newspapers for the oil-can fire to keep them alive another night in the bitter cold. But now he was eight blocks from Moms, and Alf, and the others, eight blocks from the packing crate he called home beneath the second street bridge, and all he wanted was to be warm again. In a North Dakota blizzard, he could be dead in a walk of two blocks, and time was running out.

Otis scrabbled with stiff fingers in one of two dumpsters behind the Broadway Deli, pain stabbing through his arthritic, humped back as he leaned over beyond his limit. He found a broken box half-filled with stale crackers, and a brick of frozen jack cheese covered with frost and blue fuzz, passing up a piece of strange meat aged black. He packed the first treasures of the day in his knapsack, and moved to the second dumpster, which was tightly closed, but not locked. He pushed up hard on the lid, stood on tip toes to look inside, and got the shock of his life.

Inside the dumpster, in a pile of rancid garbage, a man was lying in a fetal position, groaning, clutching at his stomach with both hands.

"Hey, you can't stay in here! A storm's comin', and you'll freeze to death in all that wet! Here, you grab my hands, and come out of there!"

The man, his rugged face covered with fine, blond hair laced with ice crystals, turned over, opened his eyes to look at Otis, then pulled what looked like a garage door opener from beneath his body and pointed it at him. "Go away — or — I hurt."

Otis flinched, but still held out both hands. "Grab hold. I've got a warm place not far from here, unless you want to die. Make up your mind quick. Storm's comin' fast."

The man considered this silently for a moment, then lowered the garage-door-opener and stuffed it into a tattered rucksack at his side, groaning as he moved.

"You sick?"

The man answered in a deep voice, heavily accented. "Was hungry — ate something — bad for me — down here. Want — sleep." He rubbed his lower abdomen with one hand.

"Moms has a tea for that. It's only a few blocks, but we've got to hurry!" Otis grabbed the man's outstretched hands, cold as his own, grimacing as he hauled him upright. The man got out unaided, holding the rucksack tight to him, doubling over in pain as soon as his feet hit the pavement. Otis put an arm around him, and they half-stumbled the eight blocks back to the second street bridge in swirling snow and bitter wind-chill, people staring at them from passing cars. Two drunks ending another day early, their eyes said.

They climbed down the embankment under the bridge. A wrinkled, squat, black woman was warming her hands over an oil-can fire, body covered from head to foot in tattered sweaters and a long coat that made her look like a dirty snowball, leaving the fire's warmth to waddle towards them as they approached. "What you got there, Otis?" she shouted in a raspy voice. "You done found another victim o' society?"

"He's sick, Moms. Ate something bad."

"Well, you just bring him to Moms now, you hear? Po' thing."

Otis maneuvered the man to a broken piece of concrete by the fire, and sat him down on it, holding him steady. Moms ran fat, gentle fingers over his face, checked his eyes. When she put a hand lightly on his stomach, the man cried out sharply, and sagged unconscious into Otis's arms.

"Not good," said Moms. "Man's poisoned. Got to get that out of him *now*." She shuffled over to a wooden-planked hut stuffed with cardboard and rags backed up against one concrete buttress of the bridge, and crawled inside through a blanket-draped opening. "Otis, you quick heat some water over the fire! Man can't drink this cold!"

Otis put a screen over the top of the oil drum, and managed to heat some water in a shallow pan before Moms came back with a tin cup containing a yellow powder sprinkled with bits of blue and red. Otis's eyes widened as he recognized the potion, but Moms pushed the cup into his hands. "Got to get it out of him quick, Otis, and you know it."

They made the tea, forcing it down the partially conscious man who grimaced with each sip, Moms stroking his forehead. "Quick, man. We're tryin' to save your life here, and there's no hospitals for the likes of us. Drink it all up."

A few minutes later, the man's eyes snapped open, he lunged out of Otis's grasp to his hands and knees, and projectile-vomited the entire contents of his stomach onto the broken chunks of concrete beneath the bridge.

"I've got the room. He can stay with me," said Otis.

"Just so's I take care of him. You knows nothin' of the art." Moms smiled a toothless smile, looking satisfied with herself.

"Don't have to, Moms, not with you here. Where're the others?"

"Probably out killin' someone for a quarter, but Jason's inside, with Alf for protection. Jack was botherin' him again, skinny demon he is, but he sure is scared o' that dog."

Otis got the man on his feet, helped him over to the mammoth packing crate he lived in against the buttress opposite from Moms' hut. As he approached, there was a low, menacing growl from inside the crate.

"Alf, shut up! And get back, now! I got a friend here, and he's bad sick!" Otis pushed aside the blanket covering the small entrance, pulling the man in after him. The interior of the crate was a heap of sleeping bags and old blankets, dimly lit by a single candle. In one corner a frail boy sat upright in a sleeping bag, staring fearfully, arm around the neck of a mongrel mix of German Shepherd and Pit-Bull Terrier still growling low in its throat. "You hold onto him tight, Jason. I gotta get this man warm, and we got a blizzard comin!"

Otis got the man's rucksack off, and stuffed him fully clothed into a bag, piling on two blankets for good measure. Instantly, the man was asleep, and Alf stepped forward to cautiously sniff at him. "Friend, Alf. Friend," said Otis, scratching the massive head of the animal. Alf waggled a stump of a tail, and licked Otis's hand.

"You all right, boy?"

Jason Boggs, a fourteen-year-old runaway from Minneapolis, slouched in the sleeping bag, face grim. "Better now that you're back. That creep Jack grabbed me by the balls again this morning, and Alf bit him good. He said he'd kill Alf when he gets back. And then the cop was here again."

"Luis Penuel? He's a good man, Jason. Looks after us."

"Well, he's no friend of mine since he turned my name in. Says my stepfather has left home for good, and my mom is comin' to get me. He had no right turning me in like that!"

"Sure he did, Jason. You're only fourteen, with a whole life ahead of you. This ain't no way for you to live, on the run. Don't you want to be with your mom?"

"She's okay, I guess. It's my stepfather liked to beat up on me."

"Well, there you are. In the meantime you've got Moms and me and Alf for family. We'll take care of you. But consider it good, Jason. A boy needs a real home, not a packing crate."

"It's good enough for you and Moms."

"That's our choice, boy. It's our way of life, and we wouldn't have it any other way — except when it gets so damnable cold. What I wouldn't give for heat in winter, and then pack my friends in here. Wouldn't that be somethin'?"

Jason shook his head, and smiled. "You and Moms take care of everyone, Otis."

"What better way to live, boy? It's our callin'. Now you hunker down and get some sleep. I've got me a sick man to tend to, and it's gonna get terrible cold tonight."

Moms' call came from outside the crate, a cup of a new brew laced with sugar in her hands. Three times that night they awakened the man to feed him an energetic tea with numbed hands as the blizzard raged around them.

Otis awoke with a start, nostrils frozen shut, the interior of the crate filled with icy fog sparkling in a band of sunlight coming in where the blanket had been pulled aside from the entrance. The man he had found in the dumpster was sitting up in his sleeping bag, peering outside, holding the blanket aside with a bare hand. When Otis snorted to clear the ice from his nose, the man turned to look at him.

"Snow gone — light again."

"Yes, but now it'll get *really* cold, and we need more fuel for the fire. We used up all the newspapers while you were sleeping. Feel better now?"

"I have — hunger — here." The man rubbed his stomach carefully. "How long I — in this place?"

"Three nights and two days," said Otis. "You were bad poisoned, and for a day or so we thought you wouldn't make it. But Moms knows what she's doing; we've never lost a sick person."

"Now I eat," said the man matter-of-factly.

"Wish I could help you there, but all we've got left is some oatmeal, and we need to cook that. No fuel."

The man found his rucksack next to him, opened it, and reached inside. "You bring food — I cook — here." He withdrew a metal globe, silver, the size of a softball out of his sack, pushed aside some rags, and placed the globe carefully in his tea cup on the floor of the crate before rummaging in his pack again.

Otis held up a metal canteen and shook it soundlessly. "All our water's frozen. We need a lot of heat to thaw it."

"I do fast," said the man. "Get food." He pulled out a metal platform with sloped vanes and flat bottom, placed the globe in it, then screwed a wire coil with threaded shaft into a short, ceramic receptor on top of the globe.

"That some kind of hotplate?" said Otis.

"This cook — heat us good." He reached out a hand. "Give water."

Otis handed him the canteen, then searched in his own pack for a bag of oatmeal he had hoarded for months. Found it. Held it out to the man. "Here you go. Now that you're with us again, my name is Otis Boswick. What's yours?"

The man didn't answer, grasped a knurled knob at the side of the globe, twisted it, pulled out a shaft about an inch, twisted again. Immediately, the coil began to glow, first deep red, rapidly turning to bright red and orange. The interior of the crate was flooded with heat, while Otis stared in fascination. "Well, will you look at that! Say, if you don't want to give me a name, that's okay. It's only I'd like to have something to call you by."

"I am Georgi," said the man. He put the canteen on the glowing coil, and picked up the bag of oatmeal to look at it closely.

"Georgi. That's a Russian name. Thought I recognized the accent. You one of the new emigrants? This cold probably don't seem very different, then."

"No Russian," said Georgi.

"Oh," said Otis. *And no last name, either.* "No matter, I'm just curious, is all. Like to get to know people better, but don't mean to pry. People come through here are all runnin' from somethin', some of it pretty bad, but I don't pry. Live and let live, I say."

Georgi looked at him darkly. "You take care — me. I — thank."

"Nothing," said Otis. "Moms did it all, anyway."

Steam was squirting out from beneath the cap on the canteen, making a whistling sound. Jason stirred in his sleeping bag, Alf lying on top of him. "Where's the heat coming from?"

"Georgi here had a stove with him, Jason. We're cookin' up the oatmeal. Want some?"

"Sure," said the boy. "Those crackers didn't go very far with me yesterday." He sat up in his bag so that Alf was in his lap, and stroked the dog's head. "Alf must be hungry, too."

"We'll give him some oatmeal. Good for dogs."

Georgi poured half of the sack of oatmeal into a small pan, took some rags from the floor to lift off the scalding hot canteen and stirred water into the pan. Otis spooned the steaming cereal into cups, and they ate silently in the warm glow of the coil, heating themselves inside and out, a luxury Otis could not remember since several winters before when a guy had come through with a backpacker's stove, and they had all gotten a little drunk on hot wine. That was before Moms.

After he'd finished eating, Otis filled another cup with the last of the oatmeal. "This is for Moms," he explained. "Back in a minute." He crawled outside, and walked the few steps to Moms' hut, keeping a palm over the cup. "Moms! Rise and shine! We got food here. Hot oatmeal!"

A raspy shout greeted his offer. "Don't want none, Charlie! Now I told you to stay away from me, and here you are again! Go away!"

Oh, oh. Back inside herself again, the spells getting more frequent in the last year. "No, it's Otis, Moms. Here, I'll put the food by the doorway. Your patient cooked up breakfast this morning. You cured him, Moms, and his name is Georgi."

"Charlie, I'll sic the dog on you if you don't go away! I mean it!"

There was no arguing with her when she was like this, but at least she was in the hut. On the street, in this condition, she couldn't find her way home. But in a day it usually passed over, and Otis wondered if she was having little strokes, or maybe it was Alzheimer's. He also wondered who Charlie was. He put the cup down by the hut's entrance, and turned as Georgi emerged from the crate, carrying a small, black box the size of a cigarette package in one hand. He barely glanced at Otis, walked straight up the embankment and out of sight. When he came down again a minute later, he was empty-handed. And the cup full of oatmeal had disappeared into the hut.

"We go out — get more food," said Georgi, and it was like a command. Otis was surprised by the sudden anger he felt surge inside him.

"One nice thing about my life is I don't have to take orders from anyone, Georgi, not even you. Last time I did that was in the Korean war. Climb the cliff, the sergeant said, and take out that gun emplacement. Me, with a wife and two little babies back home. But it was an order in a combat zone, and I didn't want to get shot by my own people, so I climbed the damn thing. Halfway up, the cliff come loose and down I went. Broke my back bad, and all I got to show for it was a purple heart I hocked for food years ago. Lost the wife, and the babies, get lousy disability checks barely enough for me and my friends to live on, but I make do, and I *don't* take orders from *anyone* anymore. You got that?"

Georgi looked at him somberly. "You soldier — in battle?"

Otis looked away from those dark eyes. "A long time ago. When I was young."

Georgi put a big hand on Otis's shoulder, and squeezed gently. "I soldier, too. I do accident, too, in — ship. Georgi not hurt, but friend — my friend die, and he buried far to — home. No battle — we only look — friend dead. Now Georgi go home — friends find. Georgi stay alive — find food. I help Otis, who saves life. You show how?"

"Who are you?" asked Otis, wiping his eyes.

"I soldier — like Otis. We get food together. Come." He put an arm across Otis's humped back. "We go where you find me?"

"No. I have some money left, and it's too cold to stay out long. Fresh food is cheap, but it can't get frozen. How long will your stove run before the fuel is gone? We'll have to keep the crate warm inside."

"Run long time — to snow gone — fill with — water — run to snow come again. I show how."

"Never heard of such a stove. You bull-shittin' me?"

Georgi laughed, then, a big, deep-throated chuckle, and hugged Otis to him. "No — shittin'," he said.

They walked ten blocks to a Seven-Eleven store that was accustomed to doing meager business with street people, the owner a friendly man who had known hard times himself, and occasionally paid them for odd jobs around the place. The owner wasn't there, and the clerk, a young girl around seventeen, eyed them apprehensively until Otis put his rumpled dollar bills onto the counter. A five-pound bag of potatoes and a box of oatmeal took everything he had, except for a nickel and three pennies.

Georgi scooped the coins up in a big hand. "I keep — remember Otis?"

"Sure, why not? Can't buy anything with it, anyway." He watched the coins disappear into Georgi's pocket.

They strolled back to the bridge, Otis pointing out the parking lot that had once been the Zephyr bar, a place to talk to friends, to belong, now gone. Across the street another bar, the Pink Pussycat, was being torn down along with an old hotel he had lived in for two years until it had been condemned. Slowly, but surely, the good folks of Fargo were forcing them out into the streets, back alleys, and under the bridges to freeze and die in the long winters. He had heard their favorite saying, of course: forty below keeps the riffraff out. Or kills them.

Sun-dogs were out in the icy air, two pillars of fire on either side of a sun low in the southern sky. They walked out onto the second street bridge to watch the Red River, a narrow channel of deep, black water winding through ice. Georgi carried the groceries in a paper bag, listening silently as Otis pointed out where he had found a body the summer before, half in and out of the river. "Old guy, just passing through. Some kids probably knifed him for fun. For the pure hell of it! Sure not my kind of people, none of them!"

Georgi shook his head sadly. "There is cruelty — with people — all place."

"Only for some of us," said Otis, and his head had turned sharply to the left to watch a police car pulling up below them, alongside the embankment. Two uniformed officers got out of the car, and picked their way carefully down the snowy slope. One of them was Luis Penuel. "Oh, oh, they're comin' for Jason. Get out of sight!" Otis pulled Georgi back from the edge of the bridge. "If he sees you, Penuel will want to know who you are, and where you come from. He's a friend, but he checks up on everyone who comes through here. Do you want that?"

"No," said Georgi firmly. "I here only little while, until — no trouble, Otis."

"Then don't let them see you. Wait up here until they're gone. I'll come back, but I've got to go down and see after Jason. He's only been here three weeks, but Penuel traced him, and his mom wants him back home."

"I wait here — you go," said Georgi.

Otis squeezed the big man's arm, then walked the length of the bridge, and fell down twice before reaching the bottom of the snowy embankment. Alf was barking angrily from inside the crate, and Moms was hugging Jason, the two officers pulling at his arms. Moms waved as the three walked towards Otis, and there were tears in her eyes. "You be good to your mom, you hear?" she cried.

Jason waved back to her, and he was smiling when he came up to Otis. Luis Penuel put an arm around him. "His mom is at the station cryin' her eyes out. She wants him back real bad, and it looks like a good situation for Jason, now, Otis. Thanks to you and Moms, he's going home in one piece."

Otis looked at the boy. "You want to go home, Jason?"

"Yeah. But I'll never forget you or Moms, and what you did for me. I'm gonna miss Alf, too. Mom says she'll get me a big dog when I get home, and I want one like Alf."

"Alf is special, all right. C'mere, boy." Otis held out his arms, and Jason was swallowed in his embrace while the officers found other things to look at.

"Do somethin' for street people someday, will you?"

"I promise, Otis. Take care of yourself — and Moms, too. She's still actin' kinda funny."

"You betcha," said Otis, releasing the boy, swallowing hard as one officer led him up the slope to the patrol car, and out of sight. Luis Penuel stayed behind a moment, an arm around Otis's hunched shoulders.

"He'll be fine, Otis. Just fine. And you watch out for yourself, too. Jack Cain is back in town. I saw him stumbling around by the tracks this morning, yelling at air. He gives you any more trouble you let me know, and I'll throw him right in the can. Got it?"

"Sure. I'll let you know. Anyway, Alf scares the hell out of him."

"Yeah, but Alf don't carry a knife or a gun. You watch out for that guy, He's pure, evil mean." Luis slapped Otis on the back, then climbed the embankment, and in an instant the patrol car, and Jason, were gone.

Moms was standing by the oil can, staring at the flames, when Otis trudged up the slope to find Georgi again. When he got to the top, he saw Georgi next to the span, balancing on snow, the little black box in his hand. He was wedging it into the rocky ground by the bridge, and carefully covering it with a tangle of frozen brush, looking up as Otis came close.

"Whatever that thing is, I sure as hell hope you ain't no Russian spy. I busted my back fightin' communists."

"I tell Otis. No Russian," said Georgi. "Jason gone, now?"

"Yeah, home to Minneapolis with his mom. No more freezing cold nights for him. A warm house, where boys oughta be. I'll miss him. Good kid."

Georgi picked up the grocery bag with one hand. "Otis feel better when eat. I cook — you show how."

Otis turned to start down the hill, taking a tentative first step, when suddenly, Georgi grabbed him from behind, sitting down with him, and sliding on his back all the way to the bottom, his excited shout echoing beneath the bridge.

"Both of you's crazy!" yelled Moms.

That night, with light snow falling, the three of them stayed in Otis's crate, warmed by the glowing stove, and feasted on boiled potatoes with one of Moms' special teas.

The following morning, Jack Cain returned to their camp.

The morning was clear, but breath-freezing cold, a foot of light, powder snow on the ground from the night before. Stomachs full, Otis and Georgi sipped hot tea in the warm crate, Moms still asleep, a shapeless mound in one corner. Alf watched them mournfully, curled up on Jason's sleeping bag, from which he had not moved since the boy had left. Georgi had shown Otis all the operating details of the stove, including where to fill it with ordinary water when the heating rate got low. He had tried to explain the source of the heat, talking about atoms sticking together, and the unbelievably hot gas somehow contained in a golf-ball-size volume within the globe. He drew diagrams, and strange chemical formulae, one Otis recognized as the one for water. The high school education he had not finished, before fleeing to break his back in a foreign war, was only a vague memory to him, now, and he found himself befuddled by most of Georgi's careful teaching. I should go to the library once in a while to read a newspaper, he thought, and catch up on what's going on in the world.

Georgi leaned against Otis, a sly grin on his face. "If Otis take heater, and what I draw here — take to great teacher — scientist — show this —

can be rich — not live like this. Have much — money. Good for Otis."

Otis laughed. He thought little of money, because there was little of it to think about. Money was a transient thing, like most of his friends, like Georgi, and the stove. It appeared and disappeared from his life, without predictability. It was better to live a day at a time, and he had learned not to dwell on what could be, or what could have been. During his hard life, he had become a fatalist, coming to grips with the program laid out for him. His life was meant to be the struggle it was, for whatever reason, and he had accepted it. And so he dismissed Georgi's humorous fantasy with a laugh, knowing that a small part of him would think about it some more. What would it be like to have a lot of money? He could do all sorts of things that—

"HEY, YOU BUMS! WHERE'RE YOU HIDIN'? I COME BACK TO KILL ME A DOG!"

Moms bolted upright in her sleeping bag. Alf's eyes narrowed, a growl rattling in his throat. "Jack Cain," whispered Moms. "Otis, he's back again. I thought we done rid o' that devil."

"Who?" said Georgi, suddenly tense.

"You stay in here, both of you. I'll go out, and talk to him."

"You're crazy," said Moms. "Man's drunk, and spoilin' for a fight. Leave 'im be."

"Come outta there! I hear you mumblin', and I can hear the dog, too. In one minute, he's dead!" A bottle crashed against the side of the crate, and Alf started barking hysterically. "That's it! Send Alf after me! One swipe of this knife, and his head's gone!"

"You come in here, Jack Cain, and I'll put the hex on you," yelled Moms. "You stick a head in, and I blow a powder on you make you blind, and suck your breath away, turn you blue, and put that knife in your own gut! You get out of here, now!"

Footsteps outside, then something hard and heavy hit the side of the crate. "Ain't afraid of you. Crazy old bitch! I want that DOG!" The words were nearly drowned out by Alf's barking and snarling, froth spewing from his mouth, teeth bared. Moms grabbed the big dog, and hung on tightly.

"I have to go out," said Otis grimly.

Georgi grabbed his pack, fumbled inside it. "I come with Otis."

"NO! This is between Jack and me, and it's *my* dog he wants to cut up. You stay *put*." Otis turned, crawling quickly outside before Georgi had a chance to answer, then stood up painfully, and faced Jack Cain a few feet away from the crate. The man's face was scarred and pock-marked, head bare, eyes puffed nearly shut from days of solid drinking. He was dying before Otis's eyes, a wasted skeleton of a man, army-surplus fatigues hanging tent-like from his thin frame, mouth twisted into a sinister grin that made him a specter of death itself. In one hand he held a large Bowie knife, waving it lazily at Otis's face.

"You still got that pretty little boy in there?"

"Jason's gone, and he ain't comin' back. You can't hurt him anymore, Jack."

"Shi-it, I kinda hoped for some fun after I carved up your dog — with this." Jack took a stumbling step forward, and now the knife was very close to Otis's face.

"I don't have any quarrel with you, Jack, and there's nothin' here for you anymore. Why don't you just leave?"

"Hey, you don't own this place, old man; now, you bring that dog out here so I can get it done quick, and *then* I'll leave." The cold blade of the big knife touched Otis's nose, then waved away again.

"I won't do that, Jack."

"Yeah! Well, then, I gotta do it another way." Jack made a short lunge, slicing a gash in Otis's cheek so that he cried out.

Alf was crazy, now, thrashing around inside the crate, Moms screaming. "I can't hold him, Otis!"

Otis felt warm blood running down his face. He circled to his left, away from the crate, stooping to grab up a chunk of broken concrete with one hand.

"Come on, Jack. You and me," he said, voice shaking with fear, hoping the others could somehow escape while Jack's back was turned.

"Hey, the old soldier. That's pretty good, Otis. Well, how about a little bayonet drill?" Jack lunged, Otis stumbling backwards, swinging the concrete chunk wildly, and missing the death's head by inches. Before he could recover, another lunge was coming, the knife sweeping past his face, and back again in an upward thrust. Otis swung weakly, punching Jack in one shoulder as he felt the knife burn into his left side. He staggered backwards, grabbing at his side, and dropping his only defense as Jack grinned wildly at him.

A loud voice boomed behind the man with the blood-stained knife.

"JACK CAIN!"

Jack jerked around in surprise, dropping into a crouch.

Georgi had emerged from the crate, the garage-door-looking thing in his hand, now pointing it at Jack.

Otis gasped for breath, pain flooding his left side. "It's my fight, Georgi," he said weakly.

"No. Now it Georgi fight," said the big man.

"You want some of this?" Jack lunged towards Georgi, the knife a spear before him.

The garage-door-thing flashed green, lighting up the entire underside of the bridge, and Jack Cain screamed. He dropped the knife, and fell writing to the ground, the heels of his boots digging grooves in frozen earth."

"You like pain? Here — Georgi give more." The weapon flashed again, and now Jack was shrieking, foam flying from his mouth. He flayed the ground with his arms for minutes, as Otis watched in horror, then curled up in a fetal position, and moaned.

Georgi picked up the knife, tossed it over to the entrance of the crate, then grasped Jack by the hair, and pulled him screaming to his knees. "Here, I show you something. I show you what happen you come back here again. You look at big rock — by where fire is." He grasped Jack by the hair again, and twisted his head in the direction of a two hundred pound block of concrete by the oil can they used for a fire. Jack's eyes were nearly closed, his moaning pitiful even to the man he would eventually have killed.

"You look, now," said Georgi, and then he fiddled with the garage-door-opener. Pointed it. Fired.

The flash was bright red, concentrated in a narrow beam that struck the center of the rock. The concrete flashed yellow — and disappeared. Jack cried out, tears flowing down his cheeks as Georgi leaned over to look at him, their noses nearly touching. "You come back again — I do that to you. Now — you go."

Jack Cain stumbled to his feet, and fled from their camp — forever.

Georgi helped Otis back to the crate. The knife blade had gone in and out of his left side at a shallow angle near beltline, and the wound was bleeding profusely, but inside of an hour Moms had him bandaged up, and resting comfortably next to the stove, Georgi hovering over him. Moms left her patient for only a moment in order to conjure up a new poultice in her shack. While she was gone, Otis, drowsy with pain, looked up at Georgi, scanning his rugged features and dark eyes in the glow of the stove. "You sure ain't no Russian spy," he said softly. "You sure ain't nothin' from around here."

Georgi looked at him sadly. "I tell you — far to home."

And it was in the twilight of that very day when Georgi's friends came to take him away.

Moms had filled him with tea, and his bladder seemed ready to burst. Otis wiggled carefully out of the crate, and relieved himself against the bridge buttress. Georgi had started a fire in the oil can, and draped a towel across the top of it to dry. Moms was shuttling back and forth, moving her pharmacy into Otis's crate, mumbling to herself all the time about too many things to do. She was never happier than when she had a patient to take care of.

Otis zipped up his pants, and turned to say something to Georgi, freezing into silence at the look on the man's face. Georgi was looking past him; head tilted upwards, white teeth showing in a huge smile. He lifted both arms over his head and waved wildly, laughing. Otis spun around; saw two men descending the embankment, one of them carrying the little black box Georgi had hidden by the bridge. They waved back to Georgi, scrambled down the slope, and ran towards him. Both were dressed from head to toe in skintight, brown knitted suits, black belts around their waists hanging heavily with metal canisters of various sizes, reminding Otis of Rangers he had seen in the war.

Georgi ran to meet them, embracing each man with a huge hug, lifting them off the ground. Comrades. Otis's heart sank. Georgi's friends had found him, had come to take him away from them. But the look on the big man's face was pure joy. It must be happy for him, thought Otis. He has found his people again.

The three men talked in low tones, occasionally looking at Otis. *I'm being talked about.* His side was hurting again, and he sat down on a concrete chunk by the fire, feeling a sudden emptiness, a sense of loss. Friends were so temporary, friendships so fleeting in his life. Why must it be this way? But then he did have Moms, and Alf, and wasn't that enough? Not good to want too much, Otis. But, oh, how rapidly this big man from a place far away had become a friend of his.

Georgi broke away from the other two men, who remained where they were, and walked quickly to the crate. "I talk with Otis. Otis wait there." He ducked inside, and came out with the little weapon he had used against Jack Cain, but nothing else. The stove — the pack — both were still inside the crate. "Say nothing. I talk." He knelt before Otis, put a hand on his shoulder. "I tell — much lost — in river. Can't find. I leave things — you keep — for make Georgi live so friends find. I go home, now — remember Otis — my friend."

Moms came up behind Georgi, looked at Otis's face, and tears welled up in her eyes. "You's goin' home, is that it?"

"Yes. Friends find."

"Goin' home, goin' home, we's all goin' home one way or 'nother. You remember Moms now, too, you hear?"

Georgi reached out and took her hand in his, then squeezed Otis's shoulder with his other hand before standing up. Otis looked up at him, and smiled.

"You sure you ain't no Russian spy?"

Georgi laughed that deep-throated laugh again. "No, Otis. Russia — close. I go — far — far to home." He made a grand sweep with one arm. "Good — bye, bye." He turned suddenly, and walked back to the other men. They stood in a tight cluster, one of them fiddling with the little black box. And then suddenly it was as if a black sheet wrapped around them, appearing out of nowhere, blinking once — twice — then a flash of white light filling it, neutralizing it to nothingness, along with the men inside.

The bright flash left spots before Otis's eyes. He blinked. Looked. Blinked again. Georgi and the others were gone. Moms clapped her hands together. "Lord, I has seen the doorway to heaven! I has seen your angels come to take our friend to yo' holy person. I praise the power o' the Lord! Amen." Moms turned, wiped her eyes, and shuffled back towards the crate. "Someday, he'll come for us, Otis, but you git back inside, now. Tea's heatin', and you don't need getting' chilled out here."

Inside the crate, Otis turned the stove down until the coil glowed dull red, then snuggled in his sleeping bag, and sipped hot tea. For the first time in days, Alf left Jason's bag, and stepped gingerly past Moms to lie down by Otis, heavy head in his lap. Otis stroked Alf's head, and exchanged a smile with Moms when the dog sighed.

Georgi had left him the stove for a reason. To stay warm? Or to get rich? After what he's seen that day, Otis was sure there was no other stove like this one — anywhere — not on planet Earth. But to get rich meant dealing with people who weren't in his world, either, people who would find a way to steal the secrets in Georgi's diagrams for themselves, the same people who wouldn't part with a quarter for a street person, the ones who sneered at them through the windows of their passing cars.

His reverie was interrupted by a shout from outside.

"Hey, Otis! You in there?"

"That you, Two Feathers?" He hadn't seen the big Sioux for months.

"Yeah. Freezin' solid out here, Otis. Got an extra bag for the night? Gonna leave for Minneapolis tomorrow."

"When's the last time you ate?"

"Oh, two, maybe three days. Got a bag of raw beans with, but nothin' to cook 'em up. You got somethin'?"

Otis looked at Moms, and she nodded her okay.

"Well, you just get yourself in here, and bring the beans! We've got enough heat in here for everybody!"

What if humankind colonizes another star system? Doubtless, the new world we inhabit will be changed. Or will it? Doubtless, living on a planet unrelated to the earth, our home and cradle of life, will change us. Or will it?

LIFE AFTER

C. M. Daniels

"Mona Lisa! Please, just talk to me. That's all I want. Please!" He was drunk, again, and decided to bring his traveling production into her yard tonight. "Mona Lisa, I love you! I'm sorry. Please!"

Mona Lisa Browne had all of the lights out and tried to take refuge in the innermost room of her modest wooden home. She hated hearing him so upset and fought the shriveled tiny part of herself that still wanted to go out there and make things better. But, it would never be better. She filed for divorce the day after it happened. He'd been so drunk he passed out when he was supposed to be watching their infant daughter. He'd smothered their baby girl to death.

"Mona Lisa!" he cried, flinging himself against a wall. He'd worked himself into hysterics. "Oh, God! It was an accident! I love you!"

She moved to a window and opened it a few inches. "Do you want me to come out there and arrest you?"

"You know I didn't mean to hurt us. Especially, didn't mean to hurt *her.*" Snot and tears streaked his grubby, formerly handsome face.

"Go home, Donny," she ordered.

He reached up to try to touch her. She slammed the window shut. That led to an even greater outburst. Mona Lisa had no choice but to put on her jeans and boots and give her former husband an escort to the town jail, where he could dry up until his next bender.

"*Baby,* you're so beautiful with your hair down."

She had him shoved up against the wall and wearing cuffs before he could come up with another classy line. After tying a bandana through his mouth so he couldn't speak, she gave him a poke in the back to get him moving.

Damn that circuit court judge, who even if he hadn't been a family friend, thought Donny suffered enough from the senseless death he'd caused. Stupid drunk only got two years.

He screamed against his gag, formless declarations of love and sorrow muffled. Soon enough, he'd switch gears again, his only concerns being when and how to secure his next drink.

"Sheriff Browne, if I'd known Donny was on the warpath again, I'd have come and got him."

"Don't worry." She signed and dated the ledger, saying she'd been in and made a deposit in the back. "You're here alone tonight, Charl."

Donny started hollering from the cellblock. Charl looked from the noise to his boss. "Can I shoot him? I hate it when he gets like this."

"Shut up you damned baby killer!" Another voice carried out. Morose, the local pickpocket, was in again.

Mona Lisa didn't want to think about it. She was afraid she'd tell Charl to go back there and blow Donny away. "Usual business tonight, I hope?"

"I wish. Got a report on the Jennings' place. There's been a murder up there. The Mastersons are keeping an eye on things, so we can go up in the morning and see what happened."

She almost asked why he didn't send someone with the information sooner. It didn't matter, with only lantern light, she had to wait for daylight to examine the scene. Only Dr. Shirley had flashlights, and she wasn't fond of lending out the fragile old devices.

"I'll see you tomorrow," she said to her deputy as she moved toward the exit.

"You want one of the mounts out back?"

"No thanks. Luna Major is still bright enough for me to see my way home." She left as Donny and Morose started in on a screaming match.

Blowflies were already dining their way through the corpse when Mona Lisa and Deputy Charl walked into the kitchen. The Jennings place was up for sale, and none of the family was living there. A caretaker, Tangent Murphy, was supposed to keep the property presentable.

"So, Sheriff, does this look like Mr. Murphy?" Charl only asked because he'd never met the man.

The body on the floor looked like a body on the floor. Decomposition was at a point where the features were bloated, making visual identification difficult. Tangent was known to wander off the job for a few days at a time. Bob Masterson found the body, only because of the smell he'd noticed while rounding up stray livestock.

"We'll have to compare notes with Dr. Shirley after she does the postmortem. I'm not making any conclusions, yet." She looked around the room, seeking out traces of the killer.

"I never pegged the Jennings as tech hoarders. Come and look at some of this stuff." Charl called her to the main room.

"Looks like they robbed the ship blind. Does any of it still work?" Nothing she saw in the kitchen approached the panels, screens, and consoles taking up the backside of the living area.

Charl had to remove his hat, to fit his head between the equipment and the wall, where he could see the power sources and cords. "All the hookups were pulled and the battery covers pried off. I'd say all the cells are missing."

This was too familiar. In the last couple of years, there were a handful of suspicious deaths in Mona Lisa's jurisdiction of Anatone County, where victims were found near caches of barely functional electronics.

"They didn't even take the movies with them." He held up a case of motion picture chips, each one neatly labeled and tucked into its slot.

"We'll have to get Gary out here to see if any other components were pulled. As a former engineering technician, he knows this stuff better than you and I ever will." She returned her attention to the body. Manner and cause of death were easy to determine, as there was a buck knife protruding from the victim's chest.

"Let's get our friend out to the wagon." She called Charl into the kitchen, and they pulled some sheets out of a bag packed with items just for death scenes. "He needs to have a talk with the Doctor."

On their way back into town, Luna Minor could be seen rising above the horizon. Mona Lisa never thought much of it. She was born on the ship, not knowing that a moon, which shone in the daytime, and a different one that came out at night, was not considered normal by some.

The horses began to act up. A rank odor saturated the air. "Ugh, tarquas."

"I don't think the animals we brought with us from earth will ever get over that smell." Charl pointed out a herd of the native land mammals to their right. The hose-nosed quadrupeds provided a lot to the people of Omak Three.

"What did you learn from the Mastersons?" she asked.

Charl coughed on dust kicked up by the horses. "Not much. They rarely saw Tangent. The Jennings sold off their livestock years ago. All they needed Tangent for was to keep an eye on the house."

The Jennings' property was separated from the Masterson's by at least fifty acres. Mona Lisa started comparing notes about the recent killings. Marlette Combs was found out behind her shed, which contained a lot of pilfered engine room components. As an engineer's mate, she once had access to vast amounts of tech. John Boyd was killed in his bed, a sizable collection of small valuables were missing. John's daughter made mention of a pouch full of small batteries. He'd amassed quite the selection and was sure to tell people of the tiny batteries' importance in keeping the few remaining high tech devices on Omak Three functioning.

"Drop the dearly departed and I off at the Doctor's office."

"Sure thing, Sheriff," Charl said. "You want Rolland and I to cut Donny or Morose loose?"

Ugh, Donny, she thought. "No, let them stew for a while."

The sounds of a small child crying to her mother echoed throughout the clinic while Mona Lisa sat in Dr. Shirley's office. She began working on the death scene report and wondered if her own little girl would have sounded like that.

"I'm almost ready in the surgical suite." Shirley stepped in and went to a locked drawer in her desk.

"I love a good autopsy in the morning." Mona Lisa joked. She hated postmortems.

"You know what? So do I." Shirley was serious. She clattered around, eventually standing back up, brown glass bottle in hand. "Meet you in there."

Mona Lisa put her notes back in the death scene kit. Curiosity caused her eyes to wander, catching a glimpse of the sick toddler. Poor baby.

The naked corpse, presumed to be Tangent Murphy, was on the operating table. "Thank some god I don't have to try and do any sections or slides on this one."

Autopsies had to be Mona Lisa's least favorite part of her job. Shirley didn't have staff enough for an autopsy assistant, meaning Mona Lisa stepped up to fill the role.

"Well, gown up and dive in."

"I don't mind bodies when I'm not crawling around inside of them." The dead were relatively harmless, and Mona Lisa had a strong gut, meaning things could have been much worse. The more she thought as the procedure moved forward, the more she realized she'd rather be crawling through a corpse than dealing with Donny.

"Any theories?" Shirley asked as she removed the knife from the man's chest.

"Tech," she replied.

Shirley cocked her head in question. "Isn't this guy a bit young to be caught up in that?"

"It wasn't his," Mona Lisa replied. "We think this is Tangent Murphy. He was keeping an eye on Jennings' old ranch. The house was pretty typical, save for the main room. It looked like half the damned ship was in there."

"I don't know about people these days. Our parents' generation is obsessed with the gadgets of the past. Our youth are out robbing trains. And us, we're trying to hold it all together."

The Y-incision was cut and the sternum removed. Odors of decomposition got stronger. Even though this was the only building in town with electricity, there wasn't enough energy for the kind of ventilation system a real morgue needed.

"I heard about Donny last night." Shirley put a big handful of what Mona Lisa could only identify as guts into a basket and hung it on a scale.

"Who didn't? The entire town could hear him out there."

When Mona Lisa married him, he hid his problem well. Like an idiot, she thought she could save him from himself, until the night he changed from harmless but loving drunk, into the perpetrator of negligent homicide.

"You don't think it's going to hurt your chances for reelection next year, do you?" Another bunch of guts went into the basket and got weighed.

Mona Lisa snorted. "No, there isn't anyone crazy enough to want this job."

"True. I'm not seeing any gross anatomical defects, save for the piece of metal rammed through his chest. I'll sign off on manner of death, homicide. Cause is exsanguination via sharp penetrating trauma to the upper torso." Shirley had the entire chest cavity and abdomen hollowed out. "I'll let you know the smaller details in the report."

Glad to get away, Mona Lisa started shrugging off her surgical gown. "You know where to find me."

Another look at the little girl on the sick bed only added to the apprehension of going back to her office and dealing with Donny. She retrieved the death scene bag and made for the front door.

She felt the sound before hearing it. A vehicle, with a self-contained internal combustion engine, was speeding into town. There weren't that many cars around. She decided to stick to Dr. Shirley's porch to see what the big fuss was about.

It figured Rich Denholm was behind the wheel of the smelly, sputtering beast. He skidded his machine to a halt and flung open the door so it whipped against the fender. Rich started to pull his unconscious wife across the seat.

"What happened to Jeanie?" Mona Lisa grabbed the woman's floppy lower extremities, helping guide her into the clinic.

"That's none of your damned business, Sheriff." Rich was one of the town's more prominent citizens. He was loud and stubborn, while somehow staying on people's good lists.

She helped place Jeanie Denholm on an exam table before heading into the surgery to retrieve the Doctor.

"If you can't help her, Whisper, I'll have no choice but to take her to the ship," Rich said.

Shirley bristled at the use of her first name. The theory about parents giving their children strange and unique names as a way of starting new traditions for Omak Three sounded nice. When those children grew up, they had their own ideas on the matter. "I'll do all that I can."

Mona Lisa decided to leave before she said something to set Rich off. She didn't have all day to listen to him cry about wanting to bring their humble town out of the "dark ages." Omak Three was working extremely hard to create the industries that would allow for the kinds of utilities and infrastructure Rich moaned about. Rather than wait, Rich wanted to go to the ship and gut what was left, making events happen on his timeline, to the detriment of others.

"Gary and Charl went back out to the scene." Her other full-time deputy, Rolland, said as she walked into work.

"How long ago?" She unlocked her office, just off the main area. The Sheriff's Office was not a large outfit.

"About ten minutes after you got back into town." Rolland popped a couple of knuckles. "I don't think Charl knows how to sleep."

"Cayman's on the schedule for tomorrow evening. Hopefully, Charl will go home for a few hours." Mona Lisa wondered where Charl got the energy and stamina to go nonstop like he did. "Are our guests behaving?"

"Morose sure keeps Donny quiet."

"Thank the gods for small tokens." She stepped into her tiny office, shut the door, and hung up her hat. There was a lot of paperwork to get done.

Sunlight came in through a narrow window, cloaking the entire room in a warm yellow glow. There was something about this lovely color that offered comfort and clarity as she wrote. She was finishing up her description of the autopsy when a strange detail popped into her mind.

Jeanie Denholm, while sickly pale, had marks on her body that were either burns or bruises. They were square, not the type she could have picked up in a fight with another person. They were too strange to come from impacting a surface.

A sketch of the blemishes was enough to show and ask people about. She had a very vague idea of what may have caused the injury. Mona Lisa, like most of her generation on Omak Three, was born on the ship and was barely five years old when it made planetfall. However, the placement of the marks struck a chord somewhere deep in her memories, and she knew they only could have come from something stolen from the ship.

"Rolland, does this look familiar to you?" He was a few years older than her and had a much better recollection of their time in outer space.

"I'm not sure." He took a second look at her drawing. "Has something to do with ship components, beyond that, I don't know."

Donny's parents had been big-time tech hoarders. Her ex might have some idea of what she was looking for. She went back to the holding cells. Morose lay asleep on his cot. Donny was seated on the edge of his, staring off into nothingness.

"Mona Lisa." His voice cracked. "How are you?" He looked badly in need of a drink and a shave. "Why am I here, Baby?"

"Disturbing the peace." She thrust the paper at him, sticking it through the bars. "What makes marks like this?"

His eyes tilted up, gazing through the paper, right to her. "Let me out of this cage, and we can go talk about whatever you want. I'll take you up to our favorite place on Lake Silver."

The mention of their old stomping grounds sent some of the oxygen from her brain. "Donatello, unless you look at this and tell me what I need to know, I'll let you sit in here until New Years."

"I'd listen to the woman, baby killer." Morose was up and feisty.

Donny scowled at his neighbor and snatched the paper. "Your opinions aren't wanted, tarqua brain."

"Is that the best you can do? Lawyers are supposed to be smarter than that."

"Enough, Morose. I hear you spew another barb, I'll put a tarqua in there with you." Mona Lisa positioned herself so neither man saw the other.

Donatello Freemont, when Mona Lisa first met him, was the Assistant County Attorney, far from the pathetic creature he'd turned into. The Sheriff and the Lawyer, now there was a good couple.

"Whoever did this, used the wrong kind of nodes. These are conductors. Sickbay nodes are supposed to be put at the points you've got listed. Looks like there's a cobbled together regen chamber out there that's frying people, instead of healing them." He handed the paper back and tried to run his hand over hers. "Mona Lisa, my love, please set me free."

She immediately turned and left. It was time to get out of the building for a while.

George Turner, long retired head ship's physician, lived in the next county over. Her deputies could take care of things for a day. Beyond her own questions, Shirley sent along a list. Jeanie Denholm was in a bad way.

After checking in with her counterpart, Sheriff Zephyr Reyes, she rode out to the Turner's house. She hoped the old doctor was around. George's wife, Abbey, answered the door. Soon, Mona Lisa was out in the garden, having tea with the couple.

Abbey, a former bridge officer, recognized the burns right away, as coming from comm panel circuitry. On occasions when power surges overloaded the transistors and surge protectors, those panels could explode. People hit by hot circuits showed marks like Mrs. Denholm's.

The doctor asked about Shirley, his former student, before confirming what Donny said about regen chambers. Someone was substituting the wrong parts for the specially designed and insulated nodes used in medical equipment. He said a lot of things Mona Lisa didn't understand. She was unfamiliar with how the sick bay miracle machines worked.

"Without seeing the patient myself, and only working with the notes Dr. Shirley sent over, I'd have to say that the woman is in a minimally aware vegetative state. She could wake up tomorrow or linger for years."

"That's awful, George." Mona Lisa latched onto something Rich said to her. "Could the ship cure her?"

"I don't know. We were capable of some pretty awesome things, but this is a mystery. As you know, there's only the one surviving regen chamber and a dwindling power supply."

Mona Lisa knew that detail well. Just before she was to marry Donny, she got shot three times in a hostage situation that turned ugly. She only survived because Charl got her in their emergency law enforcement automobile and drove as fast as the machine could move, bringing her to the ship moments before she would have died.

"For something like this, Rich needs to take his case to the Ship Council. I don't think they'd take Jeanie, not in the shape she's in now." George shook his head at the whole situation. The Ship Council followed stringent guidelines about who was placed in the chamber. True emergency cases were given priority.

Abbey said, "We should have come up with the Council long before we did."

"I know," Mona Lisa commented. The Council was created in

response to the mass looting of the ship and worked to save what was left of it from being completely destroyed.

"Most everyone who knew Tangent Murphy says he was the nicest guy on the planet." Charl was in one of the chairs that barely fit into her office.

"And what I've found, Sheriff Browne, is that Mr. Murphy looks to have been killed so that every single power supply, charger, and battery could be removed from that front room. It was a delicate job. They wore gloves." Gary, from his spot in the doorway, held out his write-up. "All that equipment was meticulously broken down and put back together again."

"Hardly any of this stuff is good these days. Hell, you can't even melt much of it down, thanks to the toxic byproducts it produces." Charl added.

Gary said, "It's not worth killing over."

"And, I went back over the last two tech murders." Charl set the files down on her desk. "It looks like similar things went missing at each one. When we find Tangent Murphy's killer, we'll be clearing three cases."

Mona Lisa wished she knew more about the great starship that brought her people to Omak Three. She knew of a handful of surviving engineers, and none of them lived anywhere near the small towns that picked the ship apart. The best she had was Gary, and he wasn't afraid to admit that as a technician-turned-cop, he didn't have all the answers regarding the ship. "Well, who has generators? Maybe someone's got a big enough generator to make use of some of this stuff."

"We can safely leave Dr. Shirley out." Gary pointed across the street. "She only uses hers for the refrigerator, some lab equipment, and the ventilator."

She reached inside her shirt pocket and pulled out the drawing she'd shown around the day before. "Burns like this are caused by a jerry-rigged regen chamber."

Charl looked close. "You'd have to have a big damned generator for something like that."

Gary, still hanging back in the doorway, perked up. "Regen chambers have all kinds of fail-safes in them. Each one of the nodes has its own small backup power supply, just like the heating and cooling, oxygenation unit, and other modules that make up the operational components of a chamber. If any single one of these independent backups goes out, the chamber won't function properly."

Mona Lisa stood. "Charl, take Cayman or Pristine and start looking for places with big generators. Greg, I need you to make me a list of what goes into those backup power supplies. I've got a funeral to go to."

Tangent Murphy had kept mostly to himself. Mona Lisa was one of the few people to stand at his windy graveside. There were no family members and no friends, just a handful of townsfolk out to pay respects to a member of their community. The only one crying was the wind.

Rich Denholm was one of the people in attendance just so he'd be seen and to gather sympathy for Jeanie. This saved Mona Lisa from having to track him down.

"Pity Mr. Murphy had to succumb to such a senseless death, Sheriff. Any idea who might have done it?" Rich cared nothing about the young man in the ground. He just wanted to be the one to hear things first.

"We're working multiple leads." She fought to keep her hair pushed out of her face, and stuffed most of it under her hat. "How big is your generator?"

Rich regarded her with a barely hidden disdain. "House lights, fridge, entertainment center, but not all at the same time. Mine's not fancy. The same still I use to fuel the car runs my generator. Why?"

"I'm looking for one big enough to power a regen chamber."

A laugh started deep in his throat. "Don't you think if any such generator existed, that I would be the one around these parts to own it?"

"I'm asking because of what happened to Jeanie."

His false amusement evaporated. "My wife is ill with some common bug, nothing more."

The wind nearly took her hat off. "We'll talk more about this later, I'm sure."

She didn't expect him to come right out and say where this generator was, but she made him nervous enough to know he was starting to worry. A talk with Dr. Shirley confirmed that Jeanie wasn't getting better. The woman was going to get much worse. While doing a physical on Mrs. Denholm, Shirley found multiple lumps in the woman's breasts. If she'd presented to the Ship Council with a cancer diagnosis, they would have put her high up on the list for the real regen chamber. Now, thanks to some malfunctioning impostor, there wasn't enough of Jeanie Denholm left to save.

"Damnit, Rich. If you don't tell me where this thing is, and who runs it, there are going to be a lot more people getting hurt, just like Jeanie." Mona Lisa nearly had to arrest him to make him talk to her again.

"I refuse to speak to you without my lawyer present." Rich finally spat back.

"How about I put you in a cell on attempted murder charges? That's what it will take to lure any attorney in here who'd be willing to work with you." She thought she had him cornered. It made sense in her mind that Rich had the chamber and the generator to go with it.

"I'm not saying a word."

"Then I hope you like your cellmate." She read him his rights and walked him into the jail. "You've got your choice, Mr. Denholm. Morose the thief, or Donny the drunk." She removed a key ring from her belt.

Donny stood up and started to sob like a child, which only served to set Morose off. Insults began to fly.

"What about the empty ones?" Rich stood stiffly, still more upset about Mona Lisa's accusations than for being jailed for nearly killing his wife.

"Not an option."

Rich chose Donny, which was what she wanted. Her ex was so set on clawing his way back into her good graces, he'd let her know every time Denholm let out a belch.

"Mona Lisa, you know how much I love you."

"Stow it, Donny."

She walked off the cellblock and left a deputy in charge. It was already dark out, leaving her not feeling so bad about wanting to go right to bed when she got home.

The Ship Council gave Gary access to the real regen chamber schematics, which brought together the murder of Tangent Murphy and the unfortunate state of Jeanie Denholm.

"What am I looking at?" Mona Lisa had a stack of metal disks on her desk, ranging in size from pebbles to legal tender.

"They're batteries," Gary said, as a horse whinnied near the office window.

Her brain kicked up a vapor of a memory involving her father doing something with these tiny things. "I think my dad called them coin batteries."

Gary nodded. "One of the most vital parts of the independent systems power backups are these coin batteries. They were common aboard the ship, but now that we've been here for going on three decades, it's hard to find any that still hold a charge."

The little objects seemed so small and unimportant compared to the generator she was looking for. Gary flipped one like a coin and caught it in midair. "A regen chamber needs nineteen of these to function properly. The Ship Council gave me a disturbing statistic that only one in forty of these now has enough power to work, and fewer of them will still take a charge. Good ones are difficult to find."

"Looks like, for some people, they are worth killing for." Batteries, generators, and nodes, all things from the past that turned deadly. "Gary, what happens when there are absolutely no coin batteries left?"

"The last chamber aboard the ship will be as useless as most of the technology that crossed the stars with us."

The places where bullets tore through her started to tingle.

Morose was released after serving out his month. Donny went out and was right back in that night for a drunk and disorderly. Mrs. Goldberg found Donny taking a leak in her garden. She tried chasing him off. Instead of leaving, he became combative.

Rich eventually found a lawyer to post bail. A law enforcement search of his property revealed an outbuilding crowded with coin batteries, power sources, and other regen chamber specific bits and pieces, but no actual chamber. The most damning part was a spare square-shaped conductor. Mona Lisa hoped Rich didn't decide to run off into the wilds rather than face the consequences of his murderous ways. Unfortunately for her, the vast expanses of land on Omak Three loaned themselves to people getting lost forever.

Bellows echoed into the front of the building. She could hear it through her closed office door. Donny was crying and carrying on for her. She ignored the noise, choosing instead to focus on preparing evidence for the start of Rich's attempted murder trial. Jeannie would convict him, while Tangent's case was more circumstantial.

Charl knocked and politely waited for her to summon him in. "Maybe you should go see what Donny wants. He's saying Rich told him some things. I think it's a ploy, but who knows?"

"At least I can go back there without Morose adding to the situation."

Donny was still spouting off when she stopped in front of his cell. He was in rough shape. A blackened eye and an ugly scab on his cheek were the consolation prizes from a fight he got into before tripping into Mrs. Goldberg's garden. "You'll love me again when I tell you what I've heard. You'll love me so much, you'll have to take me back."

"Tell me what you heard. And keep it simple." Mona Lisa backed away from the hand extending between the bars. "Donny, start talking, or you're going to find yourself bound and gagged."

The arm retracted and a mellow expression filled out his features. "He remembered that I'm a lawyer."

She wouldn't correct him. He'd been disbarred and was banned from ever practicing law ever again. "Keep going."

"He wanted to know if he could be sent to jail for building the regen chamber. When his wife started getting sick, he started collecting parts. I told him he'd still go as an accomplice. Baby, here's where he says all the charges against him should be dropped. Jeanie came up with the chamber idea, he says, making her impending death a suicide. I told him no, he'd still go." Donny was so proud of himself. He probably expected an award.

"Did he say where he was getting these parts?"

Eyebrows danced and the gears in Donny's brain ground together. "Naw, just that he'd paid a lot for the pieces. I think he might have a stash of gold bars hidden out on his property, meaning he could buy just about anything he wants."

Donny still reeked of alcohol, and she didn't know if she could trust a single word. "Let us know if you remember anything else."

"Don't I get a kiss goodnight?"

A second, more in-depth search of the Denholm place was stretching into the third day. There was no being nice. Rich wouldn't admit to anything, not even trying to save his wife.

Mona Lisa went up to the house, hoping to finally extract something from Rich. He started talking to her about his house, how he painted it a garish red as a thumbed nose to the neighborhood associations of his youth. She accepted his offer of tea and sweets. She tried not to stare, as it was always strange for her to be in buildings with electricity. The light was tinny and devoid of life.

"One day, Sheriff Browne, we'll all be back to living in the manner of which we are accustomed. There'll be no more of this Alien Frontierland hell we've been mired in."

She looked at the dull glow from a lamp. The artificial light aboard the ship was white and crisp, nothing like what Rich wallowed in. "You know what my questions are. If you cooperate with me, I'll have a chat with the County Attorney and see if we can't arrange a more lenient set of charges."

He ran a finger around the edge of his teacup. "You would have loved Earth, before the last three years with the famine and the bombs, of course. The technology we had was amazing. We were practically gods."

And now, humanity's been reduced to a remnant population, barely eking out an existence on a rock called Omak Three, Mona Lisa thought. "Judge Davis will be able to give the fairest sentencing guidelines to the jury if you just give us more information about what you've got going on here."

She wasn't getting through. Like Donny, Rich was in his own world.

Deputy Rainbow entered the residence and summoned her back

outside. She left her teacup and stepped out on the back porch. Charl and Gary had found a body. Luna Minor was in full phase, offering more light than dusk provided.

Standing at the foot of the grave, formerly covered by Denholm's automobile, Mona Lisa saw familiar clothing on an unrecognizable corpse. "We finally know what happened to Siberia Anderson."

The local high school student left his home a little over a year previous. His mother thought he'd gone to a friend's house. Siberia never returned. It was easy to tell it was him. He always wore his deceased father's old coveralls from the ship. Name badges and mission patches were still clearly visible. Ever since he was tiny, Siberia wanted to become a ship's engineer, just like his father.

"Rainbow, you know where the death scene bag is in the wagon. There're a couple of lanterns in the utility box too. Start processing the grave," Mona Lisa said.

Charl pulled himself up from his perch on the dirt. "This kid knew the ship, way better than Rich did."

"But he probably wasn't aware of the special type of nodes needed for the regen chambers. He used what he could find." Gary tried to stay comfortably away from the grave. "The kid used to bother me all the time for information."

"Charl and I are going up to the house to arrest Rich. See what else you can find."

Something in her sleep told her she wasn't alone. Dreams flashed into reality. The .44 she kept under her pillow was drawn and cocked.

"Sheriff, it's Charl!"

She lowered her weapon. "What are you doing in my bedroom?"

"You weren't answering your door."

The intense deconstruction of Rich's property had sucked her energy dry. "What time is it?"

"Three a.m."

Damn, only two hours of sleep. "What's wrong?"

She swung her legs over the edge of the bed and fumbled for the box of matches on her nightstand, quickly lighting the oil lamp. With a little more light in the room, she could see Charl's face, not just his outline in the beams of Luna Major shimmering through her living room window.

"Donny was screaming and carrying on like he always does, so

Cayman didn't pay much attention."

"Don't stop," she said, as she climbed into yesterday's dirty clothes.

"Rich hung himself with his shirt."

"Shit." She'd had everything removed from his cell, but let him keep his clothes. It got cold in the jail at night.

"Shirley tried to resuscitate him, but couldn't bring him back." Charl had kept his back turned as Mona Lisa dressed. "Maybe you can get something out of Donny since he saw it all."

"Who knows? He might even be coherent tonight."

Cayman and Dr. Shirley had the body wrapped and tied in linens by the time Mona Lisa and Charl arrived. Donny sat in the corner of his cell, knees drawn beneath his chin. His whole body shuddered.

She took her former spouse into her office, where they could talk without interruption.

"Do you still keep a bottle of whiskey in your locked drawer?" He wasn't making eye contact.

"I don't have any ice." She recited the old joke. There was no harm in letting him have one drink, especially if it would get him talking.

"That's fine." Donny white-knuckled the armrests as she withdrew a bottle and a glass, both dusty, from their hiding spot. He licked his lips as she poured.

She didn't let his obsession with his first love hurt her feelings anymore.

"It was fear that did it, Mona Lisa." He nearly swiped the glass from her hand before she set it on the desk. He slugged the whiskey down in two rapid gulps, then held up the empty. "This was what made my job tolerable when things got crazy and I was in over my head. I was so scared. My world was falling apart."

She poured him another.

"You went out on a call that night and told us not to wait up for you. It was my first time completely alone with her. I was so terrified, of everything, so I made sure my glass didn't have a bottom. I laughed. She laughed when I played with her."

Mona Lisa's insides twisted as he talked.

"I remember how when she smiled, she looked just like you. I thought I was loose enough I was doing a good job." Then, he woke up near dawn, with his wife hurling him across the room. More than one life ended that night.

"Rich was talking like we could have saved her from my fuck-up if we'd had access to some emergency medical tech. He wouldn't say anything else about it after that, just wanted me to let you know, he left a letter for you, in a cabinet in his kitchen."

The whiskey went back into the drawer. Mona Lisa wanted to find

Rich in the afterlife and beat him senseless for even suggesting that her daughter died after she had come home to find her precious baby cold and lifeless.

"I'm sorry my cowardice cost us everything, Mona Lisa. I wish I could have done better by you."

She looked across the desk, into the eyes of the man she once loved more than anything, and realized at that moment she felt nothing for him. Love, rage, hate, pity, it was all gone. She took him back to the cellblock. Neither one of them spoke.

The letter said it started years before Jeanie got sick. Parts collection was easy enough at first until it came to the rarest and most specialized items. Siberia Anderson eagerly helped with the project. Rich promised the kid a big piece of the potential profits from the chamber until the student wanted to get other techies and hoarders in on the process, to make parts easier to find.

Siberia was killed to keep the regen chamber a secret. Tangent Murphy and the other two hoarders were murdered for components. Jeanie was a vegetable because Rich cut corners and wanted to get down to the business of taking away the Ship Council's patrons and monopoly. He was going to charge a premium for medical services and make a fortune. The idea was for Jeanie to be the spokesperson of success to bring customers in.

Rich never hinted as to why he committed suicide. He'd signed his letter like the whole regen chamber ordeal was nothing. Life on Omak Three moved on.

"What are you up to, Mona Lisa?" Charl had come over to the house to give her the times for Jeanie Denholm's funeral and memorial dinner.

She had crates from her storage room strung about the living room. Piles covered the coffee table in front of her. "I'm going through the baby's things, trying to figure out what to give away and what to toss."

Charl stood beside her and placed a friendly hand on her shoulder. "Are you sure?"

"We can't all be ruled by what's happened in the past."

"Tell me what I can do." He lowered himself onto the sofa and looked at the tiny toys and clothes. "To help."

She turned her head to look at him. "Don't let me back out and wallow in what might have been."

He didn't need to speak to tell her he'd hold her to her word.

"It's time," she said.

C. M. Daniels

Drop a cowboy in London and he's a might tad displaced. Drop a schoolgirl from Osaka into Amsterdam and she won't see the forest for the knees. Drop a resident of Vicksburg, Mississippi into Brooklyn and you might get this tale from Leona Ahles.

THE ANGLES OF NEW YORK

Leona Ahles

When the cacophony of the evening traffic quieted to merely an occasional annoyance and fewer academics came in for their roasted bean libations, the clock hanging on the back wall finally chimed. I had just placed a cup of New York-style regular coffee in front of a young man with round wire glasses, and served him an automatic smile and "Mississippi" when he asked where I'm from.

Every single day at least one Brooklynite customer commented on my own accent. It didn't take long for me to stop saying, "I grew up near Vicksburg, Mississippi," or attempting conversation altogether. Sometimes regardless of what I said, or didn't say, people would begin treating me like some hoosier.

If only one could take orders without talking. As long as I didn't have to give up singing, I thought for the twentieth time that day.

I counted the chimes as I returned behind the counter. Several apprehensive moments passed until the seventh bell finally rang. By leaning over the counter and painfully craning my neck I could just barely see the entire avenue through the front window. Rounding a corner down the street walked my cue, a Southern salvation to my coffee blues.

"I'm leaving for the day!" I shouted over my shoulder.

"Okay, take care!" resounded a voice from the supply room.

I yanked at the strings behind my back, whisking the apron over my head. I tossed it to a nearby hook with practiced ease as I finally stepped away from the espresso machine. Then brushing the door aside I darted across the street.

I could still see him, silhouetted against the evening light filtered between buildings in the distance, his shadow lengthened and followed steadily behind. Of course, I recognized the familiar shape of his violin case, but I knew Roark's stride: a relaxed gait that seemed at odds with his vibrant smile, but together created a demeanor capable of initially hiding all his quirks. He had always walked like that. All of him was too far ahead of me, and I couldn't catch up before he marched into that same old brick building.

I hopped the steps and pulled open the double doors of the multi-use center. The offices and classrooms on the first floor were closed, but I could hear low voices and the setting of glassware from the restaurant and music lounge that had just opened immediately to the left. Over a thousand times now I had run through that spacious lobby where local art lined the walls, and I'd never had the time to really explore or learn the building's history.

Up the iron and marble staircase to the right, I followed our daily path. The steps were worn in the center with the weight of several decades' worth of footsteps, so instead I always hugged the railings. Perhaps in an effort to be the catalyst in creating level steps once again. I think it was the third time up these steps and past the late palladian windows that I had wondered aloud to the other band members if anyone else did the same. Roark had honestly contemplated my question while the rest of them only smirked at me and shook their heads. Our pianist, Dan, laughed so hard it echoed throughout the building.

I swung around the bannister on the second floor to where someone played a piano for either a late music lesson or dance practice in one of the studios. I had once thought that since we had easy access to the classes, I could take lessons to further improve my singing. For unknown reasons, however, I was turned down. Dan had also tried to be the pianist for the dance classes, and received the same result. So we never turned towards the studios, but kept ascending the stairs.

Two more flights and I breathlessly pressed against an unlocked heavy metal door marked "Fire Exit Only." Warm yellow light rode in on a fresh rooftop breeze that rushed around me, enticing me out of the elderly halls. Up there I felt like I could almost fill my lungs without car exhaust. I let the wind blow my day's troubled dust away and welcomed the sight of a surprisingly unobstructed sunset. Because of that, I once thought we were lucky to play at this location. I selfishly took one more moment to simply stare at the sky before turning towards two figures leaning on the parapet.

"Oh, Dan! You're sure here early," I said as I walked across the concrete roof.

"No, you're just late," he grumbled around a cigarette.

The other turned and dipped the brim of his plaid cap for me. "Good evening, my lady!"

"Good evening, Roark!" I could never help but return his wide, flashing grin.

"Just say 'hi,'" Dan said.

Mr. Sulky-puss, Roark mouthed, nodding towards Dan.

"Hi. How're you doing?" I asked Dan, gingerly patting his shoulder.

"Fine and dandy. Peachy. What else would I be?"

"Merry? At least jake?" Roark suggested, before suddenly bursting into laughter.

I looked away before Dan's laser glare could burn my retinas.

"Where're Tom and Eugene? I didn't see them on my way here."

"Eugene's already laying out downstairs doing God-knows-what with someone we'll probably never see," Dan answered. "At least we got to meet," he counted on his fingers, "the third before last, I think."

"And Tom hasn't arrived yet," added Roark.

"He might have taken an extra shift at work, then." I suddenly felt I should have stayed longer at the café.

"He can't be the only waiter at that stupid Greek place. And really, how much lamb can people actually stomach?"

"It is odd for him to stay so long, since usually he's the first one here, but things are tight lately," I said.

"What's the point when one more shift won't make a difference?" Dan mumbled. He exhaled a cloud of smoke.

A quick change of conversation seemed prudent, even if just slight.

"So how are you this fine evening, Roark?"

"Indeed, 'tis a fine evening for an extraordinarily long walk when you haven't two friendly copper coins to rub together, much less to spare for a cab. Or the subway. Or a ride from a gangster in an armored convertible. Whichever might be cheaper." He gently took my hand. "But rest assured, I am as fit as my fiddle and healthy enough for such a walk every day."

"You positive about that?" Dan asked. "You're looking pretty thin."

"Positively positive! Unless that makes a negative. I was never one for mathematics."

"Just words. Lots of words. To excess. Honestly, you should've just been a professor."

Roark raised a finger to scold Dan. "As Rudyard Kipling stated in his genius locution, 'Words are, of course, the most powerful drug used by mankind.' They are the obligatory opium of human existence, in which I willingly partake. 'The limits of my language means the limits of my world!'" He spread his arms wide as if to encompass the entire city. "Or so is my shared Wittgenstein philosophy."

Dan moaned. "Oh, for lands sake. 'You speak an infinite deal of nothing.'"

"And I am satisfied with schooling you," Roark added.

Recently I had seen such conversations between these two end in fist-fights.

"Y'know, the sunsets just aren't the same here," I said, attempting to shift the conversation again.

And then wished I hadn't. Because it was true. Wisps of gray and purple clouds floated across plain yellow that bled upwards into the remaining blue. No pink or orange or hints of gold this evening to warrant the term "pretty." No glowing reflection off a warm nearby river. The sun itself had already begun to dip below the first false horizon of far-off skyscraper roofs.

"Stop complaining about the weather," Dan said.

"Are the planet's rotations considered part of meteorology?" Roark asked.

Sometimes his questions rarely needed acknowledgment.

"Nothing in this Yankee city has anything on home," Dan continued. "Except maybe the variety of food, I'll give it that. But the damn cold still gets to me."

"As a whole, though, I feel at odds," Roark said.

"Me too," Dan surprisingly agreed. "We tried to create this Venn diagram life but the middle won't mesh."

"And if that's honestly the case, then I'm worried about the overlap," I added.

Roark cocked his head. "Venice could be nice," he pondered aloud, and we ignored it.

"Y'mean by coming all the way up here to follow a dream based on a certain someone's false dichotomy?" Dan asked me.

There wasn't a day while I mixed lattes and watched students and entrepreneurs that I hadn't thought of my responsibility regarding our current, piddling state. I did not need his poorly concealed spite to make me feel even more guilt.

"Yeah, that." I answered shortly. "And looking back—"

"We're not supposed to do that!"

Roark's sudden outburst made us turn in shock. His face contorted into a mix of anxiety and anger and something else I actually struggled to read. I clasped his raised hands.

"Sweetie, everything's alright." Although, I didn't know of what I was reassuring him. The continuance of our lifestyle in general? Even I wasn't sure of that.

Adopting an unusual serious air, he held onto my hands tightly. "All those old adages and modern motivational phrases constantly bombarding us via the Internet remind us not to look back, don't turn around, we're not going that way. However, such sayings are effective just to an extent before they become cliché and disregarded. But truly, what's done is done." He gestured widely at the sunset cityscape. "We're here, so … "

"So we may as well make the best of it?" Dan raised his voice bitterly. Now Roark and I stared at him as he threw his cigarette down to stomp it out. Clearly fit to be tied, he shoved his hat back on, the brim hiding his eyes. "How much longer can we make the best of a city that has tried over and over again to break us and throw our pieces in those stinking back alley dumpsters!"

Roark stepped towards him, reaching out a hand. "Dan, wait—"

"I'm going to make sure Tom is here and everything is ready. Y'all better get downstairs soon. At the very least, I want to put on a good show tonight."

And he walked away, fists in his pockets and back hunched. He let the door slam behind him.

"Well, that stopped just short of a hissy," I mumbled.

"I was going to say, 'We're here, so for now, let's try to glean everything possible while we strategize our escape.'"

I saw Roark's shoulders round forward as he sighed before turning and smiling weakly. A breeze ruffled my skirt and blew strands of hair across my vision.

"Are we leaving, then?" My abrupt question broke the silence.

He leaned on the wall next to me again, his sea-blue eyes shining almost green in the day's last light. "Do you want to stay?" he asked, his voice low and, for a moment, the only sound I heard on that rooftop besides the distant downtown honking. Typical of Roark, it was an honest question bearing no judgment.

But I just looked over my shoulder. "I hate seeing him like this," I said.

"I will admit that it is better seeing him melancholic and irritable than fever-stricken and bed-bound, afflicted with the worst illness this northern metropolis could inflict upon a sweet Southern boy."

"But we're not boys anymore … "

"Praise the twinkling heavens you never were!" Roark interjected.

"And I'm not sure any of us have fully recovered from the numerous illnesses that New York has caused."

Perhaps Roark was focused on his own eccentric thoughts, because another silence fell over us. I welcomed it though, since the reminder that we were once children suddenly occupied my mind with past images. I could still clearly see all of us laughing and yelling, running barefoot through the reeds around the river bend as the afternoon sun sparkled off the water. Not long after we were singing and playing our hand-me-down instruments in the parking lot by the steamboat docks. Then just a few years later we borrowed my papa's sputtering old Ford pickup truck and drove all the way to New Orleans to do the same with newer instruments near Jackson Square, catty-corner from the St. Louis Cathedral. Our parents, teachers, and various authorities were never happy about incidents like that, but no one really tried stop us. Many people believed in our little band.

I caught myself smiling, though the memories that arose stung my eyes. "Also, I'm not so sure 'sweet' is the best word to describe Dan," I said before the tears had a chance to fall.

"Sweet as a sour apple?"

"That's better!" He managed to make me laugh. As usual while conversing with him, the sight of his smile eased the two-ton weight on my chest. However, not for the first time, I wondered how often he forced that smile. "But how can we get him back to a Honeycrisp? I miss when Dan's sarcasm held more humor and his existential crises were less frequent. Now, his misery seems catching, especially for Tom and Eugene. Their temperaments have been changing lately, too. So I wonder what's better for all of us now. Roark?"

"Do you want to stay here?" he asked again, a stern edge to his tone.

The sun continuously lowered, urging us to follow its lead and head downstairs to the lounge.

"Well, as with anywhere," I began, "New York has its balance of good and bad, its sunny parks and murderous subways." I used one of Roark's phrases to describe his least-preferred method of local travel.

"Some residents and fortune seekers have labored and been able to remain in the sun. Others … "

"Have not been so lucky," I finished for him. "Despite all their hard work."

Our gazes met and locked. Shifting his weight onto one arm he reached for my hand. "You know a nomad like me is comfortable with jumping the train to board the ferry to ride the plane to the next destination at a moment's notice. So whenever the logistics are settled, I'm ready. In the meantime, I'll remain beside you here for as long as you desire."

I knew that.

"I don't hate New York City," I said. "A part of me doesn't mind it at all. That isn't to say I completely like it. But does anyone really love everything about where they live?"

And suddenly everything rose to the surface: the exciting and bustling and never-ending pace of this city's life, the disappointment behind our separate closed doors, the caring only within our band, the yelling of strangers, the persistent yearning to make this work, to somehow keep pushing forward because there is no back-up plan to our music. I dropped my head into my hands, hiding incipient tears.

"God, I don't know what to do!" I shouted into my palms. "I made us come here, but now I don't know what would be right or best to do. For myself and for everyone else. I want us to be happy, I just don't know how to make it happen. I mean, I know very well we each have to create our own happiness and learn to navigate our own struggles, but some happiness from a secondary source wouldn't hurt a darn thing!

"How many times have we reformed this band now? No matter where any of us traveled, no matter what jobs we worked, something kept bringing us back together. Clearly, we all want to succeed. But we can't — I can't — ignore our individual aspirations and needs anymore. Truly, I don't want to move again. I'm getting tired. But it doesn't seem like New York is the answer anymore." My voice cracked. "And collectively, I think we're hurting now more than ever before and I hate that. I just want us to do well and be happy," I reiterated. "I want your happiness."

Before I completely ruined my makeup, Roark turned me with a strong hand and pulled me into his chest. I put my arms around his waist in an effort to return that feeling of comfort. Sadly, I only felt that Dan was right, and Roark had lost weight. So I just held onto him. Neither of us said anything. We let the traffic continue, the wind get chillier, the city go on without us. I could have easily broken down and soaked his coat with my tears, but noticing his smell helped keep me present. His was a scent I had always associated with home: musky mid-summer pavement with a hint of the clean creek water that flowed through our old neighborhood.

I felt Roark kiss the top of my head, then rest his cheek against my hair.

"Dan may be manifesting the signs first, but we all share your mental and physical exhaustion. Frequently over the years, I was neither supportive nor present. Therefore, I normally wouldn't be so bold as to share my opinion in this matter. Perhaps it's well beyond time to return to our old swampy roots and temporarily replant our feet in the Natchez Silt Loam among the magnolias until it's our season and new inspiration blooms. There is nothing," he accented that by squeezing his arms around me, "wrong with a short hiatus, if that is what we need."

"But we worked so hard to even just get here, and even harder to plant new roots. It's not that easy for us to pack up and leave, like we've done before."

"I know. This time it would certainly take a while."

Frowning, I clenched my jaw against threatening tears again. "We made friends here. And we do have a constant paying gig, even if it doesn't pay much. But thanks to it, now we know more people in the industry."

He only nodded and listened. We both knew I was yet again trying to talk myself out of leaving behind what we currently had, just like every other time.

"If we go back home now," I lowered my voice in the hopes that Roark wouldn't hear my confidence plummet, "after all this time, doesn't that mean we failed?"

I imagined our former friends and older relatives offering consolatory hugs and handshakes while shaking their heads and saying 'Well, bless your hearts.'

Beneath my cheek Roark's chest rose as he inhaled and arranged his thoughts.

"Everything we have strived for and attained in New York will not be lost as long as we maintain those connections, which will also require an inordinate amount of work. However, we are not unacquainted with copious amounts of elbow grease. At no point in our journey thus far have we relinquished our dreams, so a mass homecoming will not signify failure. Just as any mass exodus does not guarantee success. We would simply be trying our luck again in Vicksburg, and maybe New Orleans, as opposed to New York, Houston, or Atlanta. And if necessary in the future, there are several other musical cities to serenade with our jazz and confuse with our jive. As it has been previously, leaving New York will not be our denouement."

Roark stepped back to hold me arms-length. In such close proximity I had to look up to meet his gaze, and in doing so my view of the city behind him momentarily fell away. "Your trepidation is not unfounded, though. There is a lot to consider."

"But Roark," I paused to take a shaky breath. "What if I lead us in wrong direction again?"

He nodded. "I understand why you feel that way, but you did not shackle and force us to come here. We are all our own people who have made individual decisions. But a new decision now will require more collaboration between all of us. We need to actually sit and communicate with each other. We all need a chance to form and voice our opinions."

Sniffing, I nodded and rolled my shoulders back to reset my bearing. *Unlike last time. And I can't be afraid of whatever outcome*, I thought, breaking our eye contact.

Roark pushed up his coat sleeve to glance at his watch. "Well, it may not be time to leave New York yet, but we must now leave the rooftop."

Roark and I strode towards the door, and he slung an arm across my shoulders. His hand tapped my arm to his private beat outside of my hearing range.

"In fact, if we don't hurry now, the bar will open before the curtains do and Dan will drink himself under the piano. I can see him now. His head slumped against the lyre post, an arm through the brace, and using the soft and sostenuto and sustaining pedals as soundless keys while loudly singing 'Midnight on the Bayou.' Which is your job, since you perform it much better."

As Roark pulled open the door and made a show of bowing before me, I turned for one last glimpse of a dusky New York skyline. The clouds speckling the sky had lost their dull yellow edge and the white slashes of airplane contrails were less stark against the pronounced purple smog. Someone below in a classroom began strumming a guitar, the electric notes too bright for this somber view. However, the tune would suite a warmer Southern evening perfectly.

New York definitely owned a charm unique from any other place I had been. I liked that charm, but not enough to call it love or home. So with the inner hem of my sleeve I carefully dabbed the black corners of my eyes and smiled at Roark as he let the door swing close behind us.

Leona Ahles

We have all had the experience of seeing a familiar place at an unfamiliar hour, or in strange light. Suddenly, the familiar seems anything but. The person across the room cannot help but see the world from a different angle. Surely, the world seen through different eyes must seem — other.

THE GHOST OF ABILENE

Zoe Lavander

There is something about Jeong that attracts ghosts.

He isn't being haunted. Jeong knows that much. He looked up the word when he was younger and started questioning his taste in friends. "Imaginary friends," his mom teased, even though Jeong himself could clearly see someone standing beside him.

Haunting means sticking around, flickering lights, and noises in the middle of the night — everything Jeong hears are in many of the horror flicks his classmates frequent. He has yet to experience such things, but he also knows he isn't hallucinating either. How many people can claim they've walked through ghosts and get scolded by them afterwards for their rudeness when trying to apologize?

He'd bet his month's allowance that the answer is "none."

Over the years, Jeong has learned to distinguish between the living and the dead. Most ghosts, he's found, are hollow copies of their former selves. Their eyes are black — he would go as far as to say soulless — and they don't care much for avoiding visible objects, yet they seem drawn to their previous life's routine. He's once seen a ghost commute to places by taking the subway, simply because it was familiar.

Other times, though, it is harder to identify ghosts from people. Jeong has lost count of how many times his mom has looked horrified when she's found him talking to what looks to her to be random telephone poles.

By around his tenth birthday, Jeong is sure his mom thinks he's crazy. After all, no parent would bring around a psychiatrist "buddy from work" just for dinner, only to slip him a check at the end of the night with whispers of "it's just a phase" floating through the air.

But those are the perks of living in New York City, some might say. People are just genuinely odd there. Jeong thinks it's just because people want to be more sophisticated than they truly are.

Winter graces New York City this year with slushy snow. Jeong is grateful for the change in scenery, but it's still not enough to mask the scent of garbage waiting along the sides of the roads, so he still scrunches his nose when stepping outside the school gate.

The cold makes his fingers numb and his ears prickle with pain every time a gust of icy wind sweeps past him, even with many layers on. As Jeong follows the flow of people down into the subway station, his stream of thoughts goes to the scarf and mittens left neatly folded on the kitchen counter that morning.

They had smelled of Downy.

Jeong pushes through the crowd, trying to beat the afternoon rush. It pays off to be small, as he can easily squeeze between people on his way to the turnstile, swipe his card, and get to his destined platform without getting trampled along the way.

Most days, Jeong would just walk home, but his mom has been making a conscious effort lately to text him near the end of school hours to say "it is safer to take the subway". He generally hates places where everyone is huddled in one small area. It makes it harder for Jeong to discern from reality and the afterworld — too many people to concentrate on all at once for his taste.

Although, since it is his mom who asked, he is more than happy to oblige. After all, it means that she'd be home early, which makes him a little giddy inside.

Standing in line waiting for the next subway train to pull up, Jeong allows his eyes to wander. As he expects, there are too many people to note the ghosts in the area. It isn't until his eyes land on an elderly man rummaging through the garbage cans near the end of the platform before he leaves his spot and his previous thoughts are abandoned.

"Excuse me? Sir?" Jeong says. "Is everything okay?"

The man doesn't respond. He continues his searching without sparing Jeong a single glance. In an attempt to try again at getting the man's attention, Jeong tries to tap the man's shoulder lightly, only to have his fingers pass right through the sleeve of the man's knitted gray sweater.

This time, the man does look up, shock registering across his face. "You talking to me young man?"

"Yes sir," Jeong finds himself saying.

"You can see me?"

"Yes."

"How?"

"I don't know. I just can."

By this point, the man's shock turns into a warm smile. "Well, since you are here, think you can help me with something?"

Jeong shrugs. "Sure. I got the time."

"Great. I'm looking for something."

"In the garbage?"

He ignores the question. "It's a pocket watch. Has the initials *L.T.* on the front—" Then he frowns, staring down at his hands. "—But as you can probably guess, I can't really touch material things unless I put a lot of thought behind it. Think you can search in my stead?"

Nodding, Jeong moves to stand beside the man, taking his place in searching the trash. However, the longer he does, the more doubt begins creeping through his mind. Finally Jeong pulls his hands out of the trash.

Sighing, he glances over his shoulder, grimacing at the stench now clinging to his hands. "Are you sure you dropped your watch down here, sir?"

"I know it was here," he says, making a point to show the fracture on the back of his skull. "Because if it ain't here, then I wouldn't know where it could be. I died here, so it would only make sense for it to be here."

It must have been recently if the watch is still here, Jeong realizes. But he decides not to get nosy and ask anything personal.

"Someone could have picked it up."

The man makes a face, clearly displeased with Jeong's conclusion. "Doubt it. If you don't want to help look, then go away. Don't need your help anyway."

"Alright, alright. I'll keep looking, sir."

"My name is Alfred, by the way. You can drop the 'sir' now. I'm not one for formalities. Even when I was alive, I hated them. Just because I'm old doesn't mean you need to act so damn awkward."

The man — Alfred, now, Jeong supposes — has a mouth on him. But he decides it's better not to voice that opinion and return his attention back to digging through countless burger wrappers and paper cups. Then, as if his silent prayers are being answered, a golden watch covered with ketchup emerges at the bottom of the trash. Gently picking it up, Jeong makes an effort to wipe the ketchup off with the sleeve of his coat before handing it to Alfred.

"This it?"

"Yes." Alfred runs his thumb over the engraved letters, a small smile forming on his lips. "Thank goodness."

Jeong watches as Alfred brings the pocket watch closer to his face, examining it with a relaxed expression. For a moment, Jeong feels his heart skip a beat. His eyes travel down to the ground to see that Alfred no longer has legs — the entirety of his body began to fade way. However, he doesn't have time to acknowledge the lump now forming in his throat when Alfred begins speaking to him with a soft tone.

"This used to be my wife's. She gave it to me for my birthday," he says, placing it into the pocket of his sweater. "It has her initials engraved on the cover. Louise Tager. She was an amazing woman, and I couldn't go without bringing it with me."

Then, he looks up to meet Jeong's eyes. "Thank you, young man."

Alfred disappears seconds after. Or maybe he is still there and Jeong can't see him. Even so, Jeong stands there for some time before making his way onto the main platform again. He hadn't realized it before now, but hours have passed, and Jeong is already feeling the unconscious weight of his cellphone vibrating in his pocket. Hesitantly, he looks at his screen, only to sigh at the twenty (and counting) missed calls he's received.

By the time he makes it in front of his apartment, it is well past the acceptable hours of the night.

Pulling open the door, Jeong tries to shut it behind him quietly, hoping to make an escape to his bedroom. However, he is surprised to see the hallway illuminated with the light, his mom pacing back and forth in front of the foyer. The second their eyes meet, she rushes forward, cellphone in hand.

"Where have you been?" she asks, jabbing a finger at the clock that, by what Jeong can see, reads to be about 10:35. "I thought I told you to take the subway."

Jeong looks down at his feet. "I did take the subway."

"Then what have you been doing all this time? Do you know how late it is? School has been out for hours! And you haven't been answering my calls. I was just about to call the police!"

"I'm sorry."

Silence hovers between them like an old friend. Jeong can't look at her, for he is too afraid that she can see something in his eyes that will give her some kind of clue to what he's been up to. How this isn't the first time it's happened. So he refuses to lift his eyes, his hands fiddling with the edge of his shirt.

As time passes, it gets increasingly harder for him to swallow.

"I just want to know where you were," she finally says. Jeong tries to shift his eyes down even farther past his feet to avoid his mom's intense gaze. "You could have at least called me if you were going to be out this late. Or answer my calls at least."

Then, as if to add for good measure, she says, "I'm not mad."

"I—" he begins, but clamps his mouth shut. There is no way he is going to voice out loud the events of the afternoon. Fidgeting in place, Jeong decides to go with a promise. "I'll call next time."

"Jeong, that's not the point," his mom says, gripping his hand. Urged by her touch, Jeong looks up, meeting his mom's frown with a hesitant look. "You haven't been gone for just an hour. You've been gone for more than half a day. What's going on? You haven't gotten mixed up in something bad or illegal, have you?"

"Mom, no," Jeong says, pulling his arm away. "It's not like that. Nothing like that. Just—" He sighs, balling his hands into fists. "I promise I'll call next time, okay? I'm going to bed. *Goodnight.*"

Before his mom can protest, Jeong is already running to his room, slamming the door closed behind him. He throws his backpack into the corner of the room before flopping his face down onto his bed. He resists the urge to scream into his pillow. His head is pounding and his frustration only fuels the emotions he wants to shut away when he looks at the messages on his phone, one reading "WHERE ARE YOU". Grabbing his pillow, he presses it to the back of his head, praying for sleep.

The next morning comes faster than Jeong would have liked. Before his nerves and guilt can begin to develop in the pit of his stomach, he finds the kitchen bare. Another note lays on the counter, the words *"Please come home early"* sprawled across the pink post-it in a hasty scribble. Knots twist in his stomach as her remembers his mom last night. Jeong then makes a silent vow that today there won't be any distractions. Plenty of ghosts can find ways to move on into the afterlife without him butting in. Pretending to be normal for one day won't hurt.

When Jeong steps out of his apartment building, his face is blasted with cold air, knocking black strands of hair into his line of vision. The snow on the edges of the sidewalks has almost completely melted away, leaving puddles in its wake. There aren't many people walking around — for this, Jeong is quite glad — so he decides to shove his iPod along with his headphones into his backpack. Leaving three hours before school starts is the best idea he's had in months.

He pushes his bangs away from his forehead before pulling the hood of his parka over his head. Taking one of the arm straps of his backpack, he slings it over his shoulder. Jeong then makes his way down the street, making sure to keep his eyes glued to the ground to avoid any possible ghost sightings. This time he has done his socks a favor and gone with rain boots instead of his usual worn-down sneakers.

He is halfway to school when he suddenly hears a scream coming from the park across the street. Head snapping up, he searches for the cause of the ruckus when his eyes land on a young girl clinging onto one of the branches of a tree. Without as much as a single thought, Jeong runs towards her, completely oblivious to the strange looks he is receiving from the stranger he passes along the way.

"Are you okay?" he asks, rushing to stand underneath her. "Don't let go. Can you climb back up?"

"I-I think so," she says. However, the second she goes to wrap her legs around the branch to hoist herself back up, her hands immediately slip.

Whether or not Jeong is anticipating this, he is already there in a flash. The girl screams before crashing into Jeong's arms. He half expects to drop her, or to completely crumble to the ground along with her, but neither happen. Instead, he nearly lets go of her because of how light she is.

It is like she weighs virtually nothing at all.

Eyes wide, Jeong looks closer at the girl who is now in his arms. She is staring back at him with a wide grin, showing off her crooked teeth. Her white dress is a bundled mess beneath his clenched hands. Although, there is no way for Jeong to ignore the obvious paleness of her skin or even the black color of her eyes, he still tries to deny the hints at first glance. The fact that he can touch her is a little off-putting, but there is no doubting the girl is a ghost.

Jeong lowers his arms just enough for her to hop out of his embrace. She twirls once when her feet touch the grass, blonde hair floating across her back. After finding stable grounding, she peers up at Jeong — for she is a good foot shorter than he is — and proceeds to point at his face, bursting out into tearful laughter.

"Your *face*. I wish you could see it right now. You look completely awestruck," she gasped, spreading her arms wide. "And who goes around picking up *dead* girls? Talk about lame!"

Heat immediately rises to Jeong's cheeks. His face fixes into a scowl while trying to keep his humiliation from showing too much.

"I didn't realize you were a ghost when I came over here to save you, okay?"

"You can't 'save' somebody that's already dead. That's impossible."

"I know that!"

"Obviously you didn't."

Giving up on their original conversation, Jeong finds himself asking, "Why can I touch you?"

The girl shrugs. "How should I know?" Crossing her arms over her chest, she rolls her eyes. "Personally, I'd rather know how some random kid can see me."

The term 'kid' makes Jeong raise his eyebrows. "Aren't you younger than me? You look about eleven."

"I think you're missing the point here."

A huff of laughter escapes him. "Like I would tell some crazy tree-climbing ghost girl about myself."

Narrowing her eyes, the girl swiftly takes one of Jeong's hands, gripping it in her own. "Okay then. My name is Abilene Foster. Most people call me Abby though. There. Now we're friends. So tell me."

"That's not how it works."

"Just tell me already!"

"It's not like there is a real reason for it. It's been like this since I was little."

"But that's so *boring*," Abby complains before sitting down on the grass. Jeong watches her eyes scan the area before focusing on something behind him. "You go to school?"

Following her gaze, Jeong sees his backpack by the trunk of the tree, probably having been discarded sometime during the falling incident. A feeling of self-consciousness flooded him. Yanking his hood, he rakes a hand through his tangled hair, shrugging.

"Yeah. I just started middle school."

"Did I make you late?"

Jeong doesn't bother to look at his phone for the time when he answers. "It's fine, really. Skipping one day isn't going to kill me."

Abby doesn't say anything more after that. Letting out a sigh, Jeong holds out his hand. "My name is Jeong Tae-Woo."

The introduction isn't anything special, but Abby's black eyes seem to be sparkling as she shakes his hand. Cocking his head, Jeong goes along with the gesture for a moment before asking again, "How is it that I can touch you?"

"Maybe because I'm still fresh," she suggests. The comment sounds so bizarre that, at first, Jeong thinks he misheard her. One look at her face tells him otherwise.

"You just died?"

"Almost a week," she says. "But that's not what I meant. I'm still fresh in people's minds. Like, they are still thinking about me — mourning me — that sort of thing."

Whether or not the reason he can physically touch her is because she is "fresh" doesn't particularly matter to him. All it proves to do is make his stomach queasy.

"I think I get it." Gesturing towards the tree, Jeong asks, "So did you

… you know … die here?"

Abby shakes her head. "Nope. At a hospital. I was in surgery, I think."

"Then why are you at this park?"

"Because this is the last place I came with my parents before stuff happened."

The vague response registers firmly in Jeong's mind and he immediately leaves the conversation where it is. Snagging his backpack, he plops down beside Abby and flashes her a reassuring smile. He pulls out his iPod and waves it in the air.

"Want to play some music?"

Although it hadn't been part of his plan originally, Jeong ends up staying at the park with Abby. He lets her talk about whatever comes to mind — which turns out to be mostly about books she's read or TV shows she's watched — and somewhere along the way, they had fallen asleep.

When he wakes up, his phone is vibrating, a list of missed calls from his mom awaiting him like a punch in the gut.

By the time Jeong finally reaches the apartment building, it is already past ten.

Getting home late two days in a row isn't getting him any brownie points, that's for sure. Especially when he hasn't gone to school for one for them. It wouldn't have mattered as much if his mom was working the late shifts like she normally does, but, since she isn't, he can't come up with a reason why he'd be out as late as he has been.

This time, his mom yanks open the door before Jeong can lay a finger on the doorknob. Her black hair is a mess, short ends twisting out of her bun. The longer she stares at him, the redder her face becomes until she finally drags Jeong inside, only to deposit him on the couch in the living room.

Placing her hands on her hips, his mom scowls. "Did you bring your phone with you today? I thought I told you yesterday I wanted you to at least answer your phone."

His eyes shift down to his feet and he says nothing.

"The school called," she continues. "They said you didn't show up. Where have you *been?*"

This is the same conversation he has been trying to avoid this morning. All the questions make him feel nauseated. Clasping his hands together tightly, Jeong tries to ignore the aching of his head.

"Hanging out," he whispers.

"Where?"

"The park."

"With who?"

"No one."

"That's a lie!" his mom says, grabbing Jeong by the arm. He looks up at her in shock. "Do you know how worried I was? I care about you—" Her words die for a second before she narrows her eyes, stating more firmly. "I care about you. You know I do. And I love you. I really do, Jeong. But I'm not a mind reader. If you don't tell me what is going on with you, I won't know anything."

"No matter how much you love me, it won't make a difference. Just believe what you're told, like you've always have, and forget about it." The words stun even Jeong. And, for a moment, he is just staring at his mom with such rage that he continues, "Stop acting like not knowing some little detail about me now bothers you. You think that now that you don't work late and that now you are home more often gives you some entitled right to my life again? *It's so annoying.*"

The words sting. That much Jeong can see from his mom's face. Jeong knows he doesn't mean the words, nor were they true. Even so, he doesn't take back what he says.

"We're both tired," she says, releasing her grip on him. "You should go to bed."

Jeong complies, and, surprisingly, she doesn't follow him.

The next morning, the same pink message lays waiting on the counter. Jeong takes the time to crumble it in his hand, ready to chuck it into the garbage when his mom's hurt expression wheedles its way inside his head. His hand shakes at the memory. Slowly, he lowers his arm and shoves the note into his pocket before grabbing his things and heading out the door.

Jeong finds Abby sitting against the same tree he'd seen her fall out of. When she sees him coming down the sidewalk, she calls out his name while waving her hands in an exaggerated motion. Instead of allowing him to sit beside her, Abby stands up, taking his arm and dragging him to a nearby bench.

"The view of the lake in the morning is really peaceful to look at," Abby explains, smoothing out her dress as she sits down. "My parents and I used to have picnics here. But, I guess it was a lot warmer then, with it being summer and all."

Jeong takes a seat on the other end of the bench, placing his backpack in the space between them. Although it is hard to see through the morning fog, the lake is beautiful. The scenery of bare trees only adds to the mystic feel of the park.

"So," Abby begins. "You wanna talk about it?"

Jeong looks to his side. "Talk about what?"

"Don't play the innocent card with me. Something happened, right?"

Sighing, he shrugs, resting the back of his head on top of the bench. "Just a petty fight with my mom. Nothing serious."

"What kind of person is your mom?"

"The kind to worry too much, but goes and works twenty-three hour shifts at a hospital."

"She a doctor?"

"Nurse," Jeong says. Then clarifies, "Head nurse."

Abby stretches her arms above her head, looking at him from the corner of his eyes. "That's cool. Lots of responsibility."

"That's why she's never home."

"But I thought you said you fought with her yesterday?"

Rubbing his eyes, Jeong says, "She's been coming home early the past two days. Same with today, I think."

"What was the fight about?"

"She was asking where I've been and stuff. Butting into my business. I kind of just snapped." Jeong starts rubbing the cuffs of his parka, suddenly finding them clutching his skin to be irritating. "She doesn't know I can see ghosts. So when I have to lie to cover it up, the situation kind of falls flat on its face. Usually she just accepts it and moves on but sometimes it turns into a blowout between her and me. Like yesterday, for example."

This time, Abby says nothing. She lets her hands fall back into her lap, a frown tugging on her lips. Her gaze shifts back to the lake.

"Have you ever thought about telling her?" she asks.

"Lots of times," Jeong admits. "But each time I try to, I just see my mom's face and think 'she'll send me to a facility for crazy people' and I chicken out."

"I don't think she would do that."

"You're probably right."

"Then?"

Tilting his head, Jeong smiles at Abby, who is puffing out her cheeks in a pout. "I said 'probably'. Meaning, I don't know what she'd do if I told her." Without leaving Abby time to reply, he says quickly, "So what about your parents? What are they like?"

"My dad is a goofball while my mom is always super serious," she says, relenting to the sudden change in topic.

"So I take it your family is close?"

"The tightest ever!" Giggling, Abby twirls a strand of hair between her fingers. "But then I got sick and most of our picnics ended up being in my hospital room after that."

Jeong pauses, cautious as he asks, "What illness did you have?"

"I had a tumor," she whispers, pointing to her head. "Near my brain."

Any hint of a smile disappears from Abby's face. Her head tilts down, her legs dangling off the bench. Jeong stays silent, watching as the fog slowly begins to clear. By the time she speaks again, the park is beginning to fill with joggers and dog walkers. The possibility of going to school is long gone so Jeong turns to her as she grabs the sleeve of his jacket, showing her a reassuring smile.

"It was hard. Like, really hard," Abby continues. "When I went into surgery, I never got to say the things I wanted to say. My parents were just so positive. 'Don't say anything, sweetie. We'll see you soon.' But that never happened. As you can see." She gestures quickly at herself. "I'm a roaming ghost who can't move on because she has regrets. It's pathetic."

"Would telling your parents what you wanted to say help?"

The surprise that shows on Abby's face isn't lost on him. Jeong is biting his lip. He is doing it again, butting into someone's — more importantly, a *ghost's* — business without thinking again. The one thing he promised himself he wasn't going to do anymore, especially not today.

Abby narrows her eyes at him. "How? I can't exactly talk to them. You're the only one that can see me, Jeong."

Running a hand through his hair, Jeong's eyes drift towards his backpack that is beside him. An idea strikes him then. Unzipping his backpack, he takes out one of his spiral notebooks — algebra, he thinks — then, digs around for a pencil. Abby watches him curiously, leaning sideways to take a peek at what he is doing.

When he finally finds the materials he needs to go with his plan, Jeong flips his notebook open to a blank page. "How about you write a letter to you parents?"

She eyes him reluctantly. "I'm not that great of a speller."

"Then, you talk," Jeong taps the back of his pencil against the paper, smiling. "I write."

"Seriously? Okay, so. I want to tell them that I was happy. I was glad they are my parents. That I love them very much and—"

"Wait," Jeong says, laughing when Abby puffs out her cheeks in response to being interrupted. "I can't write that fast."

They spent the next two hours sitting on the bench. Abby talks nonstop, excitedly filling the contents of her letter with reminiscing stories, heartfelt thank you's, and many I love you's to put even a Casanova to shame. Jeong doesn't mind it — although he does have to tell her to slow down every once in a while — he enjoys hearing about Abby's experiences. He just hopes that the purpose behind the letter would shine through when her parents read it.

"Finally," Abby says, rubbing her hands together, smiling. "Let go of me. Move on. I love you both and you deserve to be happy. Just because it didn't work out with having me as a daughter doesn't mean it won't work out ever."

Jeong doesn't know what to say to her after that. So he silently rips the pieces of paper from the spine of his notebook, neatly folding them together until they are in a decently sized rectangle. Abby hums in approval, excitedly wrapping her arms around Jeong's neck from behind.

"Thank you," she whispers.

For a moment, Jeong can't breathe. A lump forms in the base of his throat, making it hard for him to swallow. "Do you have to go now?"

Even without an elaboration, they both know what he means. Abby moves back around the bench so now she is facing him. She smiles, the biggest one she's shown him by far, and places her hands on either side of his cheeks.

"Talk to your mom," she says. "She'll understand."

"She won't. She'll think I'm nuts," Jeong argues, but is silenced when Abby presses a finger against his lips.

"Promise me you'll tell her."

Abby doesn't release him from her hold until he nods, muttering a simple "I promise" under his breath. Her laugh echoes around them, being carried away by the wind. Jeong closes his eyes. The next time he opens them, a folded piece of paper lays in his lap and Abby is gone.

Slowly unfolding the paper, Jeong fights back the urge to slap a hand against his forehead because *of course* he's the one who will be delivering the letter. In the folded paper is an address scribbled with fine handwriting. One glimpse at the street name makes Jeong realize the house was not so far from the park. He doesn't feel like moving though. So, for the next hour, Jeong sits on the bench, looking out over the lake.

After clearing his thoughts, Jeong pulls on his backpack, shoving the folded letter into his pocket, and follows the directions on the piece of paper.

It turns into roughly a fifteen minute walk from the park's entrance to the little red mailbox with "Foster" etched into the side. He hikes up the steps to the door and — before he can possibly change his mind — rings the doorbell.

A thought pushes its way into his head the minute he hears the soft chimes inside the house. *What am I supposed to say? Hi, my name is Jeong. Your daughter turned into a ghost and I talked with her and helped her write a letter for you.*

The idea sounds ludicrous. It is then Jeong realizes he hasn't really come up with a plan or any type of explanation as to why he is in front of the Foster's home.

I should have just stuck the letter in the mailbox, Jeong thinks, whipping his head around to face the driveway. *But what if they think it's some prank?*

Then again, why would Abby's parents believe some thirteen-year-old saying he can see ghosts? Won't they think it *is* some overbearing prank either way?

However, Jeong doesn't have time to come to a decision. The door opens, revealing a woman who looks to be in her forties. Her appearance is the first thing Jeong notices — for Abby looks like she is her miniature — and he is lost for words. Anything he has thought up to say to Mrs. Foster up until that point flies out of his mind.

Blue eyes seem to be sizing him up as Jeong feels himself sweat under her judgmental gaze.

" … How may I help you?" she finally asks.

"I, um," Jeong stutters, the letter in his pocket suddenly feeling like a ton of rocks. The only thing he can think of is to tell the truth. "I was a friend of Abby."

Mrs. Foster's expression softens explicably. Opening the door wider, she gestures for him to come inside. Wordlessly, Jeong complies, only to find a slim man poking a head into the hallway entrance.

"Honey, who was at the door?" is probably what the man is going to ask before trailing off mid-sentence to stare at Jeong. He figures this is Mr. Foster (with how his smile is almost a mirror of Abby's and all). Jeong can practically feel Mr. Foster's curiosity burning holes onto his freezing skin with the way he is being stared at.

"Abby's friend," Mrs. Foster says behind him, "from school."

Not that the assumption bothers him, but Jeong feels himself sigh. At least now he doesn't have to worry about the whole "how I knew your daughter" act.

Mr. Foster's smile stretches across his face. "Oh, really? He looks a lot older, though."

"I get that a lot," Jeong interjects quickly.

"Why don't you wait in the living room?" Mrs. Foster offers, guiding him over to a leather couch. "I'll go make you something to eat. You look hungry."

"I'll go pour us some juice," Mr. Foster says.

Before Jeong can refuse, Abby's parents have disappeared into the kitchen. At least now he knows where Abby's overly welcoming personality comes from. It almost makes him smile.

One look around the room makes it obvious that the Fosters are a close-knit, take-a-picture-of-everything type of family. The walls are filled with framed photos of Abby from the time she is little to — what Jeong expects to be — the time before Abby's illness had gotten her admitted into the hospital. There is one photo in particular that catches his eye. It is the one by the banister, a small picture of Abby under a tree.

"I took that picture on one of our picnics at the park," Mrs. Foster's voice says from behind him. It is then Jeong realizes he had been slowly making his way over to the banister to get a better look. Turning around, Mrs. Foster is wearing a small smile, holding a plate of freshly cut apples.

"You liked to go on picnics a lot?" he asks.

"Abby always enjoyed it so much when she was little that it became normal to go on one every week." Then, she laughs. "She was always climbing that tree. We were afraid she was going to fall out of it."

"That does sound like something she would do," Jeong finds himself saying, and, he too, is joining in on Mrs. Foster laughter. "She is so spontaneous."

The room has suddenly fallen into silence. Jeong begins to worry if he has said something weird. *Wouldn't a friend know these things?* But Mrs. Foster's wide eyes assure him that she is simply surprised.

"Abby was such an optimistic girl," she whispers. "Even when she got sick the only thing she showed was a smile."

Jeong freezes when he hears her clear her throat, rubbing her eyes with the back of her hand. The smile she shows afterward is delicate, small, and strained.

"Excuse me. I forgot napkins!" Mrs. Foster says, rushing back into the kitchen. The scene makes Jeong's stomach flip.

Taking one last look at the picture, he takes out the letter, placing it on the coffee table before heading out the door without a single word of departure.

Upon returning home that night, Jeong feels a deep sense of déjà vu. He opens the door, the living room light flickering on this time, and his mom sitting in an armchair, arms crossed over her chest. Jeong hasn't noticed the past two nights, but beneath his mom's eyes are thick bags. Her face is thinner — paler — and she looks as if she will break if she tries speaking.

She looks exasperatedly at him for a moment before she presses her hands against her face, mumbling, "Is this going to be a common occurrence?"

"I don't know. Are you going to be coming home early from now on?"

"That was the plan," his mom says. "Unless you don't want me to?"

He doesn't respond at first. Thinking back on the past few days, all that comes to mind is Abby's smile and Mrs. Foster's grief. Not to mention his mom — who has continuously waited up for him into the late hours of the night — never pressing him for a reason why he has been acting oddly.

Jeong can hear Abby's voice, as if she is still whispering in his ear, reminding him of the promise he made to her before she disappeared.

Taking a step forward, Jeong takes one of his mom's hands, hoping the smile doesn't look as strained as it feels on his face.

But he needs to do this.

Drawing in a breath, he locks eyes with his mom who is waiting patiently for him to speak.

"I need to tell you something."

Zoe Lavander

What is to become of us? Will we colonize the stars? Will we perish in nuclear fire? Will we bioengineer ourselves into contented stasis? Will we choke the earth until it no longer forgives our stranglehold? Here is one answer: Wrangel Island.

WRANGEL ISLAND

William Engels

The Child is father of the Man;
And I could wish my days to be
Bound each to each by natural piety.
—William Wordsworth

It was a happy day for Mrs. Donna Lufthammer of 11 Pristine Drive, Oak Park Village, Ann Arbor. She had spent the morning and much of the afternoon seated on the ottoman before the window of her LuxeDecor bedroom, pecking away at her Alienware 17 laptop as she placed orders for her daughter's ninth birthday three weeks away. She had enjoyed these world shopping tours ever since Anita was a baby and, with the list growing longer and more exacting each year, the fun just kept getting better. Halfway down the list of eighteen items, she'd already made several circumnavigations. There had been the usual new birthday party wardrobe and accessories from Brooklyn's, latest X Box model and smart phone, both ordered directly from the Seoul Samsung office again, but with item ten she'd had to look twice: a life-size play kitchen, dining room, and stocked pantry set! The titanium frame model from Spielwarenmesse in Stockholm looked promising. She envisioned it outside on the vast manicured lawn, near the sculpted boxwoods, Anita bustling about with full plates and cups amid her circle of friends. Or, maybe she should go east again with the plastic one from the Guangzhou Qixin firm in China?

Anita was the joy of her life, a fledgling brunette, perk-nosed beauty, all of the mother twenty years younger. She liked school and excelled in her studies, just as Mrs. Lufthammer had as a student. She had her quirks, it was true, a runaway imagination and a somewhat morbid sensitiveness to her surroundings at times, traits the mother did her best to keep hidden from the neighbors. Only this morning she had said something about a strange visitor in her room last night. She'll outgrow these idiosyncrasies by her teens, Donna thought.

But now a wind had arisen, chasing clouds in, and, before she knew it, rain was streaking the panes in long lines. "Just in time," she murmured. Fierce gusts pushed the delicate branches of the ornamental Japanese maple in the garden one way then another against the glass. She got up and drew the blinds. She shuffled out of her velvet nightgown and slippers and stepped into her room-sized dressing closet. Mrs. Lufthammer would have to brave the weather in picking up Anita from school.

"Mamma, who was the little girl who came to my room last night?" They were in the brightly lit, Garrison Hullinger Interior kitchen just after getting back. She poured her daughter's cup of Serendipity 3 Frrozen Haute chocolate mix and pushed it across the polished marble counter to her.

"Little girl?" She would feign innocence.

"The girl. Oh, her face was so thin and white! And she had this bubble." Anita demonstrated, encircling her head with her hands.

"Oh, that must be your dream. Wasn't there a space movie about that?"

"No, Mamma, I saw her just like I see you now. She came to the side of my bed, like Nurse Judy when I got sick. She tried to talk, but her voice was so soft and the TV in the living room ... " Anita's own voice trailed off.

"Is loud. Yes, dear, so Daddy can sleep. You know that. Well, let's not worry about this girl, shall we? You tell me if she comes again, but I'll bet last night was the last one." And she turned Anita's thoughts to the size of the cake and kind of decorations she wanted for her birthday.

Three days later, after increasingly anguished reports from her about the nightly visitor, whose message was still undelivered, Mrs. Lufthammer decided to brave a run-in with her husband. Seated with him in their snug, wainscoted living room after a dinner of Ecuadorian cuisine ordered fresh from the Quito merchant in town, she broached the subject during a commercial break.

"Donna, why do you go along with such foolishness, acting like there really is a visitor with a message? You know how she can be about some things."

"Carl, I've tried not to, but it's really starting to bother her. Maybe if she could hear her, I mean, think she heard her, it would calm her down."

"Well, tell her to tell her friend to talk louder, or take off her space hat. I'm not going to risk a sleepless night with the TV down or off, if that's what you mean. I've got to drive thirty miles to work early in the morning. And, on top of that, deal on my headphones with that nonsense coming at the Saltillo plants about waste compliance."

"I was thinking that, if she could sleep, just for tonight, in one of the guest bedrooms upstairs … "

"Don't you see what I'm driving at? Any giving in to this business is not a good idea. There's no telling what it might lead to. Just try not to pay any attention; then it will go away. That's the best thing. Now, if you'll excuse me." He got up from the tooled, Moroccan leather sofa. "I've got a lot on my plate tonight. That raw goods order, you know, for the 300 Dodges they want by winter. Imagine!" And he retired to his executive's office in the basement den.

She sat on alone, oblivious of the TV. The thought of being rid of the whole worrisome to-do in one stroke, and in time to be able to finish shopping for her daughter's birthday, wouldn't go away. No, not for all her determination to play out her usual role of compliant wife. One concession, that was all, and things would settle down to their normal course. How dare she think of standing up to Carl, though?

He was asleep when, still inwardly debating, she took her daughter, with some bedding, up to the guest bedroom nearest the stairs. She was careful not to bring up the subject of the girl, however. After a restless night of repeated wakening to imagined voices and footsteps upstairs, Mrs. Lufthammer made her way back the next morning to wake Anita before school. Her anxiousness seemed to increase the closer she got to the room. Would she find her more settled and less delusional? Oh, she hoped so! She still wouldn't mention her strange friend, but wait for her to say something. Reaching the bedroom, she was startled to find Anita awake, yet still lying in bed, her eyes bright and intent on the ceiling.

"Good morning, Dear."

"She talked to me, Mamma!"

Donna caught her breath. "Talked to you?"

Anita sat up suddenly. "Mamma, did you buy anything for my birthday yet?"

"Well, yes, a few things. Why?"

"Mamma, I don't need anything else."

"Excuse me?" A surge of grief shot through Donna's heart. Surely she must have misheard her.

"I don't need any more gifts, please."

She sank down on the bed beside her daughter. "Why, Anita! What on earth?" She wanted her back, the child who on every birthday couldn't wait to see if she'd gotten everything on her list.

Anita's eyes were fastened with fierce attention on her mother's.

"Oh, Mamma, if you could see her, so little and crying. 'Please, stop it!

Save us!' She kept saying that. 'Tell them to stop it! Before it's too late!'"

"How, 'stop'? Stop what?" Donna had drawn back involuntarily, a movement of self-preservation.

"I don't know. It's like stop something we're doing and stop something terrible that's about to happen."

"I see. And did she say you shouldn't have gifts for your birthday and how that's supposed to help her?"

"No, Mamma. Only it's like we're, well, sisters. I get something, but she can't have it and she cries. Like Bryan and Brianna, you know, our neighbors. I'm the big sister; I'm stronger so I get there first and she can't sit there. Or I took it first, so I get to play with it and she can't. And it's like I have everything, Mamma, and she hasn't got anything. That's how I felt. I can't explain it. Only, I feel awful having so much stuff."

Stranger and stranger! "This girl. Did she tell you who she is or where she's from?"

"I think she said 'Angel,' 'Angel Island.' Something like that. She kept crying, Mamma."

In spite of her dismay, the whole fanciful business was beginning to suggest more than mere fantasy to Mrs. Lufthammer. Had her daughter been sent a dream messenger from the ghettos of Calcutta or Nairobi? She couldn't account for that space hat, though.

"Mama, I want to sleep here again tonight. Can I?"

"Absolutely not!" Back to reality after her foolish notion of a heaven-sent emissary. A sickening fear gripped her stomach. Carl was right, as usual.

"But, Mamma, I have to! There's so much more she needs to tell me. About who she is and where she lives. About what's going to happen to her."

No, she couldn't imagine risking continued encounters with Carl's wrath. She was still shocked at her boldness in defying him last night. But, then, her old idea returned despite the evidence in support of Carl's. Giving in to Anita seemed the only way out of their predicament. After an evenly matched tug-o-war between her fears and wish to recover the daughter she knew, Mrs. Lufthammer settled on a compromise: one more night in the guest room.

"Just one more, is that clear? Find out whatever she needs to tell you tonight. And, Anita, don't mention anything to Daddy. Now, it's time to get dressed for school. No more delaying. Have your mango juice and cheese croissant. I ordered more of your favorite cocoanut butter."

"Oh, and Mamma? One more thing. Can I please walk to school this morning?"

More craziness! Where will it end? And what if the neighbors see her? "Dear, why don't you let me take you in the Rover like always? It's another four blocks after the gate, you know."

"I don't mind. *She* walks everywhere."

Donna was going to ask her how she knew this, but, wanting to be done with it all, merely gave her consent "since it's nice outside for once."

In the guest bedroom before school the following morning, the information flowed in — as fast as the flushed daughter could report it. The girl had cried less and shared a great deal about herself and her situation. It seems a terrific storm the likes of which had never been seen was about to strike the island, whose name, the mother noticed, Anita now pronounced with an "r." Rangel, it appears, was a sort of ecological oasis, a world of unheard of plant and animal diversity. Surrounding it at intervals were gigantic towers that protected the island from the deadly air that was destroying plant and animal life elsewhere. As best Mrs. Lufthammer could make out, the towers emitted gases or powered winds that neutralized, filtered out, or drove off the toxins in the air. Though these towers had apparently withstood many savage hurricanes in the past, they were not expected to stand up to a storm of the magnitude of the one now approaching. Sentinel, outlying winds from the storm had already begun to arrive and were countering the work of the towers, letting in noxious particles. That's why the people wore a bubble over their heads, and carried a tank, something they also did during bad hurricanes. The storm they were now facing, though, was expected to wipe out the towers, toppling them like a child would stacks of blocks. Nor was there much hope for the vast sealed-off greenhouses and factory barns, major food sources for the island. All of this likely meant starvation for many, since the towers and other structures couldn't be reconstructed, and more plants and animals raised, in time to provide sufficient food.

"The worst thing, though, is there's hardly any place for them to go," Anita told her. That was the immediate cause of danger, for the housing on the island, mountainous apartment buildings where everyone lived like ants in hills, wasn't expected to hold up before the winds. It appeared that the buildings had been steadily added onto over the years to meet the demands of an exploding population and were easy targets for such a powerful storm. The situation had grown more desperate in the last few days as factions arose over who was to be admitted to the island's limited shelter space, the network of underground tunnels and chambers that wound beneath the apartment buildings. They were no doubt designed and constructed in an earlier day, when the population was much smaller. There had been several demonstrations and outbreaks of violence. The girl, in fact, had lost a younger brother.

Donna, who had found it all rather intriguing, in spite of herself, felt genuinely concerned. "Isn't there anywhere else they can go?"

"She said there are other islands where they also have towers and you can breathe, but they don't let you in."

"Oh?" Islands. Where you can breathe. What in the world? Or, what out of it?

"She said the islands are always fighting each other. You see, they don't have enough room."

Now that does sound familiar. "And they can't go to other places, I mean besides the islands, because of the air?"

"Yes. Besides, she said the storm was everywhere. All of the islands, the whole world, Mamma."

"All this sounds awful! But what does she want us to do?"

"Well, she wants me to tell people, you, my teachers, my classmates, everyone, about her visits and what she said."

"And that's supposed to stop the storm? I don't understand."

"Oh, and there's another thing. She told me her name. You'll never guess: Anita! Just like mine!"

"Anita!" The mother's face blanched. Why this sudden dread at the sound of her own daughter's name? Then the idea of dream projections, parts of one's own personality embodied in symbolic characters, came to reassure her. Yes, it was a dream after all!

"That's interesting, Anita. Amazing that you both have the same name. Well, she certainly had a lot to tell you, didn't she? Now, it *is* time to get ready for school. No more delaying."

"She told me how she got my name, Mamma. She said, 'I'm Anita because your name's Anita.'" Mrs. Lufthammer thought the room was swaying. "'And I'm your great-granddaughter.' But I didn't understand that part. Anyway, that's what she said. And she asked me to tell you and everybody that, too.

An uncanny explanation was suggesting itself. A descendent crying out from a future world imperiled by our reckless fossil fuel consumption. She had heard before the warnings about increasingly severe weather. There was Katrina, Harvey. She let Anita walk to and from school again.

That afternoon a call came from the school Administration Office. It seems Anita had been very excited today and was saying a lot of things to the other students and her teacher about a dream or something. No cause for concern or immediate action, just, if she could meet with the principal sometime soon. She made an appointment for the next morning. And began nerving herself for a private emergency tête-à-tête with her husband that night.

After dinner, while Anita was in her old room, with the door closed, Mrs. Lufthammer stood in the kitchen cleaning up and thinking about what she would say to Carl.

"Hey, Donna, come and take a look at this!" His voice came booming from the living room.

A story had just come on the nightly news about a school shutdown after unrest in Camden, New Jersey and a warning issued by the Phoenix, Arizona school board. Children, and a handful of teachers, at the schools were saying a student had received warnings about a brewing storm of unsurpassed fury threatening life on our planet in the not-so-distant future, warnings by a strange child who showed up at night and claimed to be the student's great-grandchild. Someone had compared the storm to the asteroid that scientists claim wiped out the race of dinosaurs on the earth. The newscaster switched to an anchorman in Phoenix for an interview with one of the two children and his parents.

"Wow! It's a regular epidemic of lunacy, Donna! And with Anita and her 'visitor,' we nearly caught it right here in Ann Arbor!"

The social temperature ran high in the two communities. There was footage of both student-led rallies calling for a crackdown on fossil-fuel burning in the manufacturing and transportation sectors and of counter-demonstrations staged by local businesses. "The havoc to our planet forecasted by the two students is indeed so dire," the newscaster concluded, "that hundreds of concerned citizens have 'gone green,' making lifestyle changes such as walking or biking to work almost overnight. Local authorities are investigating underhanded activism by environmental groups behind both children's stories. NBC News, Washington."

"Yeah, I want to know who's been messing with my kid's brains, too, by God! 'Gone green.' Ha! Gone nuts. Absolutely incredible! You see what I mean, Donna, about not playing along with kids' fantasies. Aren't you glad now we didn't pretend to believe her? She thinks she hears the same nonsense, and we get to join the other loonies on national TV!"

Maybe, she thought, it's better to wait. See how things turn out. Hopefully, Anita's letting out the secret yesterday at school won't lead to anything. My visit tomorrow morning with Mr. Kilpatrick will help. I'll tell her to keep quiet. But, then, what if she talks tomorrow anyway? I'd be facing an even worse blow-up.

"Carl?" she began at the next commercial break. "Please understand I was only trying, in a different way, to get Anita to calm down."

"Yeah."

She let out her breath slowly. "I mean, in letting her sleep in the upstairs room."

He turned abruptly to her. "You let her sleep there after what I told you? So," his mouth twisted in mockery, "you *did* believe her."

"No, Carl, I just thought the visions would stop if—"

"'I just thought,'" he mimicked. "And I'll bet they haven't, have they?"

Her silent shamefacedness told him they hadn't. He rose. "And so it's her turn now to blab at school!" He grabbed her shoulders. "She's been telling them all about her freak visitor from the future, hasn't she?" He shook her.

"Oh, Carl!" she sobbed. "I thought it would help."

"Hasn't she?" he fairly bellowed, still shaking her as the tears flowed, wetting their purple flokati rug. He towered above her, raising his fist before her face. She fell back in terror onto the couch cushion. The half-full Wedgwood china dishes on the teak table jumped as he brought his fist down beside them with a crash. "Looneyville! That's us. I'll keep her at home." He muttered to himself, his chest heaving. Then it was all suddenly very funny. "Hee! Hee!" He sat, unable to stop. "Haw! Haw!"

"Listen," he finally said, turning back to Donna, who had sat, motionless, choking back sobs the whole time. "The future. It doesn't even exist yet! The present's the nearest thing to it there is!" There was a malicious gleam in his eyes. "But even supposing, just for the sake of argument — quit crying for a moment and listen to me for once! — even supposing kids could visit us from the future. That means the future they're from is already set, doesn't it? How did that future come to be what it is? What made that future they're in? Everything that's happened between now and then. Cause and effect, a fixed, iron chain! You can't break that chain. 'Oh, I think I'll pull out this link and stick in a different one,'" he mocked. "No way, folks, I'm sorry. If there's a storm coming where they are and if, which I don't believe, it's all because of global warming or climate change or whatever they're calling it nowadays, how are we supposed to stop it? There's no turning back the wind, like we were magicians or something."

Sickened, but at the same time stung by his cool, logical dismantling of what she'd been half ready to believe, she tried to block him out, put herself back in that happy morning, so far away and long ago, it seemed, when she had ordered half of Anita's birthday presents.

"OK. I'll tell you what, Donna, and I mean this." He had reverted to his earlier tone. "You keep Anita home from school tomorrow or I'm going to check her into the Michigan State Fun House the first chance I get."

"What?"

"I'm not going to be made a laughing stock before the whole world."

"Are you out of your mind?" She had risen, pale lips half whispering, steadying herself on the sofa back.

"Ha! I think I'm the only one who isn't out of his mind. Let her either sit at home or in the psyche ward until she gets this foolishness out of her head."

"Oh, God. I can't believe this is happening. You wouldn't do that, Carl. Not to Anita; she's not to blame. And what will the neighbors think if they find out she's—"

"A mental case. Exactly. Better to have the neighborhood's gossip than the whole blasted country's, I say. Now, you think about what I said. I'm going to bed." He turned back after reaching the door. "And one more thing. Don't forget that I can access the camera in the garage any time I want. If I catch the Rover or the Ferrari going anywhere, you can bet I'll sure be at the school in a jiffy."

She collapsed, buried her head in the cool, worked leather of the sofa to stop her whirling brain. Yes, this is what comes of wifely rebellion. She couldn't make sense out anything that had happened over the past five days. And what sense did the days ahead promise to make? His argument disproving the children's reports came back to her. What a fool she'd been, well, almost been. Yes, the future world reported by the girl claiming to be Anita's great-granddaughter, assuming the future could be reported, was a fixed, unalterable product of all that had taken place before it. Why would the girl come to us in order to change what's already determined? The present and the future are inextricably linked. Oh, she was weary of her whole idiotic life.

That night she dreamed she and Carl with Anita as a toddler were walking on a crowded beach somewhere. Suddenly, the winds picked up and people began screaming and running away from the shore for higher ground. News had spread that a tsunami wave of unheard of size, a brute, sheer wall reaching up to the sky, was fast approaching the land. Donna looked out over the water. The advancing waves, each one bigger than the one before it, stretched back in an unbroken series as far as the eye could see. She took Anita in her arms and, ignoring the desperate shouts of Carl ordering her to come back, waded into the water. She held her close, keeping her own back to the pounding waves as she steadied herself for each successive onslaught. When she looked up, she saw huge, windowed towers had sprung up all along the strand. Thousands of faces were peering at her and Anita through the windows. Beneath one tower stood Carl, ant-like, waving his stick-thin arms. She had the sense of some great purpose, a noble, saving mission that justified endangering herself and her daughter in this way, though she couldn't tell or remember afterward what it was.

It was early morning when she awoke from the dream and sat up in bed. In the darkness, their plush bedroom with the silver-gilt wallpaper looked simple and stark. Carl lay asleep. The TV droned on in the living room down the hall. Her thoughts returned to the incidents of the past several days and she noticed they seemed less disturbing now. She calmly took up the thread of Carl's clever argument last night. Yes, our actions have created the world known to those children. Present and future are joined in that great iron chain of cause and effect. But, and her breath came shorter at a sudden new departure, can't our future actions affect their future? OK, our future actions are already over with, if seen from the vantage point of the future, but could their effect not yet be felt by those in the future? What are our future actions? Mrs. Lufthammer felt the weight of awful, cosmic-shaping choices settling on her shoulders. Then, a new thought struck her. Why, if they are in the future, then they must know what we will do! And if they know that, they must know the outcome for them! Oh, so they know we're not going to change and that destruction awaits them. But why, then, would they bother to send the children to us? Only, and she clasped her hands in the excitement of the new turn she was making, if they know we are going to change, at least some of us! Their coming back to us is itself an event in the causal chain! An amazing thought! The question arose why, then, the girl had cried so much on her first several visits. Mrs. Lufthammer disposed of it as best she could: either because the girl wasn't told by whoever sent her or, more likely, it would add to the persuasive power of her appeal.

Her brain was spinning again; it had been an exhausting intellectual exercise and, for her, unprecedented, at least in the years since she dropped out of college to marry Carl. And what did she gain from this effort except weariness? She couldn't be sure her thinking made sense either, especially after all of the mental turmoil she'd been through. Lying back down, she tried to sleep, then, after a while rose quickly, picked up her laptop from the dresser, and settled onto the ottoman where she had done her world-wide shopping errand for Anita. Typing "Rangel Island" in her browser, she found a "Wrangel Island" in the Arctic Ocean. That made sense, if things were warming up. It must have undergone a great deal of transplantation of plant and animal species, of florescence and cultivation, since our time, judging from the images she opened of harsh, arid plains and mountains. The report on one webpage that the island had an unusual degree of biodiversity and was a strictly protected eco-sanctuary, though, meant that it would have been a good choice for setting up a microcosm, a self-sustaining refuge for humans and other life forms. And what about this? "Scientists believe that the island was home to the last wooly mammoths on earth," she read. Could this bit of natural history be part of the girl's message?

Mrs. Lufthammer was more divided than ever. She wanted to believe in the messenger, had looked for ways to, but the responsibility of believing frightened her. No, she knew she'd never risk her daughter's going to a mental institution; Anita's part in carrying out the mysterious girl's mission was over. Or, at least for now. If it was determined that enough of us will change our lifestyles to save the island, Anita doesn't need to act, not yet anyway. She can stay home today, maybe tomorrow if Carl hasn't cooled down. There'll be time to act. What's the point of inviting disaster? If a further thought also occurred to her, that maybe Anita will also cool down, she didn't admit it to herself.

She woke, disappointed, to the sound of her daughter's voice around 7:00 am. She had hoped Anita would make the task of keeping her home easier by sleeping in.

"Guess what, Mamma. She talked to me again last night, in my own room! And I could hear her!"

It's not going to go away. "I thought you said the TV was too loud." Was all that trouble she'd put herself through in letting her sleep upstairs unnecessary after all?

"She said the winds weren't so bad, so noisy now. It wasn't the TV, or only the TV, Mamma. I couldn't hear her because of the wind. Also, she didn't cry again either."

Donna couldn't tell why, but the news about the milder winds tugged at her, called forth a new emotion or capacity in her. She wanted to ask what else the girl had told her. Instead, she set herself to preparing an explanation about why Anita wouldn't be going to school today. She wanted it to sound, without the benefit of the snow, like a snow day announcement.

"She thanked me, Mamma."

"Thanked you?" But she somehow wasn't surprised.

"For telling my friends and teachers at school yesterday."

Donna felt a tinge of shame, and that pull again. She wouldn't hold back now. "Did she tell you how that helped her?"

"She said it was because of me and other kids that the winds were quieter."

She recalled the news last night, the new choices so many were making because of the children. A link in the great causal chain was being forged. Her dream, almost forgotten, now came back to her. "Do you think the storm is going away, then?"

"I don't know, Mamma. Only she thanked me and said I mustn't stop telling people. Do you think it's going away?"

Her asking and the sweetness and trust in that face hurt her heart. She felt the waves' pounding, but counter-waves surged through her at each stroke and she was holding her daughter close. She saw all those towers above the shore and what they stood for. "I think it is, Anita." And then, "Now, it *is* time to get ready for school. No more delaying."

"It's OK if I walk again?"

"Of course, Dear. In fact, I'll walk with you." She had a word or two to say to Mr. Kilpatrick.

When Carl came home from work, rather earlier than usual that afternoon, his look of resentful triumph reassured her that he hadn't yet heard about the commotion Anita's sharing today had created at school. The local news station had been called after a series of walk-outs threatened to empty half the school. Donna had been told she might be hearing from national TV. She hovered near their polished, Sterling-plated land phone in the hallway in order to be there first, like the bigger sister Anita had spoken of. Sure enough, at about 5:30, while Anita was in her room and Carl in the living room, the musical bell tone sounded.

"Who was that?" Carl called out after she'd hung up. It was time, she thought. No more delaying. She crossed to the living room. "NBC. They want to interview Anita about today's disturbance at the school. The anchorman said he'll be here in one hour." Silence, except for the TV, like the interval before the next wave. She braced herself.

"Disturbance? You're lying! She never went to school! I had the garage up all day on my phone."

"We walked."

Just beating him in the race to Anita's room, she closed the door and turned to face him. "You're not taking her anywhere." He stepped back, unsteadied with surprise. When in the next moment he raised his favorite fist before her face, she stood there motionless, like an unshakeable tower. He turned and stormed off, muttering oaths, down the hallway and stairs to the basement den. She heard the door slam. Mrs. Lufthammer went to the living room and picked up the TV remote control on the coffee table. She couldn't remember the last time the TV was turned off while Carl was at home.

Political intrigue is rife with figureheads, scapegoats, and puppets. But who pulls the marionette's strings? Conspiracy theorists are never at a loss to suggest candidates for the shadowy masters who invisibly control the fate of nations. Here is a fresh take on who is in charge. It's less sinister than average. Or, is it?

THE ELECTORAL COLLEGE PROFESSOR

Jay Dearien

The elevator doors opened.

Holding a box of doughnuts in front of her, Geneviève stepped out to face the entrance to the department. The pane of glass set into the wooden door read *Department of Memetics*. Careful not to drop the doughnuts, she twisted the doorknob with her free hand and pushed her way through the doorway.

They paid me well, she thought, but it was hush-hush. I'm sure they gave me a fake name. How can they justify coming out for a sit-down with an obscure college professor while they are still in session, trying to decide the election? They hired me as a consultant on the Vice-Presidential vote, but we can do that remotely. Whatever they're playing at, I have a feeling they won't take no for an answer.

She followed the hallway left at the door to the department secretary's office around to the small, dingy faculty lounge.

Geneviève set her sugary burden in the center of an oblong table near the sink counter and contemplated it, and the human behavior experiment it represented.

These are the bribes, she thought, and the anchor for all the behaviors, the memes, in my experimental memetic system. If people follow the rules, they're allowed a doughnut. But they also have to keep each other in line. People will sneak doughnuts if nobody bullies them for it. And somebody has to spread the memes to new people. I'm amazed at how well it's worked. Designing and implementing a memetic system to make a group of people behave in a certain way has proven to be remarkably easy.

A whiteboard marker was the first thing she found to write on the cardboard box in large capital letters, IF YOU'RE WEARING SCHOOL INSIGNIA, HELP YOURSELF.

She tugged on the lapels of her corduroy jacket, revealing a T-shirt which read, New International University of Nebraska.

I'll get a cake doughnut later, she thought. It's the jelly-filled ones that disappear the quickest.

She turned toward the coffee service and muttered, "Bloody typical."

One carafe was empty and the other contained less than a cupful of stale sludge. She savored the irony of the sign over the machine, urging, 'If you finish a pot, please make a fresh one.'

They don't make signs against things people don't do, she thought, or encouraging them to do things they do anyway.

A wizened aluminum-framed chair crouched next to the mini-fridge. Geneviève tossed her backpack onto its drab Naugahyde upholstery, patched with grey duct tape. The fridge was surmounted by a tiny black microwave oven, which in turn supported a tray containing a hodge-podge of coffee mugs of different shapes and colors.

She retrieved her own antique cup, emblazoned with the 'Unrecognized Genius' from Matt Groening's original 'Life in Hell' comic strip days, and filled it with tap water. The blinking green numbers on the microwave display switched to a fifty-nine second countdown as Bongo the rabbit pirouetted inside the light-filled diorama.

She flung open the cabinet above the coffee machines to reveal a desultory menagerie of coffee bags, once pregnant with gourmet coffee grounds, sagging against one another. Most of the bags containing little if any coffee, she shook each into the virgin-white lingerie of the filter basket before tossing them into the trash. She contemplated the meagre brown heap of grounds for a moment, then filled the machine with half a pot of water and set it to brewing.

Another professor wandered into the lounge.

"Oh, excellent," he said with relish. "Doughnuts."

"Oh, hey, Steve," Geneviève said. "We'll have coffee in a jiffy. I'm afraid I could only scrape together enough for half a pot."

"Oh, yeah," Steve Humphreys replied. "I've been meaning to bring some in."

It was all Geneviève could do to keep from rolling her eyes.

The microwave dinged.

She yanked open the fridge for a small carton of cream, emblazoned in Sharpie with the name 'Gene' and the words 'Steal & Die.' Her cup now warm, she dumped the hot water down the sink, dashed in a bit of cream, and filled it with coffee. As she raised it to her lips, she realized that Humphreys had been contemplating the box of doughnuts and the simple rule scrawled upon it for a painful interval.

He doesn't have any school colors or insignia on, Geneviève noticed. Even Humphreys follows the rules scrupulously, if self-consciously. It's quite amazing, really, considering what a disaster the coffee pool is. "Hand me a cup and I'll pour you some coffee," Geneviève offered, thinking, I want to see how he weasels his way through this.

Humphreys' hand lingered on the large, green mug in the center of the tray.

The department head, Barry Dingle, has a thing about that green one, Geneviève thought, and everybody knows not to touch it. I remember the last time. Even the department secretary was embarrassed to have to go to Humphreys' office and get it back from him. But she went. And he'll never live that one down. The name 'Humphreys Bogart' stuck, probably for good.

Humphreys passed her a mustard-colored mug and she filled it.

"Cream?" she asked. "Since I've got it out."

"Oh, would that really be all right?" Humphreys asked in mock protest.

You don't fool me, Steve, Geneviève thought to herself. I know perfectly well you use my cream all the time.

She passed him the milky-brown potion with a knowing smile.

Humphreys stood and sipped his coffee. Geneviève could tell he wasn't hanging around just to enjoy her company.

Here it comes, she thought.

"Damn," he ventured, "I forgot it was Tuesday when I left the house. But I've got a school tie clip in my office — does that count?"

"I'm not the referee," Geneviève said, while thinking, The point of this experiment is to see if it's self-regulating.

She hefted her backpack and turned to leave. She caught Humphreys dropping his eyes to the box on the table and snatching up a frosted jelly-filled doughnut.

She was overcome with the urge to goad him.

"So, Steve," she said, "today's the day we get the results on that diaper marketing campaign in Idaho Falls."

"Ah, yes," Humphreys acknowledged, gesturing with the doughnut, "that new product they're test-marketing in the Burley-Rupert area. What makes you bring that up?"

"If you recall," she replied, "I bet you a dinner at Ahmed's that my adjustments would yield a five percent increase." I would've bet him real money, she thought. Gambling isn't illegal anymore, of course. It's just considered gauche in the department. Still, I would love to see him fork over a pile of hundreds or write me out a big, fat check in front of everybody.

"I'm confident my original design is optimal," Humphreys said. "In fact, I wouldn't be surprised if your modifications actually decrease overall revenue."

I can always count on Steve Humphreys to deploy the most facile of immunomemes, Geneviève thought, tricks for deflecting things, making an attacker look foolish. He's living proof that a tawdry response can make one appear intelligent, absent any actual thinking whatsoever. As long as I don't let him upset me, he's a treasure trove of experimental data. He doesn't want to be seen as a cheater. He wants the cake of a memetic stamp of approval from his fellows, but also the pleasure of eating that cake, or doughnut, in this case. No amount of rule-bending seems beneath him. I would've never thought such a simple system could yield so many surprising results. That's macromemetics for you.

"Well, just be ready to pay up," Geneviève said as she headed out the door.

The mail holder on the wall next to Geneviève's door was empty, except for yet another memo about the coffee pool.

It's amazing how people cheat in that system, she thought. An economist would say it's an externality, and a psychologist would call it social loafing. Both true, but neither tells us anything useful, which shows the limitations of both those fields, and how memetics carries on where they fall short.

She scowled at the plain double-spaced paper, which collectively shamed the department for taking the last cup of coffee and not making more while exhorting everyone to bring coffee and cream from time to time.

Professor Barry Dingle is such a hack, she thought. He's head of the Memetics Department, for God's sake. He isn't even *trying* to build a memetic system to coërce people into enacting the desired behavior. He never brings up the most obvious memetic iconic anchoring object, a coffee cup. That MIAO is practically the unofficial symbol of Alcoholics Anonymous, for instance, coffee being the drink of choice at AA meetings. I once saw a couple of cups with their handles interlinked on the cover of an AA magazine, captioned 'Dating in Alcoholics Anonymous.' Using the symbol in a novel way can immediately convey the idea of two AA members hooking up. Dingle should know that shaming with no offer of reward for good behavior is poor memetic design. Depersonalized messages and vaguely defined requirements with no specific time parameters lead to residual memetic debt, the feeling that 'I've done more than I have to, so I deserve another cup, or two,' and of course, 'I did it before, so someone else should make the next pot.'

She folded the paper in half and raised her eyes to the frosted pane of glass in the door, imprinted with the words, Geneviève A. Thomas, Professor of Memetics.

She contemplated her key for a moment, thinking, You're a MIAO too, before sliding the key into the lock and pushing her way into her tiny office.

She dropped the memo onto her desk and swung her backpack down next to it.

The coffee pool is an interesting problem in memetics, she mused. It's more challenging than this Vice-Presidential thing these Electors want me to consult on. For one thing, the coffee pool lacks *marking*, because you can't tell by looking if somebody's allowed to take a cup of coffee or not, so there's no clear bullying opportunity, hence, cheating. There's little *engagement*, either, since you can make a pot or bring in a bag of coffee without anybody noticing, making memetic rewards unreliable. In my doughnut memeplex, by contrast, the clothing and doughnuts are clear iconic objects, providing immunomemetic anchoring sites for any number of bullying behaviors to shame cheaters. The whole time you're enjoying your doughnut, you get approval since you're still clearly wearing the clothing. The system is particularly virulent since it not only provides the reward of the approval of one's fellows, but also a tasty treat. And there's no residual memetic debt associated with the transaction. Wearing the school insignia is all that's required, and the doughnut is the clearly defined reward.

Geneviève rounded her gunmetal desk and flopped down into her well-worn office chair. She fired up her computer terminal and began unloading folders and notebooks from her backpack.

At least these people coming in person means I can do a live presentation and field their questions, she thought. It suits me. I hate polishing up a document. Something tells me the less of a paper trail, the better. Perhaps that's the point of their visit.

She closed her eyes and massaged her temples.

The nature of power is still a hot topic in macromemetics, she thought. Professor Barry Dingle is a perfect example of how power leads to laziness. The illusion of power is that you can ignore the laws of macromemetics and simply command things to happen. Using punishment to force behavior is inefficient. Barry puts out memos, his minions try to enforce them, but when people police themselves, keep each other in line, they are harsher and more strict than any despot could ever be, and work harder for the rewards from their fellows than for the occasional smile from the Great Leader.

Geneviève fantasized about what she would do with the department if *she* had the power. She opened her eyes and looked at the white coffee cup sitting on her desk.

Unrecognized Genius, she mused, chuckling to herself. That's me. Sooner or later, every memeticist falls prey to the delusion that if only she had power, or if those idiots in power would listen to her, everything would …

She felt a flutter in her chest.

The Vice-Presidency. They could be coming to draft me as a new candidate! If so, they must have the power to nominate me, and the influence to get me elected.

She flipped open her notebooks and folders and set to work organizing her notes into talking points she could use with the Electors.

The Electoral College went its own way in deciding Presidential elections a long time ago, before I was even born. No more 'rubber stamp' on the popular vote. Electors actually meet, debate, vote, and fight it out until they select a President and Vice-President. Elections had been ridiculous 'beauty contests' for too long. Wealthy conglomerates bought the votes while preserving the thin veneer of democracy. It reached a breaking point when the rich and powerful themselves began shamelessly taking power, with elections a mere formality. The Electoral College stepped in and took back control, often choosing people not on any State ballot, or even written in anywhere.

Geneviève looked up from her desk at a rap on the glass of her office door.

"Yes? What is it?" she asked.

The department secretary poked her head in and said, "Some people from that college in Washington are here to see you."

The secretary held the door open and two women and one man filed into the cramped space.

"Hello," Geneviève said, rising from behind the papers heaped in front of her. "I'm Geneviève Thomas. And you are?"

The older of the two women, wearing a pale purple suit dress and apparently the leader of the group, spoke up, "It's a pleasure to meet you, Professor Thomas. I hate to be rude, but it's probably for the best if we not tell you our names. We represent a group that is trying to break the deadlock in the Vice-Presidential vote. Can we talk for a moment?"

"Certainly," Geneviève replied. "Please sit down. Can I get you anything?"

"No, thank you," the leader lady said. "We'd like to hear what you have to say with the minimum fuss possible. As you know, this is not an election with a strong majority for a Presidential candidate, where that same majority could easily settle on a Vice-President. It's taken an inordinate amount of coalition-building to get a majority for Floyd Garner as President. Most factions have compromised, giving up a lot, but not for nothing. What's left is to haggle over is the Vice-President."

"Is the Vice-Presidency all that important?" Geneviève asked, while thinking, To anybody who's not placing bets in the gambling industry, that is.

"Oh, yes," the younger, round-faced woman replied. "It was the Democratic Convention, not the Electoral College, mind you, but part of the compromise that got Kennedy nominated was that LBJ be the Vice-President. He said it was 'the closest he would get to the Presidency.' Prophetic words, in the end."

"Sounds like what Hillary Clinton should've done with Bernie Sanders back in 2016," Geneviève half-joked.

The male Elector spoke up, "Who knows how that might've turned out? The point is the Vice-Presidency isn't nothing. It's the last scrap the smaller factions of a coalition have to fight for, for their place in history, for their chance at the Presidency, maybe in the next election."

Geneviève thought, They're more unhappy with Floyd Garner than they're letting on.

She cocked her head and said, "So I take it you're one of the factions that didn't want Flip Garner in the Oval Office, and you're worried you're going to come away empty-handed."

The woman in purple replied, "This has turned into a Dark Veep election. A coalition has been cobbled together to elect Garner, but it's anybody's guess who's going to be Vice-President. Garner inches closer with each vote, but a different name comes up as top pick for the Vice-President, with nowhere close to a majority. If Garner wins in the next few votes, we'll have a President, but without a majority the Senate chooses between the two strongest Vice-Presidential candidates. The Garner coalition could fall apart if things drag on much longer, and then even the Presidency would be up for grabs. It would be the first time such a thing happened since the Electoral College asserted itself. The fear is that if the Senate gets involved, the Electoral College will become irrelevant again, and the whole country will plunge into chaos."

They don't care about the coalition, Geneviève thought. The whole Electoral College knows what's at stake. When time runs out, if this woman has a viable solution, even if nobody likes it, they'll vote for it rather than go over the cliff together.

"You mean," Geneviève said, "that public faith in the electoral process would be undermined or even completely destroyed."

The leader lady nodded grimly, then explained, "We need your help, Professor Thomas, to secure a majority in the Vice-Presidential vote before the Garner consensus falls apart. How can we get the Electoral College to settle on a single Vice-Presidential candidate? We don't really care which one, so long as it saves the coalition, but we'd be thrilled with a candidate of our own choosing, if that's at all possible."

There it is, Geneviève thought. They're looking for a new candidate. Do they want me because they think they can control me? I'll give them more than they bargain for.

Geneviève began, "The basic memetic principle at play is who gets to do the talking. The College as a whole has a collection of memes which members may deploy, with each voting faction having additional memetic inventory of their own. There needs to be more memes about your candidate than your opponents. It's quantity, not quality."

"What do you mean, Professor?" the male Elector asked. "We need only be able to say *more* about our candidate? Can you explain how that works?"

"It's the principle of 'packing the meme space,'" Geneviève explained. "Create a bunch of memes that are easy to use, and importantly, don't expose you to immunomemes, also known as bullying opportunities. People love to yack, yack, yack, and do things to impress each other, and they hate to clam up when things are tense and they might put their foot in their mouth. If a person can drop a reference that resonates, even a little bit, makes them seem well-informed, gives others the chance to riff off of it, and is sure not to come back to bite them, they'll do it as much as possible. It drowns out the opposition."

Maybe it's time to start feeling them out a little, Geneviève thought.

"For example, would you consider an academic for a candidate?" she asked.

The two younger Electors stared at her in silence, then glanced at one another nervously.

The older woman held Geneviève's gaze before replying, "Certainly. How might that work?"

Geneviève put her fingers together and said, "For example, saying something like, 'Yes, yes, candidate X is interesting, but candidate Y is an academic, not a politician,' is relatively innocuous, asserts a tautology, and doesn't really attack anybody, at least not in a way that can be defended against. That's what ultimately makes your memeplex, that is, your candidate, attractive — the ability to say a lot without really saying anything."

"Are you saying it doesn't matter what we say about our candidate, so long as it doesn't backfire?" the man asked. "And these immunomemes are what backfiring looks like?"

"That's effectively true," Geneviève agreed. "Deny the opposition a bullying opportunity, the chance to deploy an immunomeme, a meme that associates the wrong kind of MIAO with your candidate."
The male Elector asked, "What's a 'meow?'"

"A MIAO is a Memetic Iconic Anchoring Object. It's simple and easily recognizable, like," she said, holding up her drink, "a coffee cup, to which a number of memes may be associated and called up without a preexisting context, just by invoking the MIAO itself. One example is when John Kerry ran in 2004 the Republican media invoked the image of the flip-flop beach shoe and successfully linked it to Kerry's supposed 'flip-flopping' on certain issues. Nobody remembers what those issues were, but that ceased to matter, since he was linked to this image, and whenever the flip-flop idea was invoked, it reinforced the idea that Kerry was unreliable and therefor unelectable. It became about the MIAO, the shoe. There may have been valid reasons to question Kerry's positions, but there were also irrational ones, ridiculous ones, even, but they were all tied to this word, to this image of the familiar beach shoe, so it could all be called up at the slightest provocation, and without any investment or risk on the part of the person invoking the MIAO."

"Okay," the leader lady spoke up, "I think I get it. At this stage it sounds like we want to hand out a lot of chances to talk about our candidate, period, without the worry of stepping on any landmines, kicking off immunomemes, or providing bullying opportunities, like you said. Correct?"

"Yes," Geneviève agreed, "and the way to do that is to pack the memespace with anodyne or tautological memes, memes that bother no one or are always true, even though they appear to actually say something. Insert memes everywhere about your candidate that appeal to everybody. Attach your memes to MIAOs in the environment so they are always present and available, and easy to invoke."

The leader lady said, "I'm guessing that in addition to drowning out memes about other choices, we want to create immunomemes, or bullying opportunities, to do with other candidates, too. Correct? Let's get down to brass tacks. What are some specific examples?"

"Despite not voting for their first choice," Geneviève began, "all of your factions have to be perceived as doing the right thing by their constituencies and by the other Electors. It's not about liking your candidate as much as not having the chance to say they don't like them. It's a kind of 'praising with faint damnation,' so to speak, which takes the form of saying something harmless about your candidate while deploying a bullying meme at another candidate, even a candidate who doesn't actually exist. For instance, 'At least we're not drafting a political insider or a dyed-in-the-wool ideologue.'"

The older woman's face took on a strained, quizzical look.

It's now or never, Geneviève thought. I want to see if there's anything here. "Hang on," she offered. "Maybe I can give you a concrete example — myself."

The faces of the Electors brightened.

"I'm a young woman," Geneviève continued, "and it's always good to get one-issue women on board. Spin me as the candidate who's most sensitive to women's issues, who else but a woman, and also as a woman who likes men, as opposed to some kind of ball-buster, then I'm hard to beat. One arguably 'good' result of the Women's Movement is that opposing the nomination of a female exposes one to a number of bullying opportunities."

"For example?" the male Elector asked.

Geneviève put her thumb to her lip, then replied, "The idea that women are somehow weaker, less decisive, used to resonate with a healthy slice of the electorate, but now only invites sexism immunomemes. A slightly more sophisticated immunomeme is 'What if she's PMSing during a nuclear crisis?' Since the US has already had a number of very successful women Presidents, one comes across as merely stupid and wrong, which are especially pernicious immunomemes."

"Why especially?" the male Elector asked. "You mean more so than the sexism one?"

Geneviève replied, "It opens an immunomemetic Pandora's Box. While it's a stretch to invoke sexism immunomemes in response to, say, international trade policy, transportation initiatives, or the National Debt, the 'You're stupid,' or 'You're always wrong,' or in John Kerry's case, 'You always flip-flop' immunomemes can be applied to anything. They're what we call non-parameterized, or omniphagic immunomemes."

"I get 'omniphagic,'" the leader woman spoke up, "as in 'eats anything,' but what do you mean by the meme having no parameters?"

"Take for example," Geneviève answered, "issues like reproductive rights, or child care, which are seen as applying more strongly to women. If a candidate is tied to the 'I hate women' memeplex—"

"Sorry," the leader interrupted, "how do you mean 'tied to' a memeplex? No candidate would choose to do this, correct?"

"Oh no, of course not," Geneviève replied, "but attacking a woman candidate in the wrong way can bind one to MIAOs anchoring any number of anti-woman memeplexes, and issues like abortion and childcare become eligible for enactment simply because they contain the parameter of 'women.' The candidate tied to the sexism MIAO is automatically on the wrong side of all these issues. If things get bad enough, the sexist candidate finds they can't open their mouth without the opposition, and even disinterested third parties, deploying memes built up over decades of activism. The misogynist candidate is forced to draw on a dwindling and increasingly impotent inventory of immunomemes with which to fight back. As jokes, catchphrases, and iconic imagery collect around the misogynist, debate stops and the opposition just talk amongst themselves about what an unfit candidate the victim is and it snowballs from there. That's effectively the life cycle of political schisms, by the way. At some point the memetic inventories of two opposing factions become totally disjoint. But you, you want to alienate the target without splitting the cohort. They have to keep talking to each other, at least about me."

The younger woman said, "The assumption is, of course, that all of these anti-woman and anti-politics immunomemes are already present, ready to be deployed. But the electorate is heterogeneous, divided, even. It sounds like we could easily split the electorate around our candidate. So the trick is to find somebody everybody likes, but for different reasons."

"Yes," Geneviève agreed, "you tailor me to appear strong on issues that each group cares about, and appropriately weak or ambivalent about issues they don't care about or oppose."

"And that's what memeticists call 'pseudomutation,' is that right?" the younger female Elector asked.

"Actually, it's 'polyvariability,'" Geneviève corrected, "although the two are often confused. Both make memes appear to come from multiple sources, to create the illusion they are already in widespread use. Polyvariability is the 'Great Taste versus Less Filling' approach, where two factions are prepared to go eighteen rounds with the other about how their reason for loving something is the right one. Upper and lower classes imitating each other is a well-known phenomenon, and would be an example of polyvariability if engineered deliberately. Pseudomutation means designing a memeplex to look like it's already mutated and evolved into multiple forms to make it seem established."

The young Elector woman continued, "Would pseudomutation ever apply to a political candidate?"

"I want to say it could, if the candidate were already established," Geneviève posited. "One example is Richard Nixon. He said of himself that he was the only one who could open a dialog with China because he had fought communism his entire career. He was involved in the McCarthy business, among many other things."

"How is that an example of pseudomutation?" the woman asked.

"A marketer would call it expanding the Nixon 'brand.' There's the Nixon who fights communism, and you add the Nixon who is tough enough on communism to talk to China. A fundamental principle of macromemetics is that memes are 'alogical,' which means that a meme may be logical, illogical, irrational, or completely absurd, and it's all the same to memetic analysis. The memeticist thinks more in terms of 'memetic pairs,' or memes deployed together, even if they seem illogical, unrelated, or contradictory. A perfectly logical meme may be paired with a completely irrational one, so long as they support one another, help one another to be invoked, to propagate. You need only look to religion for examples. The trick is to avoid poisoning the system by adding immunomemes that attack successful established memes. Nixon could have easily become a flip-flopping John Kerry by going to China. The clever memetic engineer sidesteps this by recognizing the potential mismatch and pairing the right memes together beforehand. Nixon is tough on communism. Only Nixon is tough enough to talk to Mao. Why is 'Tricky Dick' going to China? Didn't he used to be anti-communist or something? Yes, he's the only one tough enough on communism to not be manipulated by Mao. We avoid linking the 'Nixon hates communism' and 'China is communist' memes, and instead pair the 'Nixon is tough' with the 'China is tough' and the 'Nixon can't be bamboozled by communism' memes. These become immunomemes that defend the new, expanded Nixon memeplex. You can use pseudomutative design to set your candidate on top of a divisive issue, in a stronger position, playing both sides against the middle. Let's say I have a reputation as an anti-abortionist. In order to make me sensitive to women's reproductive rights, I could create a new thing, a 'Zero Abortion' stance, and there's a buzzword for you, a MIAO. So I'm still against abortion, but I'm also about preventing women from getting into a situation of needing or wanting an abortion. In actual practice, that might be only slightly less impossible than whatever the pro-abortion camp wants, or than outlawing abortion completely. The point is that it provides a host of immunomemes to allow me to really shit on the other two positions from a place that is difficult to attack."

"What could that look like? Can you draw us a practical picture of such a memeplex?" the leader woman asked.

"You could think of a number of submemeplexes," Geneviève began, "that narrow the immunomemetic inventory the other sides can use down to 'I want to force women to have unwanted children,' or 'I want to kill babies.'"

"It's like some kind of parasite, or a guerilla war, where you use the enemy's strength against them," the man marveled. "Could you walk us through a specific example of how this might be done?"

"Sure," Geneviève replied. "You can derail both sides with a MIAO like 'abortion trauma,' or 'abortion scarring,' which may or may not exist, but you can spin a whole submemeplex around it. You force the pro-abortion and anti-abortion camps to talk about your meme, that women can be traumatized by abortion and shouldn't have them. It's a weapon the antis will use against the pros for you for free, establishing the MIAO."

"And the anti-abortion camp?" the man prompted.

"You can derail their fetal heartbeats and sanctity of life with, 'You're not the only one who knows cannibalism is horrible. It's a famine, people are starving, literally killing and eating each other, and you're milking it for political gain. How dare you?' That's one of many immunomemes that could be constructed within this memeplex. You could beat both sides over the head about how neither is working to prevent unwanted pregnancies, but you don't call it that, you focus on the poor women and girls who wind up killing their babies or facing the clothes-hanger-of-the-back-alley abortionist."

"Okay, but that sounds a bit simplistic," the younger woman protested. "A lot of voters aren't in favor of sex education, for various reasons which are closely tied to their views on abortion. It seems like what you're saying just ignores that, but the voters won't."

"Okay, okay," Geneviève said, "you have a point, but the idea is to sidestep those sticky points. Let me be clear that I'm talking about engineering a solution to a political problem, and not about solving a real-world one. I maintain that I require macromemetics for both, but I must also be in power for the latter. Rather, one heartbeat away from holding the reins of power, which is what we're talking about right now. To answer your question, I'd try a number of submemeplexes. For instance, 'We have to prevent a woman from getting into the situation where she would even consider an abortion. It's really too late at that point and we've failed her as a community. Whether you're pro-abortion or anti-abortion, if a woman is alone, standing in front of an abortion clinic, then you've already failed her. Building more abortion clinics doesn't solve that problem. If you say you care about women and babies, but you're leaving that girl alone there, then you're just a Pharisee.' Oh, and I can really beat liberals over the head with the sex education thing, since many of them don't practice sex education themselves, and probably got their sons circumcised. Beating up one side or the other makes me look good to the other side, and macromemetically speaking, it means they use my memes."

Geneviève thought, I don't know what more I can say to impress these people. This 'first date' is wrapping up. Either we kiss and say goodbye here, or we take it to the next level.

"Say," she ventured, "my students could start popping in at any moment if we don't get out of here. I don't know about you three, but I could use some lunch."

"That's an excellent idea," the leader woman said. "Is there a restaurant near here where we can speak privately?"

"Well," Geneviève told her, "there's a good Persian place down on Howard Street in the Old Market District. They could probably get us a quiet table."

They all walked out to the visitor parking lot where the Electors had parked their rented sedan.

Geneviève sat in the back seat with the leader woman.

The leader lady spoke to the Maître d' of Ahmed's Persian Cuisine and they were seated at a table in the corner, away from the windows.

Geneviève said, "Tell me, to what do I owe the pleasure of a group from the Electoral College coming all the way out here to Omaha just to see little old me? I assumed we could do without a face-to-face meeting."

"We felt it important to meet with you outside of Washington," the woman in pale purple replied. "There's a lot that goes on behind the scenes."

That's an understatement, Geneviève thought. There's a lot they're not telling me. They're taking a risk by coming here. This is a high-stakes game. The potential for monetary gain is astronomical, but it ultimately has to be about power. That's the only way to cover up winnings from long bets on the Vice-Presidential outcome. But how can control of the Vice-President's office give them that?

"I am an outsider, but I'm not entirely naïve," Geneviève began. "We're not just talking about Washington. Las Vegas is a big part of this, too, or am I wrong? If I look like a long shot, that also makes me a good bet, right?"

The Electors all became grave.

The leader lady broke the awkward silence. "Professor Thomas, as you've no doubt surmised, we have come here to draft you as a candidate for the Vice-Presidency. Obviously, we couldn't summon you to Washington without raising suspicion of favoritism and insider dealing. Our coming here is only marginally better. You know as well as I do that there's no way around the gambling angle. If we reveal you to the public too soon, we can't do the groundwork, the memetic engineering, we need to, and we destroy any chance of your actually being elected. By the same token, with the state of the election and the odds the gambling industry is making, anyone privy to our conversation today stands to make a huge sum by betting on your victory. But that's the way it has to be."

There it is, Geneviève thought as she stared into the woman's eyes. They know they can get me in. But she's not going to tell me the rest. Garner's an idiot, a puppet backed by shadow money, and they all know it. They already have plans to get rid of him after the election, replace him with me, and they want me to help them do it. It's the chance of a hundred lifetimes.

The giddy thrill she felt turned into a chill, a sudden vertigo.

If they're going to destroy Garner, maybe kill him, they can do the same to me. It's too late to back out. No, Geneviève thought with a strange sense of relief, there was never any choice here. I have to play this through to the end.

The head Elector held Geneviève's gaze, then asked levelly, "Professor Thomas, do we have an understanding?"

"Hell," Geneviève replied, "we have an agreement. I'll even shake on it."

As she extended her hand, she noticed how much it was trembling.

The head Elector smirked and took her hand in a weak grip.

Geneviève scooped up some lamb and couscous with her last scrap of bread, and said, chewing, "We should probably leave separately," and after washing her food down with a gulp of tea, added, "I can get a cab back to the university."

A mild smile crept across the lead Elector's face, and the other two looked simply relieved.

Geneviève strolled out of Ahmed's Persian Cuisine and wandered up the cobblestones of Howard Street towards the shops just at the top of the gentle rise. She looked up and down the street for a cab and, seeing none, glanced back into her own reflection in the window of a stylish boutique, her own wash-and-wear tweediness clashing with the haute couture clothing and accessories behind the glass. Sneering and dismissive three- and four-digit numbers lurking beneath each item, like little trolls under a bridge, denying her passage, now smeared into warm blurs, inviting her to cross.

Normally I never give these kinds of shops a second look, she thought, her eyes lingering as never before on the treasures arrayed within. She imagined herself slipping them around her wrists, onto her feet, around her waist and shoulders, and how that might feel.

As the cab pulled away from the curb, Geneviève rolled her head onto the back of the seat and stared up at the ceiling for a moment. She closed her eyes and took a deep breath, then fished her phone from her jacket pocket.

"Perry? It's Gene," she said into the phone.

"Genie?" the voice on the phone said. "It's been a while. Say, I'm a little busy now to place one of your crazy bets, what with the election and all."

"Funny you should mention that," Geneviève replied. "I want to put fifty large on the Vice-Presidential election."

"Are you kidding me, Gino? Do you have any idea the odds of picking a Veep vote in the College, let alone the election, for Christ's sake? Especially the way things are now."

"Let's say I do have some idea," Geneviève replied.

"Okay, I'll bite. Who's your pick for the next Veep, Professor?"

"Geneviève Ashton Thomas," she replied.

"Is this another one of your crazy experiments? No, I'm not even gonna ask. It's your funeral, Gene. Consider it done."

Geneviève said, "Wire my winnings to my numbered account at the Standing Rock, South Dakota branch of the Full-Service Native American Bank."

Talking to some people is like talking to a rock. It's frustrating. To the contrary, talking to an actual rock is relaxing because the rock is guaranteed to maintain a sympathetic silence, no matter the gravity of the sin confessed. Imagine the surprise, then, should the rock reply.

DRAGONANGEL

Guy Worthey

The Loneliness came, as scheduled. The dragons wept and clung to each other as the appointed hour rushed closer. Not literal tears, of course, for the dragons of Aquarius were mineral life forms devoid of water. Not literal hugs, of course, for the dragons of Aquarius seldom took delight in the textures of pressure on whatever exterior they presented to the universe. Therefore, they seldom morphed the necessary sensory organs to detect a hug, much less appreciate one. But, psychically, the agonies of imminent separation were palpable. The anticipated grief almost overwhelming.

Then the dragons scattered. Distraught and fearful, they dispersed, each to their preassigned latitude and longitude coordinates. They changed, in the way of dragons. They modified their physical forms, using gamma rays from their neutron sun to drive their internal entropies in the directions they desired. In this case, they each grew more dense, englobing themselves in the toughest shell they could manage.

For many, perhaps most, the Loneliness would be the loneliness of death. For some, the Loneliness would mean life, but life in solitude. That was a hideous thought for a dragon, for the dragons of Aquarius were lovers and talkers and dreamers of shared dreams.

The white dwarf swept implacably through their planet as the mathematical prophets had foretold. The nuclear flash obliterated much of the planet instantly. Much of the remaining debris exploded outwards, but not quick enough to avoid the inexorable gravity of the white dwarf. Some detritus, however, accelerated beyond escape velocity. Dark, living pellets shot starward, along with droplets of cooling lava. Encapsulated dragons spread fanlike through the Galaxy. After the shock of ejection wore off, the shock of utter silence fell. The prophecy became reality. The Loneliness began. The forever-falling dragons called and called, but no-one answered.

They hurtled rudderless through empty, vibrationless space, weeping.

The spectacular Ophiucid meteor shower surprised even the experts. Most meteor showers arrived annually, their peak dates written on the calendar, but the Ophiucids fell only once in the knowledge of humankind. Arrows of light radiated from the starry fields of the serpent bearer and streaked to earth. Their brief flashes of incandescent fury made daylike shadows pop into existence all over the Western hemisphere. Hundreds, perhaps thousands of pieces large and small struck the ground, splashing out crater scars in the patient, forgiving earth.

Father Arazon's introduction to the Ophiucids was abrupt and painful. He walked along a cool, dark track in rural Chihuahua. His weary footfalls raised clouds of dust unseen in the moonless night. The church house he shared with the two Sisters was being rebuilt, so Father Arazon lived alone for a while in an adobe cottage that belonged to one of his parishioners. It was a long walk from the Ruiz farm, where the Father had wasted his time in fruitless conversation.

Arazon glanced up at the star spangled sky. "What can I do, Holy Father? Julio will not plant oats in his opium poppy field."

The sky answered. A blue-white line traced itself across the heavenly dome, then slowly faded from view. Arazon inhaled sharply at the sight, then exhaled with a drawn-out sigh of wonder. "Too often, we walk sightless among miracles, but, tonight, I have seen."

Father Arazon lowered his eyes from the silent stars to the outline of the small house that was his destination. Contemplations of starry beauty transformed into thoughts of the comfort of the bed that awaited him.

A blue light began to illuminate the scene. The shadowy cottage resolved into sharp focus as the light brightened and brightened. Too quick for thought, the light descended into the house, as if a blue sun had come to roost at its center, sending blinding rays through the windows. The house walls became jagged fragments that expanded outwards. In a few milliseconds, the shock waves caught up with the light. The blast hurled Father Arazon backwards. The blinding light and deafening cacophony became his world. The ground slammed his aging body.

He cried out, but his ears heard only ringing. He blinked, but his eyes saw only white afterimages. His back pressed cool earth, but his front blushed with a flare of heat, as if he was standing in front of an open oven door.

Slowly, he patted himself down with numbed hands. He did not seem to be bleeding. He could feel his rosary beads, and they gave him comfort as he sat blind and deaf and bruised. The smell of burned wood constricted his nostrils. The taste of powdered adobe coated his tongue.

He spoke, unable to hear his own words, "Blessed Mother Mary, blessed Jesus Christ, into your hands I am delivered! Is it war? Is it some kind of accident?"

Only the ringing in his ears answered him. And so he sat still, and mumbled to himself as his heart slowly calmed. "Truly, Father, Son, and Holy Ghost, you have sent an angel to watch over me. I am humble and low, but yours is the glory. Blessed am I."

It seemed to Father Arazon that his thoughts echoed and stirred, like an invisible vortex of air lifting dust to become a visible whirl. He was suddenly struck with the certainty that he was not alone. Almost a spectator in his own mind, he watched memories unfold. Arazon as a boy, touching a cactus, touching the thorny crown, touching his mother's smile. The boy's lips sounded out the names of the angels as his young finger traced each wondrous inked syllable. Azrael. Gabriel. Zophiel. Severe nuns rapped his knuckles. His first mass. First christening. First last rites. The layers of experience piled high as his youthful body thickened and slowed.

Dreamers of shared dreams.

The cool Chihuahua night stole back into its own. The radiant heat faded. The smell of burning wood disappeared. The ringing in Father Arazon's ears grew less insistent, and he sat up. When he blinked his eyes, an indistinct blob of light appeared and changed shape. "An angel to watch over me," repeated Arazon. With each blink, the shining figure clarified: broad feathered wings, noble face, spotless robes, and golden eyes.

"You must be a brother to Gabriel, in your majesty and light," he said. To his surprise, he heard his own words under the ringing. "What? What? I can hear!" he shouted joyously, trying to leap to his feet. But one leg was full of pain, so he stood wobbly and almost fell over.

A strong hand found his and held him steady. The hand was warm, but hard like marble, though it moved like flesh. Father Arazon's breath caught in his throat. He looked over and up at the shining angel figure, slowly realizing that his hallucination was real, and shining tall, and holding his hand in a gently immovable, steadfast clasp.

"What is your name, Angel?" the Father queried tremulously.

The angel's mouth did not move, but his body vibrated like a struck bell, making eerie noises that flitted and danced over the musical scale. The tones pulsed and fuzzed and eventually resolved themselves into words. "Zzz ... Zo ... Zophiel ... I am called Zophiel."

Arazon half sobbed, half laughed, "Ah, ha, ha! As I imagined. All my childhood, I wanted Zophiel to be my guardian, ever since I learned his name. Your name. The angel of wisdom. And so it has come true. Zophiel. I meet you at last. Dear Zophiel."

"I am Zophiel, your guardian angel," the shining seraph resonated.

"Am I dead, Zophiel?"

"Neither of us is dead. Neither of us is alone."

Arazon clung to the warm yet stony hand. He smiled for a whole minute before speaking again. "When I look away from your radiance, I see stars. I think I can see again."

"You are weary, Arazon. You need sleep."

"I am too excited to sleep," laughed Arazon. But Zophiel folded himself to sit on the ground, and Arazon curled into the angel's warm lap.

The angel sang, wordlessly and with many voices like a choir. The harmonies entwined hypnotically. Arazon forgot his bruises. It seemed to him that he chased the fugue as it curled, and stepped from the earth into the air, weightless and free. He followed the melodies from bright cloudscapes of consciousness into even brighter regions beyond.

Arazon blinked his eyes open. "Zophiel?"

"I am here, Arazon," the marblesque lap hummed.

"Then all is well."

Dawn came. The sky lit with regal tapestries woven in blue and orange.

A faint, urgent voice called, "Father Arazon! Father Arazon!"

Arazon rose from his angel bed, and took Zophiel's hand. The angel stood, too. Arazon saw the crater for the first time. The bits that were left of his adobe manse were splattered outward from the impact site, much of it charred black. Arazon's jaw dropped. The sight was so arresting that the calling voice was forgotten for a moment, but it came back, almost at the priest's elbow.

"Father Arazon! Father Arazon! Who is that? An ... an angel? But can you come? The drug men are back!"

Arazon wrenched his head around to view scrawny Matias, a lad who lived at the farm next to Julio Ruiz's. Arazon glanced up and over to the tall angel, whose wings arched wide. Arazon answered Matias softly, "We will come. This is Zophiel, angel of wisdom."

The dusty track was long, but Arazon was already covered in dust. Zophiel flowed over the ground, smoothing it slightly during his passage. Matias's fleet fifteen year old feet wanted to fly down the road, but he held his pace to match Arazon's limping. His young eyes drifted often to the silent angel.

The dust-caked 4x4 hulked ominously by the Ruiz's small house. Over the crunching of their feet Arazon heard wails of from within the house. "No! No! No!" Feminine sobs. Was it Rosa? Arazon strode forward and reached for the handle of the closed door. Meaty slap sounds and pain-filled grunts made him pause.

Arazon ordered Matias, "Stay outside!" even as he himself pushed in. The tableau inside brought his feet to a stunned halt. Arms pinned behind her, Rosa Ruiz struggled in the grip of the shorter opium buyer. He made her face her husband Julio, scrabbling on the floor, and the other opium runner standing over Julio. Mouth agape and wide eyes uncomprehending, a small boy sheltered under the rough kitchen table. He was Pedro, Rosa and Julio's child.

The taller drug man dragged Julio Ruiz off the floor. Julio could not stand on his own. Vivid blood streamed down Julio's glazed face, staining his shirt front all the way to his belt buckle. Blood covered the fist and brass knuckles of the taller drug man.

The tall one grinned at Arazon and cocked his bloody fist back. "Come to watch, Father?" He leered at Arazon, then smashed Julio in the face. Blood flecks splattered on a shabby window and the tin pot they used to heat water for oatmeal or tea. Julio dropped in a heavy heap on the dirt floor, moaning faintly.

Rosa cried again, "No!"

"Stop!" Arazon's paralysis evaporated. He held his hands out in supplication, palms up.

The tall one frowned and loomed over Arazon, ignoring the farmer scrabbling in the dirt. He said, "Father. You're on our side. Tell this dirtbag to stop his talk of finding other buyers. Filthy cheat."

"No!" Father Arazon's heart pounded in his chest.

"Don't you tell me no!" snarled the man. He powered his brass-knuckled, blood-covered fist at Arazon's face.

It struck stone, instead. The silent Zophiel was suddenly there, a protective wing interposed between the fist and the priest. The impact clanked, brass and bone meeting mineral. The tall one screamed, again and again. Arazon could not see him very well with Zophiel there, but his screams faded out in the doorward direction.

The short one pushed Rosa away and down. She landed on hands and knees on the floor and crawled toward her husband Julio. The short one fumbled for a pistol stuck in his belt, babbling, "Angel? What the—? Crazy—!"

"Zophiel! Watch out! He's got a gun!" Arazon spun around to face the new danger and looked for a place to hide.

The short one emptied his clip, shooting wildly at Arazon and the angel. Bullets ricocheted, but Zophiel shifted his stance, quick as an eyeblink. Arazon's view of the muzzle flashes was blocked by beautiful white feathers, hard as stone.

Zophiel pivoted again. He enclosed the smoking snubnose in a cage of marble-white fingers. Part of his own hand caught in the angel's grip, the short drug man's eyes showed white all the way around. He yanked to escape, then yanked again. With a panicked bleat, he finally ripped free. Blood spurted. A severed finger fell to the dirt. The short one put his head down and ran through the door.

Abruptly, the only sound was Rosa calling, "Julio? Julio?" She stroked his hair and cradled his injured head.

Gradually, his dazed eyes sharpened. "Rosa. Oh, Rosa."

Arazon said, "Zophiel. You saved me!" He stepped to the door to watch the drug men. Each down to one functional hand, they struggled to get in their truck, and start it, and drive away. When they managed it at last, Arazon heaved a shaky sigh and realized he was trembling.

Inside, something felt empty. Zophiel stood, peaceful and tall, mineral eyes placidly watching Arazon. Rosa cradled Julio's beaten head on her lap. She looked at Arazon. And then they all remembered. They looked.

Little Pedro lay motionless under the table. His eyes, still uncomprehending and perfectly still, slowly glazed.

It was Julio's duty to lay Pedro out and pull a sheet over the tiny, cooling body. Matias ran with the news, and neighbors came. Friends all, and many of them relatives. More would continue to come over the next day or two, bringing small gifts and what comfort they could to Rosa and Julio. Arazon spoke the ancient words, "In sure and certain hope of the resurrection to eternal life through our Lord Jesus Christ, we commend to Almighty God our child Pedro Ruiz. The Lord bless him and keep him, the Lord make his face to shine upon him and be gracious unto him and give him peace. Amen."

Zophiel was present, but still. Only the angel's presence spoke to the room, his light shining even into the corners of the rustic home. Zophiel was treated as an altar. Whenever anyone made the sign of the cross, they faced his direction. And whenever they knelt. And whenever they clasped their hands in prayer.

Arazon took his leave. His own still-shaking hand holding the hand of his angel, he left the leaden atmosphere of the house and stepped into the bright day. Hours and hours had passed. Rosa's inconsolable keening echoed and reechoed in his memory.

Arazon stopped just outside the door. He didn't know where to go.

Faintly, from inside, he heard neighbors talking.

"Angel of death."

"Angel of peace."

"I heard Julio say he will plant oats."

Arazon walked, brow furrowed, in any direction away from the Ruiz's house. He glanced to Zophiel, who sparkled like a million tiny diamonds in the sunlight. Arazon said, "You are beautiful. But the explosion wasn't a dream, was it? The little house is destroyed?"

"Yes. I am sorry."

"We'll have to stay at the chapel, I suppose. Are you hungry?"

"It is cold, here. I will always be hungry, I think."

The pair changed direction. Arazon asked, "What does that mean, always hungry?"

"Where I am from, it is warmer. The warmth is food for me. I apologize. I do not have words to describe it better." The angel's lips never moved, but Arazon could feel the words buzzing through his hand as it clung needily to Zophiel's.

"There is no need to apologize, dear Zophiel. I know the ways of heaven cannot be comprehended by men. I was just worried about you. At the chapel, there may only be stale communion bread to eat."

"I do not eat bread, never fear."

They walked, holding hands. Zophiel's feet could not be seen, and he did not leave footprints. The path behind him was smoother after his passage.

The adobe chapel was cool compared with the sunny afternoon. Water and bread revived Arazon, at least in body. "Why did you come down to me, Zophiel? And what happened to the house?"

"I came. I did not choose it. I think you would say that God sent me. But if that is true, He did not explain why or how. As for your house, I fell on it. My speed was approximately forty kilometers per second. The impact hurt me, but less, I think, than it hurt you, my friend."

"The stuff angels are made of must be tough." But it was obvious: Zophiel's hand did not compress at all when Arazon squeezed, and bullets did not hurt him.

There was a brief silence.

Zophiel said, "The death of Pedro Ruiz troubles you."

"Yes, Zophiel. Wise Zophiel. You know my thoughts, it seems to me."

"Only when you dream, Arazon."

The priest studied the glowing seraph, realizing that he had a confessor. "Pedro was a happy blessing for Julio and Rosa. I married them. Such a beautiful couple."

Arazon smiled nostalgically up at Zophiel. Then his eyes filled up with tears.

He wiped them away. "They will carry on. They will have many more children, God willing."

Zophiel waited, patient until more words came.

Arazon's brow furrowed. He clenched his fists. Finally, he burst out, "Zophiel! Wise Zophiel. Why do innocent children die? I want to blame someone. I want to blame the drug lords, or the gun makers. Julio wanted to blame Julio, Rosa wanted to blame Rosa. I do not know if my feeble words helped them to shed their guilt. I want to blame Satan. I cannot blame you, dear Zophiel! Not for Pedro. But children die. From disease, sometimes, or freak accident. Who can I blame for that, except God?" Arazon looked pleadingly at Zophiel, gripping the warm marble hand with desperation.

Zophiel's face, noble and serene, regarded Arazon. The angel's eyes seemed not to move at the whites, but the iris and pupil swam to different locations on the white ball, sparkling when they moved, but still when they were still.

Zophiel took his time in answering, but Arazon didn't mind. How could he? "I am your guardian angel, now, Arazon, but before I met you I was," Zophiel searched for words. "I was a dragon. One dragon among many. We, like you, sought after God, but never found Him. And we never found an answer to your question, though we asked it, over and over. My answer is that I do not know, Arazon. I do not know why Pedro Ruiz died this morning."

Arazon leaned on Zophiel. Tears leaked down his face. "I tell people that God has a plan. Do you think that's wrong?"

"I told you. I am a seeker, like you."

"But you are an angel! An angel of God! What is this dragon word?"

"You are an angel of God, too, Arazon."

"I am a man!"

Zophiel's face flowed into a tender smile. "I am sure that species does not matter. Tell me what an angel does."

"Angels sing praise and watch over mortals and carry messages from God to people."

"You do those things, do you not? You did all those things this very day."

Father Arazon was silent. He raised two fingers to massage his own forehead. "Wisdom makes my head hurt."

"We are both angels, Arazon. You are a man angel. I am a dragon angel."

"I," Arazon stammered, a new gush of tears flooding his eyes, "I try!"

"I did not mean to make you cry, Arazon. Are you still glad that I am your guardian angel?"

Arazon replied in a rush. "Yes! Oh, yes! I hope we never part. Already, I love you like a brother. I love you like breathing."

"Something still troubles you, Arazon. Tell me about it," Zophiel resonated.

Arazon winced. "Well, now it's you. I am worried that you're not the sort of angel I thought you were. You are like a sculpture of an angel. You fell from the sky and you say that you once were a dragon. You are not, perhaps," Arazon swallowed. "Not from heaven."

"I do not have words to tell you where I came from."

"From the stars?"

"Yes, from the stars. Ordinary parts of the universe. Not extraordinary parts like heaven."

"But you look like Zophiel, angel of wisdom. And you said you were Zophiel!"

Zophiel hesitated. "Yes. I hope I was correct. I wanted to be Zophiel, because you wanted and needed Zophiel."

"I?"

"You dreamt of Zophiel. You needed Zophiel. I wanted to gift you with what you desired. I made myself into that shape."

Arazon's mouth opened and closed twice. He tapped his finger on the unyielding warm stone of Zophiel's robes, each fold of fabric carved to mimic the flow of actual cloth. "One thing is certain. You are going to attract a lot of attention," Arazon predicted gloomily.

"I am? I thought I fit in well, today."

"Yes, you will. Today was nothing. Reporters will come. Scientists will want to cut you up. My bishop will want you to be his angel instead of mine!" Arazon's voice rose.

"Calm yourself, dear Arazon. I will not go. I am your guardian angel, not his."

"Why? What keeps you here?"

"I am your Zophiel. I am not lonely when I am with you."

Father Arazon smiled and patted Zophiel's hand. "You are afraid of being alone?"

"Yes."

"It seems like a small thing, to be here so that you are not alone."

"It is a very important thing, to me. I am lucky. For me, the Loneliness is over, if you will let me be your guardian angel."

"I can be here for you, Zophiel."

"Then you are an angel to me."

"Yes, if you wish to use that word. I can be your angel, just not a heavenly one. We will face the reporters and scientists and bishops as a team."

"Together?"

"Together."

Assuming one obeys the laws of physics, it is nigh impossible to achieve orbital velocity using steam propulsion. Mark Rounds invents a clever, albeit terrifying, method for achieving the necessary delta vee, and writes a rousing steampunk yarn in the process.

MAD AS A ROCKETEER

Mark Rounds

Sir Ian Campbell, the British Empire's new Minister of the Void, charged with overseeing all of Great Britain's possessions near the earth and on Mars and the Moon, stepped onto the landing at Liverpool harbor. His formal morning coat and silk hat looked incongruous among the naval ratings' rough working kit and the undress uniforms of their officers.

"Now, you're sure this contraption is quite safe?" he asked as he looked over the compartment of the ethereal ship HMS Constance. The ship itself was not all that impressive, resembling the shell of some gargantuan gun. The crew compartment was forward with a cockpit and passenger space. There was a cargo space immediately aft that was not air tight.

"Most assuredly, Sir," said Captain Brumley. "The initial launch is entirely by steam pressure jet followed by the propulsive cannon. No more mercury vapors for the crew and, more importantly, the passengers."

"That is reassuring certainly, but what about the propulsive cannon?" said the Minister. "Surely that is an issue?"

"There were some regrettable incidents early in their development," said Brumley hurriedly, "but they have been ironed out with better ammunition and a more precise triggering. The recoil shield has also been improved. I realize the thought of being fired on by 12-inch naval rifles is daunting, but they are very accurate and it's far cheaper to fire from the ground than to engage a mercury engine."

"Oh, quite," said Sir Ian as he entered the cabin. "I am sure you have it well in hand. I have only had the Ministry for a few weeks, Brumley. An inspection of the ethereal outpost is part of my job."

"Yes, Sir," said Brumley. "The new ethereal outpost is important to our trade with Mars and the moon. I do worry about the pirates out of Venus, however."

"You're a military man," said Campbell quietly. "I'm not Royal Navy, but I did serve in the Army — during the Mutiny, you know. The men need to see their commander with them. I must go."

Brumley nodded, then dogged the hatch and breathed a sigh of relief. He had advised against this visit, but the Minister would have none of it. That being the case, he planned to pilot this flight himself. His preflight inspection had been more than thorough. He was sure that his craft was as good as British engineering could make it.

But the Irish rebels were active. There had been another bombing in London, this time it had been at the Irish Special Branch and there were VIPs among the casualties.

His inspections turned up nothing, so Brumley entered the main cabin of the Constance. He nodded to the Minister who, with the help of his aide, was strapping himself into his cushioned seat and turned to the left and went forward into the cockpit. There, his coxswain was already in his seat, buckled in, and adjusting his trim wheels.

"How does she look, sir?" asked Able Seaman Whitaker.

"She's in fine fettle," said Brumley easily. "As soon as our passenger is strapped in, I'll raise the flag."

"Looks like he's settled sir," said Whitaker looking over his shoulder. "That young pup with him is also in his seat."

"Tally ho," said Brumley as he yanked on the cord. There was no communication with the outside world with the hatch in place, save for flags, printed signs, and the occasional knock on the hull. In a window, visible to the ground crew, a shutter went from red to green, the signal the crew inside was ready to launch. The harness around the ethereal ship tightened as the steam crane began to lift it into an upright position.

"I say," said the Minister rather worriedly, "are things going appropriately?"

"Yes Minister," said Brumley in a reassuring tone, "the stevedores are merely setting the ship upright and connecting the steam hoses. It will take a few minutes to pressurize the steam vessel and we're off!"

There was a series of bumps and then an unsettling moment when it felt like the ethereal ship was swinging freely. Then, another loud thump, and the ethereal ship stopped moving. Steam could be heard hissing into the pressure vessel below the crew cabin.

"We'll have release very soon now, Minister," said Brumley. "This is the delicate portion of the operation. Once the pressure vessel is filled and the ship mounted on the pedestal, we must launch as soon as possible. Otherwise, the steam will cool and we will lose lift."

"Oh right, like a tea kettle," said the Minister brightly.

"Quite," said Brumley. "Then, after we clear a thousand feet, the naval guns will fire. Each one precisely aimed to strike the bottom of the ethereal ship on the recoil shield. The high explosive shells will push us up into the void."

The stevedores rapped three times on the hull signifying that they were ready for release.

"Settle in, Minister," said Brumley as he pulled on the signaling cord a second time. The shutters in the signaling portal went back from green to red signifying that they were ready for launch. "Things are about to get a bit sporting."

"Er, what?" said the Minister nervously.

There was no time for Brumley to reply for the steam clamp released with a loud clang and the cabin was filled with the discordant scream of escaping steam. The occupants of the cabin were pushed back roughly in their couches as the steam escaped and accelerated the ethereal ship into the sky.

"Urk!" said the Minister involuntarily as the steam was expended and acceleration quickly ceased. The first impact of the naval shells was startling, especially as the first burst pushed them through the sound barrier. Each successive blast pushed the ship faster and faster.

The shock from the twelfth explosion, rather than coming from below, smacked the ethereal ship soundly on the port side, causing the ship to tumble out of control.

"What are you playing at up there, Brumley?" asked an agitated Minister as centripetal forces thrashed his inner ear. His aide apparently did not have as stern a stomach and became noisily sick.

"Whitaker," said Brumley, ignoring the shouting Minister in the passenger compartment, "is there any residual steam in the attitude thruster lines?"

"The gauge reads about 30 p.s.i., Captain," said Whitaker.

"Not enough then," said Brumley. They were two impacts shy being safely in the void. "Use enough to stop the tumbling," said Brumley. "But save as much as you can as we might have to try landing."

"Sir," said a shaken Whitaker quietly, "we don't have near enough steam for the landing sir. We'll hit awfully hard and likely splatter across the ground like a rotten apple. Isn't there any way to get back into the void?"

"I'm afraid it's up to the folks in Liverpool now," said Brumley. "Steady on, son."

"Sir," said the breathless ensign, "the Constance is tumbling!"

"Get a hold of yourself, ensign," said Commodore Welbourn, who, while a 'wooden ships and iron men' sort of sailor, had recently been seconded to the ethereal branch of the Royal Navy. He was much more in tune with the rigging of a frigate than the trajectory of an ethereal vessel in the void. He did, however, know men. "Take a breath and give me a proper report."

"Yes, sir," said the ensign, visibly calming himself. "At least one of the propulsive naval rifles was misaligned. Its shell detonated on the forward panels on the port side. Yeomen with telescopes trained on the Constance reported that there was damage to the outer hull and that she was tumbling, sir."

"Hold fast, lad," said Welbourn, patting the ensign's shoulder. "Run and get Chief Engineer McPhearson and Professor Symthe. Be quick, there is not a moment to lose!"

"Yes sir," said the ensign who vanished through the doorway. He immediately returned with Professor Symthe in tow.

"I was watching the launch from my office," said Symthe. "There seemed to be a spot of trouble, so I thought—"

The professor's words were interrupted as the sharp featured Chief Engineer McPhearson burst into the room.

"The Constance is in a wee bit o' trouble," said McPhearson. "She didna get the last two charges from the propulsive guns and the last one that did hit was off target."

"Will she make port?" said Welbourn.

"I doubt she can even remain aloft," said Symthe, "much less attain a high enough trajectory to dock with the ethereal outpost. I haven't made my calculations yet, but the Constance will, at most, manage three circuits of earth before she hits the atmosphere and burns up."

"How long does that give us?" asked Welbourn.

"I haven't done my calculations, mind," said Symthe, "but—"

"Oh fer gawd sake," interjected McPhearson vehemently, "guess man, guess."

"If we can't get to them in a couple of hours," said Symthe, stroking his chin, "they will have started to reenter the atmosphere and affecting a rescue will be difficult."

"Right," said Welbourn. "What have we got available for rescue?"

"That might be a wee bit difficult," said McPhearson. "The Active, the only other ethereal ship with a four-place cabin, has a cracked recoil shield."

"Damn it, man," said Welbourn. "We have twelve ships on the ground and more in the void. There is always supposed to be a backup ship available for launch."

"Oh aye, there is a ship," said McPhearson, "an auld one, but a good 'un. The Resolute is prepped and standing by."

"What am I missing?" asked Welbourn critically.

"The Resolute has a mercury vapor second stage," said McPhearson ruefully. "Most of the young pilots won't fly one. They claim there are problems with the vapors when they are under power."

"But we fulfill the statutes of the Alkali Acts to the letter," said Symthe vehemently. He had invented mercury-based propulsion twenty-five years ago. The system used a high-pressure natural gas flame to boil mercury and create a hot, dense jet suitable for propulsion. It worked well enough in the atmosphere where there was plentiful oxygen for the natural gas flame, but there was a worry about the toxic effect of mercury in the ship and in the air where the mercury vapor was vented.

"Laws made by rich men," said McPhearson rising to the fight, "to keep themselves rich."

"Is there anyone who will fly the thing?" interrupted Welbourn forcefully. "We don't have time to debate politics."

"There is one man," said McPhearson ruefully, "but he is … a wee bit difficult."

"You don't mean—" said Welbourn.

"One in the same I'm afraid," said McPhearson. "He has been the pilot of the Resolute for nigh unto three years."

"This will be deucedly difficult," said Welbourn. "I beached him yesterday, you know."

"I'm aware," said McPhearson disapprovingly. "The broken mercury valve in the Resolute dosed his particular friend Lieutenant Zackary pretty thoroughly. People say he hasn't been right in the head since. Perhaps you shouldn't have jumped Brumley so, after the accident."

"What's done is done," said Welbourn. "There's nothing for it, I'm afraid. There's not a moment to lose!"

Lieutenant Colin Baker swore as he dropped his pen holder, spilling ink all over his desk. Or, rather, what used to be his desk. He had a few more things to clear away and then he was off. After twelve years in the Royal Navy and eight as a pilot of ethereal ships, he was being beached. Being put on half pay was the euphemism, but he would never fly an ethereal ship again.

He knew most of it was his own fault. He didn't suffer fools gladly, and when one of them was in a position over him, it made things more difficult, especially over the last two years. His reverie was disturbed by a knock on the door.

"I say, Baker," said Commodore Welbourn diffidently. "Could I have a word?"

"I'm a beached lieutenant with no friends in high places," said Baker.

"Sod off might suit, but I'm curious what you have to say after our most recent contretemps."

"We don't get along, that's true," said Welbourn, "but we need you to fly the Resolute one more time."

"After I told you," said Baker distinctly, "that the Resolute was unsafe to fly. After I rather pointedly cast aspersions against your manhood and challenged you to a duel. After you beached me, you have the gall to ask me to fly again?"

"We have our differences," said Welbourn swallowing his pride, "but there is an urgent matter we need to discuss. Sir Ian Campbell is flying on the Constance."

"What of it?" said Baker desultorily.

"There was sabotage," said Welbourn coldly. "Someone shimmed the last three propulsive cannons. They would go into detent properly, but they were slightly misaligned. The Special Branch is looking into it now. What that means is—"

"I know what it means!" shouted Baker. "It means you are accusing me of treason. I should—"

"Baker. Enough," said Welbourn sharply. "We don't get along you and I, that's obvious, but never have I doubted your devotion to king and country. You weren't like this when you were a midshipman and I was first lieutenant on the Indefatigable. Maybe there is something to this mercury vapor issue, but that's not germane to the present circumstance. What we need is for you to take the Resolute and rescue Sir Ian."

"The cabin on the Resolute has room for only two passengers," said Baker, his fury forgotten. "Even if I left my coxswain behind, I'd have room for only three."

"Captain Brumley is in command of the Constance," said Welbourn. "He will know what to do."

"That, he will," said Baker, pausing for thought. "I'll need to meet with Chief Engineer McPhearson. I have some modifications to make. I am going to need all the thrust I can get out of the old lady. I may have an idea on how to pull this off."

"He is waiting in my office," said Welbourn, indicating the door.

"The launch window is small," said Professor Symthe, "but if we can get you launched in the next twelve minutes, you can make the rendezvous."

"I'm ready," said Baker.

"There are still a number of preflight checks to complete," said McPhearson, holding his notebook.

"You built a good ship, Alan McPhearson," said Baker kindly, "I trust it will fly straight and true."

"God go with you, you daft Scotsman," said McPhearson favoring Baker with a rare smile. "Just bring it back in one piece!"

"Always the worrier," said Baker as he closed the hatch, sealing off further debate. He quickly settled into the command chair and set his restraints. Then with a shake of his head he pulled the cable that connected to the warning flag.

In a few minutes the steam valve popped, and the acceleration built rapidly. The Chief Engineer had agreed with Baker, and so, many of the fittings in the Resolute had been removed to decrease the weight and increase the available thrust. In less than a minute, the steam in the reservoir was expended. Explosive bolts severed the lower stage which parachuted to safety.

A carefully measured flow of liquid mercury was released into the firebox to be heated by the natural gas jets. The resulting dense, high pressure jet from the vents in the stern increased the acceleration dramatically. The turbulence followed by a soft pop that signaled the breaking of the sound barrier, once thought to be impenetrable.

The reduced weight of the ship made the handling characteristics different and it required all of Baker's attention. Soon, the burners shut down due to lack of oxygen. Baker closed the valve that controlled the flow of mercury and tapped the gauge.

Hmmm, thought Baker, *there is more than a third left in the tank. We may be able to make this work.*

Using built up pressure in gas lines, Baker maneuvered the Resolute toward the rendezvous. The trick was to come close enough to be seen without causing a collision.

Soon the Constance was visible through his forward portal. Baker could see the port side was dished in and they were losing water vapor through the maneuvering system. There were occasional bursts of steam from the forward jets to keep the Constance from tumbling. It told Baker that the crew was still alive. Baker had his hands full with the trim wheels to make sure the forward port panels of his ship were visible and the closure rate was acceptable. Too fast, and the structural integrity of the Constance could fail. The next bit was up to Brumley.

"That's the old Resolute closing, sir!" shouted Seaman Whitaker. In the confines of the Constance's cabin everyone heard it.

"Easy does it, Whitaker," said Captain Brumley. It had been a strain, keeping the Constance from tumbling and at the same time keep everyone's morale on the positive side. The Minister was made of surprisingly stern stuff, but his aide was prone to panic.

"There is writing on the Resolute's hull," said Whitaker in a more subdued tone.

"Here is my glass," said Brumley handing him his telescope. "What can you make of it?"

"There has been some scorching," said Whitaker, "but I think it says 'Vent your steam tank and jettison. Will take you under tow.'"

"Say that again, Whitaker?" said an incredulous Brumley. "You can't tow an ethereal ship."

"It's as right as rain," said Whitaker. "He is flashing his shutters red to green to see if we understand."

"Give him a green flag," said Brumley. "It's not as if we have a real choice in the matter. Use the aft nozzle so perhaps we can get a little more speed and give the pilot, whoever he is, a little more time."

Baker saw the green flag followed by a short steam jet from the rear nozzle of the Constance. They didn't get five feet per second off that vent, but Brumley was clearly trying to enhance his trajectory to give him more time.

It took Brumley longer than Baker would have liked to jettison his pressure vessel. But, in due course, the explosive bolts fired, and the tank tumbled free.

Now for the tricky part, thought Baker as he nudged the Resolute into the cavity left by steam tank. He had to close slow enough that they wouldn't lose structure integrity. With a gentle bump, Baker connected to the Constance.

Up till now, Baker had the ability to make the ethereal outpost on the vapor he had in the ship. Now, he was committed. First, he donned his emergency helmet. The tank in his chair held, perhaps, fifteen minutes of air. Then, with a gulp, he opened the mercury valve and the natural gas valve, and vented all his cabin air plus reserves into the fire box. Then he punched the ignition button. The acceleration pushed him back into his chair. Baker sweated under his helmet, working very hard to keep the ships properly aligned. All too soon, the air was exhausted, and the acceleration faded away to nothing.

Now we wait, thought Baker.

"Did you see what the Resolute just did?" exclaimed Whittaker as he looked out the aft port of the Constance.

"That would have been difficult," said Brumley, rather testily. "You are the only one with an aft-facing port."

"The pilot," said Whitaker, gesturing wildly toward the aft. "He opened the natural gas vents and then relit them. He could only do that with his cabin air! Has he gone daft? Is he suicidal? He burned up all his breathing air!"

"Perhaps daft," said Brumley, who smiled for the first time since the ship had tumbled. "He is a rocketeer after all."

A disheveled Sir Ian Campbell exited the Constance's hatch shaking his head. The tug from the ethereal outpost had not been gentle, but they were docked, and he had work to do.

"Where is the pilot of the Resolute?" asked Campbell.

"Here, Sir," said a medical orderly.

"Is he hurt?" asked Campbell.

"The air got a bit stuffy is all, Sir," said Lieutenant Baker as he struggled to a more upright position.

"Captain Brumley said no one has ever pushed an ethereal ship like that, before," said Campbell. "What possessed you to do it?"

"It seemed like a likely idea, Sir," said Baker.

"Get well soon, Lieutenant," said Campbell, patting his shoulder. "We will have need of men like you."

"Minister, if you please?" said the young midshipman assigned to guide him in the unfamiliar environment.

"Young man," said Campbell to the ensign as they were walking down the corridor. "Do you know what that man just did?"

"No, Sir," said the midshipman. He couldn't have been more than fourteen.

"Captain Brumley said he used his cabin air and all his reserve air to heat the mercury, so we could get here safely," said Campbell in awe. "The man is mad. Mad as a rocketeer!"

Mark Rounds

Sometimes that sense of otherness sits inside ourselves. How do we deal with it, when it feels like we don't quite belong anywhere? Here's a tale about a teenager feeling stuck between two worlds, and stuck in Spokane. But this isn't quite the Spokane we know (and love). Read on.

SALT WATER

Sonya Bramwell

"Come on," I whispered, tugging Pieter down the dark hall to my bedroom. He shuffled and hesitated. Navigating through a house must be as unfamiliar to him as walking on the moon. My home was as familiar to me as my own body, but I saw it fresh through Pieter's eyes. I noticed the scuff marks on the worn, patterned rug. Thick dust colonized on the picture frames hanging on the stuccoed walls. I hadn't really looked at any of the photos and album covers in a long time, but now my mind tried to categorize the complex pattern in which Dad had hung them.

Pieter paused and leaned close to one of the framed covers, his scraggly goatee practically brushing the glass. "Is that Sirena? The famous singer?"

If I'd let him, he would see that every one of those album covers on the wall were hers. From behind the dusty glass, Sirena's big blue eyes accused me for the neglect. I pulled his arm until he unglued himself. "Yeah, we're big fans around here," I muttered.

We slunk past the bathroom. A slice of weak aquamarine light pooled under the closed door and I sucked in a breath.

Crap, Mom is still awake. I pressed a finger against my lips, then led Pieter into my room and carefully shut the door.

"Are you sure this is okay?" Pieter whispered. He looked adorably frightened, his amber eyes wide and his goat-like ears flicking this way and that in nervous twitches.

"As long as we're quiet," I giggled and drew him to me. He gasped as I slid my hands under his t-shirt. I pressed up against his chest and tilted my face. "Kiss me."

"This doesn't feel right," he went on haltingly as I traced circles on the wiry muscles of his back. "Your parents might not like a guy like me in your home. Our kinds don't usually intermingle, you know."

"Ugh, come on." I tossed my head back. The plastic glow-in-the-dark stars on my ceiling gleamed their sickly green light down at me. I'd pressed them in careful constellations to the ceiling as a six-year old. I had hoped for comfort and familiarity, but they'd always been poor replacements for the real night sky. During the coldest winter months we slept in our eco-friendly cobb house instead of under the mosquito netting set up in our backyard and I would miss the stars so badly my chest would ache.

An ache like the one I felt now, less sharp but constantly present. An ache for something I could never name. A hollow in my chest begging to be filled but rejecting everything I had thrown at it over the last few years.

Wild disregard for rules? No.

Piercings and tattoos? Nope.

Drugs? No, not even the human kinds.

Sex? Yet to be discovered.

I turned my gaze back to Pieter. "Don't you want to do this?"

"Well, yes," he stammered. "But I feel like this is really forced. Like you're pushing to make a point instead of just going with the flow. Maybe that's the human blood in you." He said it as if he were trying to figure out a puzzle more than finding faults, but I pushed away from him.

"Excuse me?"

"Cressa, I didn't mean it like that." He held his hands out. "I like every part of you. But you try to live so fast, I think you sometimes run over other people in your hurry."

I stuck out my chin, my chest tightening. "You'd better get out of here then, before you get run over."

He sighed and scrubbed his face with his hands and then ran his fingers through his curly auburn hair and around his horns. In the half-light from the plastic stars and window he looked deliciously wild and alien in my human room. His bejeweled snakebite piercings glinted, daring me to kiss him even in my anger. The smell of his leather jacket and the earthy forest scent of him beckoned to my inner-self, drawing me towards him the same way it had when I first met him two months earlier in the park on Halloween night, among all the other fae.

Guilt twinged through me at his exasperated, uncertain expression. He was right. I had been pushing too hard and I shouldn't have. I could mess it up with him, and that thought hit me like a pickaxe. I liked him. I really, really liked him, more than any other guy I'd dated or messed around with.

I wouldn't say sorry, because he'd ribbed me about my parentage and that was something I'd been teased about all my life, both directly and indirectly.

"Her eyes are weird," I'd hear the neighbor human kids whisper to each other.

"She stinks of human," the fae would sneer. I was too much of one thing and not enough of the other.

But Pieter hadn't seemed to care. And he stuck around, even after I'd been prickly towards him. I hadn't figured out why, yet. He wasn't a glutton for punishment, but he seemed to always forgive my bad attitude.

I let my shoulders drop with a sigh and he mirrored me. His posture told me that he would stay, yet again, even after I'd been obtuse towards his feelings.

I sat on the edge of my bed, a warm tingle of happiness wiggling through my earlier annoyance. He would stay. I patted the mattress next to me. He ambled over, his hooves brushing the wool carpet. What would my parents say if they knew I'd brought a faun home?

I found that I really didn't care and gave a mental half-shrug. Maybe I should care. Maybe I should be a good little girl. But I was so tired of that job.

The mattress sank as Pieter sat down next to me. He took my hand. "Your house is nice. It's way more suburban than I expected."

"Is it okay? Are you comfortable?"

"It's a little confining, but kind of cozy, too." He shrugged and studied my bedroom, the pile of dirty clothes on the closet floor, the ugly yellowish-green stars, the epic number of house plants balancing on any surface large enough to hold a pot. I looked at it all with him. Was it lacking? Was I lacking?

"That's why I asked you to come here," I said with a half-grin. "I want a little bit of wild in my life. Most of the time I feel like I'm just living out my Dad's interpretation of a nostalgic childhood. He's always cared too much about fitting in with the humans."

"It's okay to want to be a part of your heritage." Pieter shrugged. "He's what, half human and half pixie?"

I nodded.

"And your mom?"

I sighed and closed my eyes for a moment. I wondered if Pieter could hear the faint splash from the bathroom.

"You know the albums on the wall, of Sirena?"

He nodded.

I nodded.

His eyes flickered as he scanned my face, his expression opening into surprise. "Oh wow, you do look like her. She's a siren! Her music is crazy popular, with humans and fae both."

"Yeah, except her real name is Ondine. 'Sirena' is her working name. We basically live off the royalties from the three albums she did, like, fourteen years ago. Well, and Dad does some pottery."

"Wow. That's sweet. But what happened to her? She just disappeared. Everyone thinks she died."

"Nope, can't talk now. My back is too itchy." I yanked my leather jacket off and dropped it on the floor. I caught the expression on his face before I pulled my t-shirt up around my head and I grinned inside the jersey tent for a second. He didn't know that beneath my shirt I always wore a halter top camisole to leave my wings unencumbered. I tossed the shirt in the general direction of my closet.

"Can you scratch my back?" I flopped face-first onto the bed behind him and flexed the palm-sized wings that grew from my shoulder blades. They were useless little things and always stuck under some layer of clothing, lying still and quiet, as if they didn't exist. If I were a full pixie I wouldn't be trying to masquerade as a human. I'd be out with all the other pixies, flying around, living outside twelve months out of the year, attending all the revels and mad dances, steeped in magic and moonlight.

Pieter's jacket creaked as he shucked it. Then his fingernails raked deliciously along my skin, bringing life back to my shoulder blades.

I groaned. "That feels amazing. Can you stay all night and do that?"

Pieter didn't answer which was unlike him. One of the reasons I liked him so much was his ability to carry on an intelligent conversation. He was rarely without words. I shifted to glance over my shoulder at him.

"What's wrong?"

"Are you serious about me staying? I don't want to cause any trouble between you and your family."

I turned my face back to the mattress, my voice muffled. "I don't care what they think. I'm old enough to make my own decisions. Anyway, what's the big deal? We never talk about your parents. What do they think about your human girlfriend?"

He laughed softly. "Firstly, you're not human. You're way more than that. Secondly, fauns aren't big on family ties. A faun and a faun met in the woods and had a baby boy faun. So, I don't know who my dad is, which is pretty standard for most of the fae. And my mom is very detached. Honestly, I'm a little envious of your tight family. I can tell it's a big part of you and I don't want to mess it up."

"It'll be fine." I fluttered my wings at him. "Now scratch, slave, scratch!"

"You're just changing the subject, little sneak." Pieter dove in and tickled my ribs. I shrieked and wiggled.

"Stop, no!"

I twisted and grabbed his wrists. "My parents," I hissed. We froze, listening and my heart fell. A thud, thud, thud sounded from the hallway and my door swung open.

"Cressa, you okay?"

The lights flashed on and I threw my arm over my eyes, struggling to sit up. A leaden silence weighted the air. I squinted over my forearm at Dad. His hazel eyes flicked between Pieter and I and his mouth was settling into a thin, tight line.

"What's going on? Who is this?"

I cleared my throat. "Pieter, this is my dad, Forrest. Dad, this is Pieter. My boyfriend."

Dad was too fine-boned, too pixie-like to loom in the doorway, but I could sense his anger rising, charging the room like a thunderstorm. He clenched his fists but said in calm, cold tones, "Pieter, it's time for you to leave."

"Dad, we weren't doing anything. It's really late and I told Pieter he could crash here tonight."

"Absolutely not."

"He could sleep on the couch." Anger lapped against the edges of my voice. Why couldn't I ever get what I wanted? Just once.
Pieter bent to collect his leather jacket from the floor. I caught his arm. "No Pieter, don't go."

"He can't stay," Dad commanded from the doorway.

"Please, Dad!"

"No, Cressa. You're too young to have boys over, especially a faun. I'm not having a dirty, hairy, sex-maniac in my house at night!" Dad snarled.

My mouth fell open and my cheeks flared hot as a fire. "You can't say that, it's racist. You don't know anything about Pieter."

"And you don't know anything about life," my father retorted.

"What's going on here?" Mom's melodic voice came from the hallway. She peeked around the doorframe, her dark green hair dripping from her bath. Her blue eyes widened.

Pieter squeezed my arm. "It' okay," he mumbled. "I'll see you later."

"I'm sorry," I squeaked. I couldn't say anything else, anger grappled my vocal cords and all coherent thought. I hoped he could accept my apology. How could I possibly ask him to stay in the house after being called a dirty sex-maniac? I hoped that he'd still talk to me after this. Pieter shuffled past my parents with his head bowed.

We all waited in tense silence for the front door to thud shut. Then I untied my tongue will a bellow. "What the hell, Dad! How could you do that to me?"

"I'm only trying to protect you. I love you too much to see you get hurt," he yelled back, his face red. His eyes were bloodshot, but they'd been like that for weeks.

"Oh yeah, sure. You must have picked up that line from one of those

TV shows you watched as a nice, normal human kid, huh? You don't know anything about me, or about what I want. So don't start pretending that you care about me now, Dad." I spat out his title venomously.

His face blanched. "Look, fauns are promiscuous and flighty. How can any father stand by and let his daughter fool around with one?"

"You don't know anything about Pieter," I yelled. "And I'm old enough to be making my own decisions. I'm sixteen, in case you haven't noticed. I've grown up while you've been busy playing nurse maid." I felt mean, my anger like a red-hot poker. But I couldn't stop, and it felt good to let it out.

"Your mom is very sick," Dad argued.

"You're not winning any points with me." I crossed my arms, forcing myself not to glance at my mother standing behind him. "I know Mom is sick. But that doesn't give you the right to choose one family member over the other. When was the last time — hah, when was the first time — you let me choose anything for myself? I hate missing all the revels and fae circles and hearing about it second hand from my friends because Mom is so sick that we can't leave her. And for what? To watch her dry up like a raisin right in front of my eyes? Forget that. Forget it. I'm out. I'm done wasting my life on this."

I tromped to my closet, ignoring Dad's suddenly bright eyes and the anger, guilt, and sadness flashing across his face. As I ripped my backpack out of my closet I heard him mutter to Mom "I can't talk to her."

"Coward," I hissed under my breath. Out of the corner of my eye I saw Mom nod as Dad slipped past her into the hallway.

I dropped my gaze and stuffed a shirt in my bag. Seeing Mom lately made my stomach hurt. Even though her hair dripped down her towel-wrapped body, her skin peeled off her in huge, dry flakes. She spent ninety percent of her time in the bath, the water carefully concocted with the appropriate amounts of salt, brine, and minerals to recreate the ocean right in our tub. Most of my childhood memories involved leaning over the porcelain edge, up to my elbows in the briny mixture, chatting to my mother and playing with toy whales, starfish and seahorses while she placidly looked on. And yet, she continued to dry out and shed weight. She got smaller and frailer each passing month.

I froze in my packing, unable to ignore her as she shuffled into my room. To see her standing on dry land was so alien. Her bare feet hardly indented the carpet. The webbing between her toes had cracked and slivers of raw flesh winked at me as she came to my side.

I glanced up at her and winced. Her thin shoulders jutted up through her hair like twin peaks. She cradled her elbows in her hands, as if she couldn't quite manage the weight of her own arms. She panted lightly, and I could hear the air hissing through her parched gills.

"What are you doing?" she asked in her mellifluous voice.

I met her huge orblike eyes, trying not to see the flakes of dry, transparent skin actively peel off her cheekbone. A thin white fleck of decomposition spun and drifted down between us. I clenched my fists.

"I'm leaving. I can't stay here anymore."

"I know this is hard for you. All of this. But think about the struggles Daddy has gone through. He was a halfling child, too. He never fit in anywhere, so he wants to make it easier for you."

I laughed a short, harsh bark. As a child, growing up in Suburbia, I had wished on every shooting star that I could be human. After every wish, I'd poke my eye and taste the tears to see if they had somehow, magically become salty. Fae don't have salt in their blood.

"But he chose the wrong side, Mom. I'm way more fae than human. I belong with them, not here in a house. Besides, it's more than that. It's—" I waved my hand in her direction.

"Me," she whispered.

I swallowed the bitterness in my mouth. I suddenly hated the years and years of worry and fear that her sickness had caused. I hated her for putting me through the forced responsibility of being a caretaker. It should have been the other way around. A child should never have to worry about their parent.

Most of all I hated the way she just laid in that tub, day and night, quiet as a lamb going to slaughter.

"I can't breathe here, Mom. And I can't just give up on my life like—" I couldn't bring myself to say it. I couldn't force myself to even gesture at her again, even with all the burning turbulence roiling in my chest.

"Give up?" Her voice was incredulous, hurt. "Like me?" She backed slowly to the bed and sank onto it, as if her legs suddenly couldn't hold her up anymore. "Is that what you think I've done? That I've just given up on life?"

I opened my mouth, then closed it, unsure. There was a fierce anger in her voice that I'd never heard before.

"I've been fighting for eighteen years, Cressa. Fighting for my life." She made a motion, a fist brought to her chest. It should have been a quick, vigorous strike with a hearty thunk as knuckles met ribs. Instead it was like watching a film in slow motion, her thin fist landing as light and silent as a feather over her heart.

"I know the iron sickness is bad," I nodded. "I know. But look at you! You're falling apart." The words squeezed out of my throat before I could stop them and I flinched at the blame and fear laced in them. Mom closed her large eyes, so much like round fish eyes with lids. When she opened them again they were bright with anger and great sadness. The expression punched me in the gut.

"I'm fighting as hard as I can, Cressa. You don't know how painful it is to keep breathing. It's taken everything I have to hide the pain from you."

I caught my lower lip in my teeth, forcing back the sting in my nose. "Then can't we leave Spokane? Dad's made you live in this place, surrounded by iron and exhaust. Can't we go to the forest, where you can get better?"

She shook her head. "It's not iron sickness. No matter where I go, I will continue to suffer."

I blinked at her.

Her words came slow, careful, intense. "It's not iron sickness. It's a curse."

"What? What kind of curse?"

"A killing curse. For leaving the ocean."

"What?" My frustration streamed out of me like water from a garden hose, leaving me empty and unprotected. "Isn't there some kind of cure? Some way to reverse it?"

Mom shook her head. "The chieftain of my clan said there would be no cure for the death I would suffer if I dared to leave the ocean. I didn't quite believe him then."

My legs went wobbly, and I sagged against my closet door. A motion caught my eye. Dad leaned against the doorframe, arms crossed. He looked at Mom for a moment, then dropped his gaze, as if he couldn't bear looking at her.

My mind raced to understand why his face was a mask of guilt and pain. Mom never really talked about her own life in the sea, before she met Dad. A nervous, painful expression would spasm over her face whenever I asked. One of the only answers she ever gave was 'I met your Daddy and wanted to live with him on land.'

I pointed at Dad. "You did this! You did this to her. You took her from the ocean and now she's cursed to die!"

"Stop it, Cressa!" Mom shouted, her powerful siren voice commanding me for the first time in years. My mouth snapped shut as she continued. "I wanted to go with him. I fell in love with him and I got to give birth to you, my beautiful baby girl. There's nothing I regret, so just stop it."

"Mom, really?" My voice cracked. I wanted to fight, but how did someone fight against a curse? I felt completely drained. I knew she was dying. I'd known it for years. But I wasn't ready for this. I walked to her, knelt at her feet and cried in her lap.

I woke with tears on my cheeks. I wiped the dampness from my eyes, wishing I could wipe away the hours of nightmares, too. All night I'd dreamed different renditions of Mom dying, all of them featuring me trying to save her in an utterly powerless panic. I was no match for an irreversible killing curse.

I stared at the cheap stars on my ceiling. In the pale morning light they nearly blended in with the off-white paint. They had never been a good substitute for the real things, never filling me with the joy and awe of the true vast night sky. My life was a flimsy imitation of what it should be. Like Mom's tub of fake salt water — never quite giving her the comfort she craved, a comfort that would be only provided by the real ocean.

Oh.

I sat up in bed.

I trotted across my room, threw open the door and paused. Little water sounds came from the bathroom. I strode down the hallway and burst into the bathroom. Mom lay up to her neck in the bathwater, her sea-green hair floating around her face. Dad sat on a stool next to the tub, holding her hand. It was the perfect horror scene, like a painting titled "Invalid and Grieving Family".

I hadn't spent much time with my parents in the past few years. I realized now with sharp clarity how hard I'd been pushing them away, trying to escape the heavy sadness that hung over them. I wished I'd been a little more kind and patient. The hollow in my chest twinged. This could be one of the last moments we had all together, if my idea worked.

"We have to go to the ocean," I announced.

My parents blinked at me, not comprehending.

"Where did you come from, Mom? The Pacific?"

She nodded.

"We don't even have to take a plane. We can get there in one day! And then you can be in the real ocean again."

Dad shifted cagily, and his head nervously oscillated back and forth.

"Go back?" Mom whispered. Her gills fluttered under her ears. They were pale and cracked, like chapped lips. Her eyes glossed over with yearning and fear.

Dad sat up straighter. "Don't say that, Cressa. That'll kill her."

"She's dying already," I shouted, my voice reverberating painfully in the small, tiled space. "Don't you see that? She's practically decomposing right in front of us and it's agonizing for her, Dad. Can't you see how aweful it is?"

Dad dropped his head into his hands, his wings rasping dryly against each other as his shoulders quivered.

I turned to Mom. She was glancing back and forth between Dad and I. "At least you'll be able to die peacefully." I gestured to the tub. "This isn't right. It isn't real. You need the ocean."

Dad pulled himself out of his hands, his face red. He had the blood of the fae in his veins, endowing him with what should be supple, youthful skin, even at his age. But his eyes looked like holes at the center of a spider's web, his cheeks hollow with ragged stubble sprouting on his chin. His once glossy chestnut blond hair hung in dull strands to his shoulders. He stank of fear, a human smell.

"No, Ondine," he choked. "We can't."

Mom laid a hand on his arm. "Forrest, I want to." She took a deep, rasping breath. "Yes. I think Cressa's right. I think the ocean will end it quickly and painlessly. I like the idea of ending where I began."

Mom's words dropped like a bowling ball into my stomach. When she said it that way, my nerves sizzled with terror. Had I just condemned my own mother to death? Dad's shoulders shook again, and he made a strangled, choking sound. But Mom met my gaze and held it for a long moment, her expression calm and determined.

I took a deep breath. "I'll call Pieter."

"Why?" Mom asked.

"He'll know how to get us to the coast."

I had hoped for a magical faery transportation circle or powerful travel potion, although I didn't know if either actually existed. My heart sank a little when Pieter pulled up in a Honda Civic with faded maroon paint. A rattling sound came from the tail end of it as it idled in front of the house.

I waved from the doorway and Pieter's silhouetted figure waved back from inside the car. He killed the engine and stepped out into the snow. In the stark winter light, at the end of our suburban street in full view of any curious neighbor's eyes, he wore a heavy mask of glamour to hide his cloven hooves and horns. I could see through it, but any human would see a perfectly unfae boy, slender and dressed in black jeans and leather jacket.

I gestured at the car as he neared. "Is that thing up for such a long trip? It looks ancient." I wrinkled my nose.

"Jackson assured me that Hondas never die. Plus, it's a 1999. It's not that old."

"It's older than I am," I grumbled. But I couldn't help smiling at his broad, proud grin. "Okay. Let's get packed up then."

"Oh, I brought you this." He held out three small white paper bags. Leather and earth and the stink of metal and car exhaust wafted at me along with the bags.

"What is it?"

"A super strong blend of faery dust, to keep off the iron sickness while we're in the car. I already took mine."

The stiff paper crinkled as I opened a bag and smelled the wild power of magic. The powder looked like pink sugar. I tipped the contents into my mouth, letting it dissolve on my tongue. It was tasteless but tingled like electricity.

A slight pressure behind my eyes evaporated. I hadn't even noticed it was there until it was gone. I sighed and smiled. Pieter nodded.

"Listen, about last night," I began.

"It's okay." He held up a hand.

"Really?"

"Really." His soft amber eyes smiled at me. "Along with our dirty, sex-hungry hair, we fauns have thick skins."

I groaned and buried my face in my hands. He laughed and kissed the top of my head.

"Come on, let's go get your parents."

We packed food and extra clothing, sleeping bags and a tent in case we had to cut the trip into two days. According to Google Maps we could make it in one day if we blasted through the four hundred miles from Spokane to the west coast, so long as none of the mountain passes were closed with snow. Seven and a half hours, not counting pit stops. I wasn't sure how well Mom would tolerate being out of the water for so long. I'd never known her to go more than a few hours.

My teeth chattered from cold, but mostly nerves as Dad helped Mom into the car. I handed him the two packets of pink dust.

Pieter drove. He'd had a few lessons from Jackson, his human friend who had the Sight.

Despite the January cold, we kept the windows partly rolled down to let in as much fresh air as possible. The stench of asphalt and rubber tires mingled with the noxious burning of metal in my nostrils. The combination made my stomach roil, even with the extra hit of faery dust. The chill puffs of wind carried the gentle hints of the natural world beyond the industrial grunge of Spokane. The cool scent of lodgepoles of the Inland Northwest melted into the brisk sagebrush of Washington's interior scablands as we passed through.

Pieter and I tried to keep a conversation going at first, but we were both nervous and my parents made little or no response from the back. I couldn't help glancing back every few miles and worrying my fingernails with my teeth.

Mom stretched out in the back, head resting on Dad's lap. Her eyes were shut, and she didn't move. Only the shallow rise and fall of her chest let me know she was still alive. That and the occasional whimper.

She reminded me of the desiccated corpse of a sparrow I'd found once in the back yard. It must have fallen from its tree and lay under a season of snow. Its fledgling feathers were matted and dull. One side was flat where it had lain on the ground, slowly collapsing in on itself. The long toes were stiffly curled in a death grip, clinging to the memory of a branch.

Mom's chapped webbing between her fingers wept red tears for an ocean long denied, much in the same way that little bird still begged for its branch long after its eyes had closed.

I turned back to watch the road, blinking tears from my eyes. My stomach lurched sickeningly. Had we made the right choice? Dear gods and seasons and powers that be, I hoped we had. Pieter offered what little comfort he could — a wan smile now and again, a never-letting-go grip on my hand, and careful driving.

We stopped for gas once, throwing ourselves from the car for the quick dash to the gas station bathrooms. Mom didn't move from the back seat. Pieter and Dad had to take a second longer to construct a glamour disguise to hide their more obvious fae characteristics. But my wings were tiny and tucked like good little girls under my t-shirt. My aquamarine hair could be mistaken for a killer dye job, so if I didn't linger under curious human stares I could get away without the glamour.

We crossed the Cascade mountain range and began the descent, the final stretch before hitting the ocean. Wintry, evergreen scented air blew through the car.

"Should we take a break?" I turned to look in the back.

Dad stared down at Mom's still form for a long moment, then met my gaze. "Just go."

On Jackson's advice we took backroads to avoid Seattle. The traffic jams were brutal, he'd said, and could trap us in the car for hours on end. Better not risk it.

Finally, I caught the briny sharp scent of the ocean, through the lush, tangled greenery of the Pacific temperate rainforests. We'd left the snow back in the Cascades. Here, hanks of moss hung from the branches like the beards of old gnomes. Deep green shadows hunkered below the thick undergrowth, heavy with mystery. The unique beauty of the forest tugged at me. The wildness crowding either side of the road called to me with an invitation to come play.

Later, I promised.

The forest suddenly ended, rupturing apart to the wide-open sky and sandy dunes of sea grass. In the air the pressure of a huge body of salt water pushed against my skin. My lungs tingled, heart jumping with fear.

Dad's shoulders had come up and his eyes were wide, like a caged, feral animal. Mom's eyes were cracked open too, as if she could feel the ocean. I was sure she could.

Pieter parked by the dunes, the rattling engine sighing into stillness. We tumbled out of the metal cage, stretching and breathing. The bitter sea wind raked through my hair. Before me stretched the vast, vast ocean. It spilled across the horizon in silvery grey, melting into the sky at some faraway point so seamlessly I could hardly tell them apart.

I turned and helped Dad. We had to pull Mom out by her legs and sit her up, and she flopped loosely like a dead fish. She took deep breaths and blinked but didn't seem to be able to move on her own. I took one arm and Dad held her around the waist and we crab-walked through the thick sands toward the water. Mom hobbled, her feet half dragging, no strength left. I'd never seen her so weak. It was like she'd already died. Except, her gills hissed frantically by my ear. Tears streamed from her round, blue eyes. She looked forward, leaning hungrily towards the sea.

My vision blurred, and I bit my lip. Look at me, I wanted to say, hug me and tell me that I'd been a good daughter and you love me very much. But she was beyond that. This was her moment and distracting her from getting to the water would be like barring a dryad from her tree, a bird from its sky, a salmon from its river. I couldn't be selfish now. I'd had years of that.

We reached the wave pounded sand, flat and hard under our feet. Mom suddenly sagged, nearly falling to her knees. I gripped harder, pulling her up and forward with all my strength. I kept my gaze locked on the sea, unable to look at the desire on her face. We had almost reached the frothy edges of the world before I realized Dad was not there. I was hauling her myself and Pieter hovered anxiously nearby.

I searched the beach wildly. I twisted all the way around and saw Dad far behind us, on his knees in the sand, face in his hands. I got it. I knew what he was feeling. This was overwhelmingly hard. My face crumpled, and a sob escaped my mouth before I even knew it was there. It came from my gut, from the aching hollow in my chest. We're we completely crazy to toss my mother back to the sea? My mind said yes, but my heart said different.

I firmed my chin. We still had a job to do. I took a bracing breath and yelled. "Dad, get up! You took her from the sea, you put her back."

He didn't move, other than the flutter of his hair and wings in the wind.

I glanced at Mom. She looked far past higher brain function, her eyes glossy and steadfast on the heaving grey water. I looked at Pieter, exasperated.

"I'll get him," Pieter offered.

"He should come on his own. He has to take some ownership, here." I scowled.

"He just needs a little support. I think he's been doing this on his own for a long time." His words stung, but he hadn't meant it to hurt me, I could tell by the heavy empathy in his voice. I couldn't comprehend Pieter's kindness, considering all the terrible things Dad had said to his face.

I hesitated, and Pieter trotted back to Dad. My gut jolted again, and tears started afresh down my cheeks as Pieter offered his hand to Dad. I couldn't hear his words, but I could just make out the soft, gentle cadence of his voice, as if soothing a wild animal. Dad slowly lifted his head, then took Pieter's hand.

'Thank you,' I mouthed to Pieter as they neared. Dad slid back under Mom's arm, his eyes red and face pale, and we finished our funeral march across the sand.

The water bit into my feet and legs with icy teeth. Mom gasped and shuddered under my arm. This was it. Her last breath. Why wasn't I more prepared?

"Hurry, get her in, get her in," I panted. It felt important to completely submerge her all at once. We jogged awkwardly the few yards to waist deep then slipped Mom into the water. Her inert body floated just under the surface, cradled by our hands. Her eyes had closed. The water swallowed my tears as easily as death swallowed life. Dad sobbed loudly beside me. My own breath stuttered and heaved through gritted teeth as the waves ebbed around us, freezing and unkind.

We held her a long time. I couldn't let go of her. It felt impossible.

At some point Pieter muttered, "I'm sorry, I can't stay in any longer. The salt."

"It's okay," I nodded. My siren blood, and Dad's human blood protected us against the salt, a tolerance already built into our red cells. But Pieter, pure fae creature, didn't have our molecular makeup and he must have been enduring the stinging on his skin from the first step into the ocean. I was surprised he'd stayed in as long as he did. A surge of gratitude warmed me. He slogged back to shore.

I couldn't feel my legs or hands anymore. They'd gone numb from the glacial temperature of the Pacific Ocean in January. My teeth chattered, but I wasn't sure if I could let go of Mom yet. Dad remained solidly in place, quiet sobs shaking him every so often.

"Maybe," I said softly, "we should let her go now."

Dad shook his head.

Then I jumped. A cold webbed hand gripped my elbow. Mom's eyes stared up at me through the cloudy water.

"Mom!" I lifted her till her face broke the surface. She blinked, as if waking from a long sleep, her eyes brighter than I'd seen them in years.

"I'm feeling a little better," she said.

"You are?" Dad asked, his voice incredulous.

"I think I'd like to float out a bit, maybe swim a little." Her mouth tilted upwards slightly.

Dad's wide gaze met mine. My heart jumped like a fish in a net. She was alive and gaining strength. What did this mean? She wriggled against my grip, almost dislodging herself with her sudden vigor. Such a contrast to yesterday when she couldn't even thump her own chest with conviction.

Dad's eyes gleamed with fear, but I nodded at him. "We have to."

"I love you," he croaked to Mom.

"I love you," she replied.

We let her go. She slid from our grasp like a snake, easily and smoothly. Her hands and feet gently stroked the water. We stepped back, then back again until we stumbled up onto the dry sand.

Pieter came running from the car with sleeping bags. "What happened?"

"She said she was feeling better and wanted to swim," I replied. I couldn't believe the words even as I said them.

His mouth dropped. "It must have been a reversed curse. She'll die only if she stays away from the ocean?"

"Or maybe," I mused, "she wasn't really cursed at all."

If this were true and she really was cured, then everything had changed. We waited on the beach, wrapped up in our sleeping bags. Pieter sat on my right side, Dad on my left. My gaze fixated on the little black dot that was Mom's head far out beyond the breakers. Every once in a while, she raised an arm to wave.

"We'll have to move to the coast. We can't keep her away from the ocean anymore," I said.

Dad nodded.

I turned to Pieter. "What about you? I don't know how to ask — We've only known each other a short time."

"I like the coast," Pieter replied airily.

Dad took a deep breath. There was a hopeful gleam in his eye that hadn't been there yesterday. "I'd like to get to know you better, Pieter. I can't thank you enough for your help today."

Dad glanced at me shyly and I smiled at him.

"When we move here, can we live like real fae? Can we live in the forest and go to revels?" I pressed.

Dad nodded again.

"And can we be a real family?"

He took my hand, eyes brimming. "That's all I ever wanted."

I squeezed his hand and twined the fingers of my other hand with Pieter's. Dad and Pieter's shoulders warmed me on either side, right down to my core, filling up that hollow place.

Lacy wavelets hissed and bubbled up onto the sand. The frigid wind slapped my hair across my forehead and susurrated through the sea grass. A few brave seagulls wheeled overhead, crying tremulously. The flat, silver ocean spilled across the horizon like melted pewter. It was beautiful in all its starkness.

How stupid were we, to think that a bathtub full of brine could ever replace this? How stupid was I to ever wish for the salt of human tears?

I smiled. This was all the salt water I needed, right here.

It is estimated by scientists that about one percent of humans have anatomical variance from the two gender archetypes, male and female. This estimate does not come easily, and it is not without uncertainty, but one percent is a lot of people; about the same as the number of people with (genetically) red hair. Why mention this? No reason. Let's read about the dormitory fire.

LEARNING CURVE

C. M. Daniels

University dormitories and fire alarms were so synonymous with one another when I was in school that the rumbling and wailing of heavy firefighting equipment rushing under my windows at night barely registered in my sleeping brain. Drunks pulled alarms for fun. Rich kids burned their noodles. A recreational smoke set the detectors off. Whatever the vigilant firefighters were racing off to tend was none of my concern. I learned to sleep through just about anything short of a nuclear blast.

Rueben, my roommate for the last two semesters, objected loudly in the hall, pronouncing to the person pounding on the door that I had a final in the morning and was not to be disturbed. Rueben was the mother hen of our floor. Knuckles on solid wood registered less quickly than my roomie's nasal whine. I was ready to tell him to go bother our neighbor Sick Insomniac Steve. "He's not going to be happy."

An ever-expanding slice of fluorescent light from the hall reflected off the white linoleum floor, allowing me to see the outline and shadowed features of my friend Naro. "Get up and put your shoes on."

I remained supine, wanting him to get the hint to go away, without having to snap at him. Naro grabbed my shower shoes off the floor and started shoving my feet into them. "What the hell?"

"The third floor of Kenyon Hall is on fire."

I pulled my legs away and sat up. "One of the girls accidentally leave a candle unattended in the lounge again?"

Naro's lips pinched. I failed to see what this had to do with dragging me out of bed to go down the walk and freeze my butt off while watching the fire department run into the building like heroes and come out grumbling about college kids. That spectacle lost its luster early on in my freshman year. "No, it's really on fire, up in flames."

His gaze tried to will me to action. Rueben hung back waiting to lavish Naro with a fat I-told-you-so. An ungodly orchestra of flashing lights and sirens approached this part of campus, growing louder. Reinforcement trucks and ambulances were about to arrive. He was serious.

"Are you going?"

"Why? So I can be another gawking body in the way? I'll let you go join the circus." I wasn't going to say it.

Rueben made an inquisitive sound, not ready to ask if I was sure. He took another step back, getting caught up in the basketball hoop we had mounted on his closet door.

"You're not even going to go see if she's all right?" Naro didn't hide his disappointment in me.

I stared at my knees, waiting for the word no to cross my lips.

"Martee is in that fire. You can't just sit here." Naro sniped. "You need to go see if she's out. You need to go find her."

Her, she, the inadequate nature of the main language we spoke in the Confederation barely had the words to describe someone like Martee. "That's the firefighters' job."

Naro hit me. I deserved it. "Get your ass out there."

I wasn't as lucky or as smart as my brother who went all the way to Earth to attend Michigan State on a scholarship. The farthest away from home I got for college was Newcastle Colony University, the local school. It was two hundred clicks from my parents' house, so it was almost like being out on my own, like my brother. Sometimes I felt like I had a lot to live up to, but when it came down to it, my parents were proud of both of their boys.

NCU was one of the best places in the Confed to study History of Colonization, my major. It was in my first history class on my first day of university that I met Martee, a fellow Colonization major. She was shy, afraid to speak up or look others in the eye. Short and slender, she could only touch her toes to the ground from the seat of her desk. I certainly took notice when I was the only person in the class she looked up at as we went around the room and introduced ourselves. She was the most delicate person I had ever seen. The professor let us go early since it was the first day. Martee knocked her notepad and stylus off her desk. I leaned over and picked it up. Our hands touched as I made the exchange. Soft skin, brown hair, stunning blue eyes. She thanked me and all I could do was stare.

The every-other-day schedule of that class made me sad that I wasn't going to see her the next morning. I went to my room and thought I'd try to start my reading. My roommate Tom came storming in. "Did you hear the news?"

"What news?" I was still trying to figure out if I liked Tom well enough that I could spend nine months locked in a large closet with him.

"There's a Glorin on campus, like enrolled here and going to classes!"

"A Glorin?" I had to admit I was curious about this person, whoever they were. "If they're here, doesn't that mean they're old enough to have gone through their change?"

"Who cares if it's been through and is in its final form? It's a Glorin."

I was slightly disturbed by Tom referring to the Glorin as an *it*. If the planet Glorin weren't the Confed's most significant source of the brains that developed interstellar travel and the fantastic computers that made it possible, it would be a closed planet due to the strange defects the first generation of native Glorin were born with. All the babies born on Glorin had ambiguous genitalia that was eventually linked to fetuses not receiving certain hormones in utero. Each child was still genetically male or female. Adolescence came and went, with the children not experiencing puberty, in effect rendering them children forever, physically. However, adults treated with hormones found that their own bodies reacted well and began self-producing. The treated Glorin underwent a late puberty with little or no effect on their fertility. Generations of this contributed to the Glorin culture. Children grew up not knowing their sex until the age of majority, meaning they weren't subject to the ridiculous gender stereotypes still at play in Confed society at large. At twenty, they learned their sex and chose for themselves if they wanted to take the hormones. As a result of this oddity, Glorin rarely, if ever left their home world until after they were adults, regardless of making the change or not.

"I've never met a hermaphrodite before. I hope it's in my classes."

"They're not hermaphrodites." I gathered my stuff together and went to my next class.

By that evening, the whole campus was in an uproar, wanting to know who the Glorin was. Six weeks later, we all learned, it was Martee.

The side of my face hurt. Naro hit me hard enough to bruise. "What are we supposed to do?"

"We don't have to do anything, you idiot. You need to see if she's okay. How many times do I have to say it to get it through your click-thick skull?" Naro hurled a pair of shoes at me.

Rueben pulled my closet open and grabbed an outfit's worth of clothes. "Stop being stupid and go."

The overhead light burned my eyes and more sirens, this time from police vehicles, went racing under my window. A pair of socks hit me in the face. I pulled the shirt over my head and didn't bother with socks or pants. I had on a pair of sweats that I liked to sleep in. The last thing in the universe I wanted to do was walk over to Kenyon Hall. "What about finals?"

"Do you want to get hit again?" Naro grabbed me by the arm and hauled me off my bed.

The three of us ran down the stairs rather than wait for the slow elevator to crawl its way up to the fifth floor. Smoke brought water to my eyes.

The second semester of our freshman year, Martee and I got to spend a lot of time with one another. We were paired up to work on a presentation. Our work sessions often turned into talk-until-we-lost-our-voices sessions. I liked everything about her. Not only could she hold intelligent conversation, but her sense of humor was second to none. We talked about our homes, where we grew up and such. When you got down to it, our childhoods weren't all that different.

The campus newspaper did a big spread on Martee, showing her pretty face to everyone. After that, I was known as "the Glorin's boyfriend." Honestly, I didn't mind the label. She never mentioned anything about it, either. We departed to our respective homes for the summer. My brother told me he was jealous that I had someone like Martee. Mr. Michigan State was not doing a good job of holding on to friends.

Through messages and emails, we kept in touch over the break. I couldn't stop thinking about her, about how she was the first person who'd ever made me feel truly alive. There were things I couldn't wait to say to her face to face when school started again. Three months felt like forever.

A sad steady bell rang, Kenyon Hall's fire alarm, through the noise of the charging first responders. We were still a few blocks away, but close enough to see orange flames coming out the windows on the top floor. City police and campus security were doing their best to set up a barricade, mainly to keep curious students out of the way. I tried to slow down, but Naro and Rueben wouldn't let me, barricades be damned.

We coughed as we closed in on the police line. They told us to go back to our rooms. Instead, we wedged ourselves into the crowd of spectators.

Sickeningly enough, a lot of the gawkers held miniature cameras up over their heads to record the incident, probably to sell to outfits like InterStar News Corp and Confed Alert Network. Damned vultures.

"Which room is hers?" Rueben pointed at the blazing dormitory.

My eyes had glued themselves to the crying, blanket huddled, collection of girls, about a hundred yards across from us. I tried to see the features on their faces, a challenge in the kaleidoscopic swirl of lights. Where was that fine-boned face?

"She's on the fourth." One floor above the inferno.

"Do you see her?"

A brand of frantic was starting to set into my systems as adrenaline leached into my body. As much as my conscience thoughts told me to screw it all and let the firefighters do their jobs, that part of my mind that loved Martee, desperately wanted to see her unharmed.

As much as I'd half-dreaded the start of my freshman year, I could have counted down the seconds until I got back to school as a sophomore. Over the break, I'd come to realize I liked Martee as more than just a friend. Each letter, call, or simple three-word message she sent, had me high, hanging on every word, daring to think of terms like soul-mate.

Together again in our second-year history curriculum, we paired off for projects, sat next to one another, and spent so much of our free time together, friends would ask about our wedding date. By midterms, I'd finally gathered the courage to ask her out on a real date. She turned me down.

Each time I asked, her answer was no. She always cited the value of our friendship, giving a canned line about not wanting to ruin what we had. It didn't seem to matter that we were beyond friendship in many ways. We finished one another's sentences, knew if one of us had stubbed a toe from across campus, sometimes we even had the same dreams.

The one compromise she made that term was accepting my invitation to the Winter Formal. The girls of Kenyon Hall made themselves beautiful. I arrived at the dorm, to meet Martee, overwhelmed by all the glitter, skirts, and coifs. She came down to the lobby, obviously dressed by friends and roommates, looking like a tiny awkward princess.

"Gabriella insisted that I borrow her falsies." Martee pointed to her much fuller chest. Typically, her slight breasts were barely visible.

I laughed. It figured, the first thing out of her mouth was the least expected. "I think you look great."

"I've never seen you wear a tie. You look very professional."

I wanted to hear handsome or even sexy. I could settle for professional. It was the same tux I'd worn to my junior prom, and it barely fit. I don't suppose anything about me was handsome that night.

Everyone we talked to that night couldn't stop complimenting Martee on her transition into the belle of the ball. Her typical mode of dress was the college student favorite of pants and a baggy shirt. After several spins around the dance floor, we were hot and decided to sit outside on one of the benches. We talked about how we hoped we were better remembered by the school to merit more than a concrete bench when we died.

Martee leaned against me, where I could smell the soap she used on her hair. I let my cheek caress the top of her head. It felt like we just sat there and watched overdressed students and faculty walk in and out of the venue all night.

Her hand on my cheek set my nervous system to zap me back to my sad reality. I was no longer looking out on the quad, but into her eyes. Lips met and parted. I was her first kiss.

"What are they doing? I thought firefighters were supposed to fight fires, not stand around and watch buildings burn." Naro was ready to start picking fights with the first responders. It was my turn to pull him back.

"Let them do their jobs."

"And just let them hang back while your girlfriend dies?"

"She's not my girlfriend. She's not even—" I couldn't finish the sentence. It didn't seem right.

Hands up in the air, Naro spit. "Screw it. You're such a piece of shit. You'll just let her burn."

Rueben glared at me, probably wishing I were the one in that dormitory instead of Martee. "I'll go rankle some cops. Come on, Naro. We'll do this ourselves."

My friends disappeared into the crowd and flashing lights.

Martee and I were signed up to do a summer session at the University of Edinburgh. We'd rented an apartment not far from the Royal Mile. Neither one of us had ever been to the human homeworld and with our "educational opportunity" there was an excuse to tour around and not be separated from one another.

During our third week of classes, we went to a pub to watch a football game with some new friends. Since she was so slight, Martee was asked to verify her age before she was served. I wanted to tell the people that she was a couple of years older than I was, and they'd let me in.

"Looks like you'll be twenty, tomorrow, Lass. Happy birthday." The keep set a pint in front of her.

New friends offered a toast. I thought back to what I knew about the Glorin. If she was away from home, she had to have been some sort of exception to their rules. She'd learned early about her nature. I understood she was a bit uncomfortable with her body, especially as we'd slowly crossed the line from friendship to something more romantic. Martee didn't have the confidence yet to let me see her naked and we hadn't had sex. I was patient with her to the point I was ready to go crazy. Modesty wasn't a crime.

We went home, drunk, waking up the next morning, curled up together on the couch. Someone knocked on the door too early for our tastes. A courier needed Martee to sign for a package from the Glorin consulate. She stood in the open doorway long after the man left.

"Is something wrong?" I pulled myself up off the couch.

"Maybe," she said. She turned to me. "I've been dreading this day."

A lump started in the pit of my stomach. There were no humorous quips we could fire off to one another to shake the gravity in her composure at that moment. "What is it?"

"It was never important to me until I met you." She started talking, not really addressing me. "I never should have fought so hard to leave early. My parents, everyone, warned me that something like this would happen, that this thing that means so much to you people could ruin something beautiful."

She stared at the package, as though its mere presence was enough to make her sick. "I find out today."

I knew what she meant, but she just kept standing there, holding the answer to something that I'd never questioned in her or myself. "Are you going to open it?"

"I don't know if I can."

"Let's go to the couch, and we'll do it together." I shut the door and led her across the room. I noticed then, she was in last night's pants, but had stripped down to her undershirt. I had all the proof I needed.

Inside the box was a beautifully padded leather folder, like the type diplomas came in. She touched the embossed seal of her world's government before flipping it open.

"Wait!" She shouted as I hurtled toward the kitchen to vomit into the sink.

She put her hand on my back, trying to comfort me. I sniped at her. "Don't touch me."

Martee withdrew her hand. "I don't want us to end like this."

I rinsed my mouth, even as my stomach threatened to revolt on me again. "I thought you went through this. You live in an all-women's dorm, use the ladies locker room. You wore a dress to the formal."

She followed my harsh gaze to her chest. Feminized breast tissue made for a deceptive profile beneath her undershirt. "Your food is treated with hormones. Almost everything you touch is some type of plastic. The average Confed environment is full of estrogen and compounds that mimic it. My body responds to it, since, unlike you, I don't produce my own sex hormones."

Her eyes averted, trying to reconnect with mine. "The Glorin arranged to have me live in Kenyon Hall, since in this state, all Glorin are physically more female than male. Could you imagine me living in the jock dorm?"

That stab at humor fizzled. How could she do this to me? I was still somewhere beyond disgusted. "What made you think it was okay to string me along for two years?"

"I didn't know how to tell you. There was never a right time, especially after you started asking me out. I didn't want to lose you."

"You didn't think that your possibly being a man wasn't going to be an issue?" I pushed my way past her and grabbed my wallet off the coffee table.

"I hoped it wouldn't matter."

"You make me sick." I threaded my belt on to my pants, stuffed my feet into my shoes, and headed toward the door.

"Please don't go." By that point, she'd started to cry. "I love you."

The police were making a real push to get us away from the scene. It was starting to get extremely dangerous. Windows were exploding, showering the neatly manicured lawns with glimmering bits of glass. I watched as Naro got into a shoving match with a cop and started to skirt around the crowd.

The huddling girls, most wrapped in their blankets and bedspreads, were surprised to see me. I looked from face to face, feeling a crushing panic when I realized Martee wasn't there. I kept hearing that no one had seen her. Catty comments came as well. I knew I was a stupid jerk, no need to remind me.

"She should have left you for what hangs off your crotch." Gabriella got in as many digs as she could. "Get out of here."

I backed away from the females and decided to walk away from all the insanity. I refused to go back to my dorm, knowing I'd have to face my friends. It was a walk around campus night. The walkway closest to that gaggle of girls lead around the back side of Kenyon Hall, over toward the science labs and engineering school.

In the four months since I'd left Scotland, left Martee crying in the apartment while she was holding that damned letter in her hand, I'd had a lot of time to think. My brother, bless him, told me I'd acted like a spoiled brat, storming off when I didn't like the outcome of the situation. That's what I did when I was a little kid when I lost a game of checkers.

My first two years of school, I'd preached about the Glorin being as normal as any other human beings. I corrected the misinformed, like my first roommate. For anyone who asked, I let them know what it was like to have a great friend who just happened to come from one of the more isolated planets in the Confederation. I remembered telling those who asked if I'd be so close to Martee if she were a guy instead of a girl, that I would stand by her no matter what. Like a politician who wanted everyone on my side, I blathered on about how it's what is on the inside that matters. I'd said you can't help who you love.

She read me, understood me, so much better than I was capable of comprehending myself. Martee didn't tell me about her age or unknown chromosome earlier because I was completely hung up on her. I was hung up on her being a her, when during our entire relationship, she'd never given much of an indication as to which gender she preferred to eventually become, if she picked one at all. The night of the winter formal, she said she wore a dress because she was under the impression that she was expected to wear one. And pronouns, we had many discussions about them. All Glorin were shes and hers. Those were the acceptable pronouns to use when not referring to someone by name or title. I didn't get that at first.

I missed the clues. I missed her. My anger was directed at myself. She wasn't my girlfriend, because I'd walked out on her. We weren't in the same classes this term since I didn't think I could face her after I hurt her like I did. Coward, hypocrite, idiot, those words almost described how it felt to lose such a great thing.

The wind started to pick up, making the flames worse for the firefighters. I felt tears begin to prick at the corners of my eyes. What was I going to do if she was gone? I trudged forward, ducking into the breezeway of the biological sciences building.

A cough, a chest deep, rattling cough echoed off the concrete and brick walls. So, I wasn't alone. I decided to change course and walk to another corner of campus, far away from Kenyon Hall and the people I knew. Looking down as I started to turn, I noticed footprints on the ground, like stalking feet walked through the dewy grass.

Just through the breezeway, stood a metal column with a blue light on top was near the entrance. I couldn't see the whole emergency com as a trash can was positioned near it. Those footprints lead that direction. Then, the cough came again.

"Martee!" She didn't respond to her own name. In the poor light, her lips looked blue on her ashen face. The palms of her hands were burned.

Her torn nightclothes bore witness to the desperation of her escape from the part of the dorm where the fire raged. Why she ran this way instead of out the main entrance eluded me until I remembered her favorite study lounge was on the fourth floor, near the seldom-used rear fire escape that let out on a back lawn adjacent to this building.

I punched the big red button on the emergency com, before getting on my hands and knees to evaluate her more closely. It took some explaining to get the dispatcher to understand I was not trying to pull a joke. Martee was suffering from burns and smoke inhalation. She needed help as soon as possible.

When the wait for emergency personnel started, I laid down on the cold ground beside her. Her hair was still dark and fine, silky between my fingers. It felt so good to touch her, to be so close to her again. My voice soft, I talked to her. I rambled, unable to settle on one topic longer than a few sentences.

"You're here." Eyes barely opened before she coughed again.

"Easy, easy," I said as I sat up and propped her against me.

Heavy footsteps and gruff voices approached. "You're going to be just fine."

She tried to touch me and withdrew her burned hand. "I'm sorry."

"Don't be sorry." Our eyes locked. "You need to conserve your energy and wait for the paramedics to get here."

I don't know if she smiled, or what, but her gaze was a soft one. Perhaps she didn't hate me after all.

"Martee?"

The noise of the approaching first responders started to thunder and echo through the breezeway. Help was immediate.

"Yes?" She whispered through a surge of pain brought on by another cough.

I touched my lips to her forehead. "I love you, too."

"Any sufficiently advanced technology is indistinguishable from magic."
—Arthur C. Clarke, "Profiles of the Future," 1961

PATTERNS OF BREATH

AND BLOOD

Antonia Overstreet

No one else tests the Wall like I do, teasing out its favorite secrets. They're afraid. But the Wall and I have a better relationship than I have with any of the Outsiders in this city.

They still call themselves that, despite living Inside for 23 years. Guess they don't feel at home here. Not like me.

I lay back on the blankets I've scattered across the floor of the Cranny, the narrow home the Wall has granted me in its depths. Patterns spin and pulse against my eyelids, twisting into new shapes to try. New secrets the Wall has to tell me.

That one.

I scramble up and swipe two fingers along the smooth wall to illuminate its milky white surface. The Cranny looks shabbier than usual in the harsh glare, and I end the gesture in a flick to dim the light.

I begin to trace out the pattern I'd envisioned, interweaving seven fingers in its complex swirls. The last stroke of my thumb opens a cavity in the Wall, and I squeal in delight. I shove the blankets aside, looking for something I can offer to the Wall in exchange for what it wants to give me. I cast aside the pebble I dug out of my shoe before. The Wall deserves better.

There. I snatch up the feather that floated down from the sky two days ago, edged in blue. Perfect.

I place the feather in the cavity, blink, and it's gone. I peer closer, into the shadows, and pout. Nothing. This is the first time the Wall hasn't given me a present back.

I sit back in a huff. That lovely feather gone for nothing. I could've traded that for something useful in the bazaar. Old Nila likes pretty things.

I stare at the Wall, and the empty cavity. How long have I been in here? I don't even know if it's day or night out there. My stomach grumbles. I need dinner or breakfast, either way. I swipe a quick gesture on the Wall to make a peephole, and peer out. Bright daylight streams down, cut by the deep shadows of the Wall. I swipe again to create an exit, and slide out into the sun.

I stand for a moment, gulping in the fresh air. I keep hoping one of the new patterns I try will allow air to penetrate the Wall into my Cranny. The Builders must have had some way to breathe in the rooms the Wall made for them.

My stomach growls again and I jolt back to reality.

It's two steps across the tiny courtyard outside the Cranny. I shimmy through the impossibly narrow alley where the Wall almost touches itself, and pop out into the Ratter District. I haven't taken more than ten steps when someone jerks my elbow.

"Taxes are due, little shadow!" comes the whisper at my ear, and I whip around. Tosu sneers at me, leaning against the Wall where the Outsiders have tacked on a ramshackle hookah bar. The rough wood salvaged from the shanty town Outside clashes against the pristine white of the Wall.

I scrounge in the pocket I stitched on for the benefit of the pickpockets, teasing out a single chip. I flip it to him, and he barely gives it a glance.

"Not enough," Tosu says. "What else you got?"

"That's it." I'm not as good as the Wall at keeping secrets, but I feel like I do a creditable job.

"You'll have to come inside then."

"What? Why?" I tug at Tosu's grip on my upper arm to no avail.

Tosu doesn't answer, just bats aside the ratty cloth hanging in the doorway of the hookah bar, shoving me inside. The dim room has a sweet stale smell that makes me sneeze.

"Good to finally meet you, Fedra." I whip around to the deep cheerful voice and twitch when I see the man. How does the leader of the Greyskins know who I am? Time to abandon the Cranny and find a new place in the labyrinth of the Wall a few days' walk away. Maybe with the Sentinels?

Tosu elbows me, and I stumble forward. "Thank you, sir." Best not to give him any more information than he already has — even a reaction.

"I have to report that the little shadow has failed to pay her taxes,

Amil, sir," Tosu pipes up. Amil flicks a dismissive hand at him, and Tosu ducks his head, stepping back.

"I hear you have a special skill, Fedra." Amil tears down a dusty tapestry hung on the back wall, revealing the vibrant white of the Wall. "I'm willing to accept a new pattern you've discovered in lieu of your usual taxes."

"I—" How did he know? I practice all my patterns in the Cranny, or at least out of sight. I skim through the patterns in my head. I have five or six patterns nobody else knows about, but the last thing I want is to give a man like this more control of the Wall. And this morning's pattern was useless. But they didn't know that.

"I suppose I could do that," I whisper, trying to sound as reluctant as possible. I look him in the eyes, then. "You're not afraid?"

Amil laughs, a delighted sound. "I'm not superstitious, nor do I think you can call a spirit out of the Wall to consume me. My kin within these walls are fools not to understand the tool they have before them. Go ahead."

I slink up to the Wall and rest my palm against it. "I can show you a pattern that allows you to hide an object in the Wall." I hide a smile to myself. I wouldn't promise anything about getting it back.

"Proceed."

I close my eyes, recalling the pattern, and begin to glide my fingers over the Wall. I forget one stroke and curse under my breath, starting over. Finally the cavity opens.

"What — what would you like me to put in?" I ask Amil.

My eyes go big as he hands me a heavy sack of coin. I'm going to need to move *really* far away after this.

I slide the sack into the cavity in the Wall, my mind buzzing in panic about what to do after this fails spectacularly.

The sack, heavy as it is, floats in the dark space in the Wall for a moment before vanishing. I try to calm my features as much as possible before turning back to Amil.

"See? Works like a charm."

"Indeed. And how do I retrieve the item?"

I lick my lips. "About that … "

If I can slip past Amil, I'll just have Tosu to contend with. He looks so dumbstruck by the Wall consuming the gold that I might have a chance if I take him by surprise. My best option is to make a mad dash back to the Cranny, and hole up there until I can formulate a more permanent plan.

Amil's brows furrow, and I tense to run, but he raises a hand to his face instead, coming away with blood. A nosebleed? Perfect timing. I dart towards the exit, Tosu stumbling toward me. I dodge, and make it to the doorway when a thud shudders the ground behind me. I glance back to see

Tosu shaking on the floor, and Amil on his knees, face covered in blood. What?

The dark gap in the Wall lurks behind them both, still open. I stand frozen as Amil topples, and Tosu grows still.

No no no no no.

The Wall did give me a gift in return. The Wall gave me death.

I run.

In the sweltering other world of Alabama, one's sweat-sticky shirt hampers free movement. The cloying humidity seeps into the brain, and even thoughts gurgle sluggishly. That's good if one is trying to avoid thinking.

TAILS

Terri Picone

Mason Dunn sighed at the pile of squirrel tails lying on the makeshift table under his carport. He was handy with plywood and sawhorses, but his work was never done. Of course, that was how he liked it. He'd been washing and rinsing the tails since sun up.

He tugged at the waistband of his pants and stepped closer, peering at the colors of gray, brown, black, and white mixed through the collection. They were unique. No two alike. Arlene had called him unique, too, but it never seemed a compliment — like everything else she called him. So why did he miss her?

A brisk wind whipped around him, raising the hair on the squirrel tails as if someone blew across the top of them. The house curtains flapped behind him, trying to escape through the open windows.

He turned the radio dial louder on the portable that hung from a nail on the nearby post. Country music. It was as deep in his Alabama blood as trapping.

Across the back of the carport, three clotheslines held tails inches apart, shortest to longest. They swung back and forth from clothespins, a mix of brown and gray and white rippling in the summer breeze like a dance ensemble in perfect rows. A new and, thus, empty clothesline waited to be filled.

He positioned the baking sheet of still damp squirrel tails onto the makeshift table. The fabric softener didn't quite cover the tails' smell, which was similar to wet dogs. Next time, he'd use more. Or a stronger brand.

The carport was almost as big as his house and served as his workshop and his storage shed. Local newspapers were piled against the house so they didn't fall over. Paper grocery bags filled with black walnuts were scattered in random places. Boards. Kindling. Bricks, stacked thirty-three high, formed a wall on the east side. Plastic grocery bags hung from a large nail on a supporting beam, snapping whenever the wind picked up.

Mason opened a new bag of wooden clothespins and laid it open-mouthed so he could reach inside without fumbling. He lifted the first tail from the tray with his square hand, placed it to the far left side of the table. Its tip nudged the line he'd drawn with a yardstick and permanent marker early that spring just like the last three springs since Arlene left. That was the year he'd gotten focused. Or busy, because what else would he do these days without her?

One at a time, he added the next size tail and the next. He rarely chose the wrong size. And if he did, he'd sweep the whole lot of them back onto the tray with his forearm and start again. He would be perfect. She might come back and then she'd see what he really was.

A distinctive clank came from under the walnut tree, and he smiled for the first time that day. Did his neighbors know all the good he did for them? The squirrels flocked to his yard, right into his traps. He felt hot and wiped his forehead with his blue handkerchief. He began to whistle as he leaned back into his job, longing for a breeze to cool him.

A sign hung from a piece of twine stretched across the front of the driveway, about a foot above the concrete. "No Trespassing." A seven-year-old girl with tangled yellow-white hair stood, wearing an extra-large men's t-shirt and pink leggings with holes in the knees. Her hair fell over her left eye and tumbled down her shoulders.

She studied the letters printed in sloppy black marker on the sign but couldn't quite put that many together to form the word. "I'll have to ask Mama when she wakes up."

But Casey knew better than to wake her. Mama had worked late last night and needed her beauty rest, and Casey was supposed to stay in her own backyard. But she was lonely in her new neighborhood, and when she heard someone whistling, she was drawn to see who it was.

She so hoped for a new friend. She was getting impatient for school to start up, and even though Mama said it would be soon, it seemed forever. She still missed her old friends from her last school: Marissa, Kennedy, and Emma. And she missed Grandfather, too.

She squinted to see where the whistle came from. The bright sun reflected off the flat roof and made it darker under the carport. She raised her arm, bent at the elbow, to use it as a visor and block the noon sun from her eyes.

There was a lot of stuff under the carport, but she finally spotted someone wearing a red baseball cap and a hunter's orange flannel shirt. A little man, and the baseball cap reminded her of her grandfather who always wore a baseball cap and was always very nice to her before the divorce.

It would be easy to step over the little fence of twine, but she thought she should read the sign first. She checked her house next door for any sign her mother was awake. The kitchen shade was still pulled down.

Finished with the tray, Mason straightened, stretched, wiped the sweat from his neck. He still felt hot. It was hard leaning over the table for very long. He felt stiff, more than usual. But at least these particular squirrels wouldn't be getting his walnuts. And trapping was what he liked best of all these days.

The trapping not only distracted him since Arlene left, but transported him back to when he was a boy, trapping and fishing to help out his large family. And back to the Sunday dinners when his mother would fry or stew his catch. He'd been trying to duplicate her recipes without luck, but at least his attempts were more satisfying than hot dogs and baked beans.

He planned to give the squirrel he'd been tenderizing in the fridge a try tonight after he was finished here. Maybe deep-fry it. Then he was done for the day. Done. To eat and then fall asleep in front of the TV.

He reached for the first tail, the shortest one. A drop of sweat trickled down his face from under his hat.

The man had stopped whistling, and she didn't want to disturb him. She knew it's always best to stay quiet, see what happens. In the meantime, she studied the letters of the words on the low-hanging sign. She wished she had her momma beside her because Mama was always patient and helped her sound out the words.

The second one was a really big word that might have something to do with trees. But what, she didn't know. She thought and thought about it until her brain got tired, and her feet scooted closer and closer to the words until the toes of her fuzzy pink slippers slipped under the sign, cutting them off at the ankle. Half hidden behind the sign.

From a telephone wire above her, a bird cawed. She jumped back, looked up. It was the biggest and blackest bird she'd ever seen. It cawed, cawed again and flew over the man's house to disappear. She stared into the sky where it went, waiting for its return, waiting for her Mama to holler her name.

He counted the tails. Thirteen. Suddenly, he felt lightheaded and, realizing he hadn't had a break for a few hours, took a slow breath and leaned on the carport support beam. He was sweating more and reached for the hankie in his jeans pocket, almost losing his balance as he did.

He looked for a chair to sit on to wait for the dizziness to pass, but there was nowhere to rest. Every chair was stacked with newspapers or kindling or bags of walnuts. His ears rang. His eyes saw light flashes. Sweat trickled down his neck. As he began to fall, he reached for the table, but in slow motion. His hand caught the empty baking sheet instead, pulling it to the cement floor with a crash. He fell, partly beside it and on top of it. His shoulder and arm scraped the concrete. And his head banged on the edge of the baking sheet. And then he blacked out.

She heard a crash and a thud, but she had been watching the black bird. Did the man throw something or did he fall? She stood on her toes. She jumped along behind the little sign on the string. Maybe she should step over it. She listened in the direction of the man and called, "Mister?" But there was no sound.

A motorcycle buzzed past her. A baby cried from somewhere in the neighborhood. But there was only silence from the carport. "Mister?" Louder. She looked toward her own house next door. Was Mama awake?

A moan came from under the carport.

"Hello." She stepped over the sign as a large cloud passed in front of the noon sun.

She didn't want to get in trouble for not staying in her yard, but maybe the man needed her. It was important to help people, Mama always said so. Casey walked along the outside of the carport, but the stacks of wood and boxes and bricks wouldn't let her see inside where the man had fallen.

She knew how to be as quiet as a mouse, just to see what is what, like when she had to be sure her father was sleeping before she snuck money and the car keys from his pockets before they moved here. She held her breath, stepped around the kindling and newspapers. She concentrated on the path in front of her, listening.

Her eyes adjusted to the darker area at the back of the carport where she thought she'd heard him; the only sound was the pounding of her heart in her ears. She stepped around more boxes, and there were strings of something hanging back there. She took a step forward to see and almost stepped on the man's hand.

She squealed and cupped her hands over her mouth.

His eyes were closed, his hat beside him, his arm flopped over his head. One of his legs was twisted under his other. Was he dead? She held her breath for what seemed like a long time. How would she know if he was dead? He really might be.

"Hello?" she whispered. "Mister?" She inched a little closer. "Mister, are you okay?" she asked, a little louder.

He still hadn't moved and didn't seem to be breathing. She would have to go wake her mother. But first, she brushed his arm with her slipper. "Hello?"

Mama would know what to do. Casey backed away, keeping watch on the man. The whole area was a mess. A baking sheet and clothespins were scattered on the floor, partly under him. The furry things hung on lines of twine, waving at her. Like the tails of stuffed-animal at Walmart.

The man moaned. "Arlene?" He lifted his head a few inches and dropped it back to the floor. "Is it you?"

Casey backed up farther, so she could run if she needed to. "No, I'm your neighbor." He didn't look scary, so little, so crumpled. But she liked to be ready.

A strong breeze whipped through the carport, blowing the man's hat several inches. One of the furry things fell to the floor and another dangled loose. "What are those . . . things?"

Mason tried to sit but could only moan and lay back down. "What are you doing here?" He grabbed at his twisted leg. "Oh, that hurts." He shut his eyes again.

She was glad he wasn't dead. "I heard you fall and came to help." She pointed behind him. "But what kind of creepy place is this? What kind of weird world? Just what are you doing with all these . . . tails?"

"Didn't you see the 'No Trespassing' sign?" He stared, held his leg.

She shrugged. "I saw a sign. But, what are those?" She crossed her arms and glared at him. "It's probably illegal."

"None of your business, little Miss Snoopy. You're trespassing. I thought you saw the sign."

"Well, I can't read the big words yet. I'm only going into second grade." She couldn't quit staring at the tails, the faint scent of clean laundry wafting in the air.

"In case you don't know what trespassing means: it means stay out, stay away."

"Or what?"

"Just go."

"I'm going. To get my mom so she can help you."

"I don't need help." He tried to stand but couldn't. "Especially don't need help from a little kid."

She picked up his hat. She ran her hand over the bill, her finger tracing the letter G. "Grandfather always wore a baseball cap."

"Hmmpf."

She stared at the hat, thinking about the last time she saw her grandfather. She hadn't known it would be the last time until later. But maybe it was better that way.

"Don't change the subject. I don't need help. I don't want it."

"I might only be seven, but I can tell when somebody needs help. You can't just live in your own little world of squirrel tails like you're the Pied Piper or something." She tossed his hat over a pile of boxes. "See, you can't even get your own hat."

A siren wailed in the distance.

She walked around the boxes and came back with his hat. She brushed off the dust, wiped the bill, and handed it to him. "And when I get back, you're gonna tell Mama and me about those tails. Okay?"

This circular tale of hunted hunters brings us to the very brink. Can murder be moral? Step into the Eye and find out.

SOLDIER Z

Bianca Wemhoff

Sirens blared down every hallway, corridor and room. Red lights illuminated the concrete walls with crimson red. My feet slapped against the plaster floors as I ran down the blinding and deafening hallways towards the TM-18 vault.

This South Dakota facility only housed one classified contraption, and something was wrong.

By dodging and sprinting past a few soldiers and scientists, I rounded a corner and saw a pair of large armored steel double doors waiting to greet me at the end of the hall. "TM-18" was painted above them. With both hands, I pushed open the doors and ran into a large room covered in concrete and metal. There was an enormous and elaborate metal ring-shaped machine connected to a long ramp on the right side of the room, opposite a glass observatory overseeing all. People ranging from scientists to soldiers cluttered the room.

The ring-like machine was about twenty feet tall and had wires, cables, cords and numerous others alike, running from it into generators or various chunks of metal welded, screwed, and bolted to the machine itself. In the center of this revolutionary machine was a swirling matter of blue and white light; almost liquid but solid at the same time. We called it the Eye, and it was the first functioning time machine.

It truly was magnificent, but, unfortunately, it was damaged.

Alarms continued to blare with the rhythm of relentless flashing red lights. I looked around and saw the mechanics and scientists swarming the machine, desperately trying to fix or stabilize the problem. The blue-white swirling then began to blink out, and sparks shot from the machine in various areas. I shielded my eyes from the sparks and heard the sound of orders being barked behind me. I turned and saw General Wilton on the other side of the crowded room in front of a few cadets.

He finished shouting orders to the group of men while I rushed over to him. The men responded with "yes sir," and ran off to fulfill their command. General Wilton then turned and saw me with eyes full of dread.

He was a bigger man, with his white brows furrowed and sweat beading down his forehead. His grey eyes were hard and had seen the worst this world had to offer.

"Soldier Z, nice for you to finally show up!" General Wilton shouted over the commotion. "Follow me!" he ordered, then proceeded to march out of the vault with me following close behind him.

We made our way briskly down the hallway, passing soldiers who looked almost exactly like me. With our BDU's, buzzed hair, and guns slung across our backs we all looked like we could have been brothers. We protected secret government facilities throughout the United States that harbored sensitive inventions and machinery created for war, but with the mindset of peace.

The General and I turned and approached a door leading to an empty bunker-like conference room with a circular white table and an assortment of chairs outlining it. General Wilton let me walk in first, then closed the door behind us, silencing the alarms outside the fortified room.

"Please, take a seat." He directed his hand towards the table.

I took a seat in the first chair and waited patiently while I watched my superior slowly make his way to the chair across from me. He had his hands clasped behind his back and his eyes were studying the floor as he stopped. His lips were pressed together, almost as if he was trying to find the right words, but they seemed lost to him.

"Sir?" I asked quietly.

He let out a quiet sigh and pulled out the seat and sat down. While intertwining his fingers together on top of the table, he looked up at me with his old and tired eyes.

"You're probably wondering why no one has told you anything yet," he began steadily, "and for that, I apologize. Only a handful of witnesses and the big guns upstairs know exactly what has happened here today. The reason is simple; I don't want to start a panic. But I'm telling *you*, because I think you can help. I trust you. But if you refuse my request, then you are under strict orders of silence, or you will be terminated; is that clear?"

"Yes, sir."

"Very well." He nodded slightly. "Then let's continue. A man by the name of Cesar Smith activated the Eye while shouting hysterically that he was going to 'wipe the slate clean' and start anew in his own way. He went about five to ten years into the future with a bomb he created. The other scientist say it has the capability and equivalence of a neutron bomb. Maybe worse."

"But why?"

"No one knows why, but for *who* he is, we know enough. He was one of the scientists who had helped to create the Eye; so, he knows every nook and cranny of that machine and what makes it tick. *Well*," he continued with a breath, "Cesar rigged the Eye, meaning, once he had stepped through that portal, no more trips to the future could be made without the risk of a nuclear meltdown and the destruction circumference of over two hundred and fifty miles. The energy core stabilizer was also compromised and will take many years to fix."

"But, sir, he went to the *future*, not the past. His actions haven't affected us yet, so why would it be an issue for how long it took us to fix the Eye?"

"You're right, but the real problem is that we have no idea where he is. He jammed our systems and we were unable to see exactly where and when he went once the trip was made. Those systems can be fixed for the next trip, but as of now, he is lost to us in time. The moral of the story is: we can't jump through the Eye and follow him without ending thousands of lives, we don't know where he is, and the machine isn't a quick fix."

"So, we're stuck between a rock and a hard place," I chimed in.

He shook his head. "Not exactly. You see, we still have the means of traveling *back* through time, just not forward. So, your assignment is to go back and—" he paused to search for the right word, "—*eliminate* the threat before he becomes the threat." He spoke delicately.

"Do you mean, sir, to execute him as a child?" I asked.

"Yes, I do. Now, according to the white coats who created the Eye, the past can be a touchy thing. They're not a hundred percent sure of what would happen if you were to walk into a reality where you already exist, and we're not taking any chances. Dr. Smith is thirty-two years older than you, so we have quite a bit of wiggle room to work with. With that in mind, we concluded that it might be ... easier for this mission and for you, if you went back to a time period where Dr. Smith is very young," he explained.

"How young?"

"I think you know."

While pressing my lips together, I looked down at the white table top and pondered the request General Wilton just laid out in front of me.

This mission was simple, yet so complex on so many levels. All I had to do was travel to the past and kill a child before he grew up and committed one of the largest genocides this world had ever seen. But could I do it? Kill a child? He wouldn't have done anything yet, but we know he will in the future. So, did that still make him guilty? Now was the time I needed to question the limits I'd be willing to go to for my country.

"I'm not forcing you to do this," General Wilton reminded me. "If you refuse, I understand, and your rank or my respect for you will not be altered. I've known you for a long time, son, and taking a child's life, even if he's destined to do something this terrible, isn't an easy task." His old voice made his words seem almost reassuring if I decided to refuse.

The room fell silent.

I knew that if I didn't accept this mission, someone else would have to fill my vacant spot and kill the kid. I didn't want that kind of guilt resting on my shoulders just because I wasn't sure if I'd be able to pull the trigger. I needed to be sure. I was sure.

"I accept."

General Wilton nodded, outstretched his hand across the table and stood up. I gripped it tight and stood as well, then we shook.

"Let's get you ready, soldier."

"Now, time travel is a tricky girl, but I'll attempt and explain this as simply as I can," the chief scientist by the name of Dr. Spencer began to explain.

General Wilton, a few scientists and soldiers, and I stood in front of him and faced the closed Eye, while Dr. Spencer kept his back to it. I was dressed in the time appropriate attire and armed with two pistols.

"When you, Soldier Z, go back in time, everything you do will change the present," Dr. Spencer continued. "This means, it is very, *very* crucial of you to make as little changes as possible. Don't talk to anyone, interact or disturb anything unless completely necessary." His old voice was stern and steady. "Now," he adjusted the glasses on his nose, "after you have completed your mission, we need you to understand that you will not be coming back; this is a one-way trip. And once you do something as major as killing a child, then who knows how that might alter the present. The Eye may never be built. Or, it might be greater; we're not sure. All we know is, Dr. Cesar is too big of a threat to just gamble with; we need to stop him before the worst can happen."

I felt everyone's side glances rest on me as I held Dr. Spencer's gaze.

"I understand."

He nodded. "Good. He's all yours, sir." And with that, he traded places with General Wilton.

General Wilton stood tall in front of us with his hands clasped behind his back.

"Once you're through the Eye, there will be no way of contacting us or vise-versa. You will be on your own."

"I know, sir."

The old General then took in a breath and stepped closer to me. He raised his right hand to his forehead and I did the same.

"It's been an honor working with you through all these years, Soldier Z," he said.

"Likewise, sir."

"I wish you the best, son. Even if we don't remember what you are about to do here today, or how many lives you're going to save, my prayers go out to you and may God be with you." He saluted and so did I.

He stepped aside and I made my way up the metal ramp. The sound of commands being said through the intercom echoed off the concrete walls.

"Starting sequence."

The Eye turned on with a low hum that you could feel through your bones. Lights dotting the massive machined flickered on one at a time and shined blue. The ring itself started to spin and spin, until it looked still, while the blue lights smeared together into one line. Then, we watched the swirling white and blue mass begin to splash out from the inside rim of the ring and meet in the center with a bright flash. Everyone shielded their eyes for a brief moment before looking back at the magnificent machine.

"Date entered. Coordinates entered. Time entered. Ready when you are, sir," the man over the intercom informed.

I looked back at General Wilton for permission to go through. With a nod of approval, I turned back to the pool of time, my heart pounding in my chest. I took in a silent breath and slowly made my way up the ramp and towards the blue energy until I was merely inches from it. I paused, stared, and then stepped through it.

It felt like the air inside my lungs was yanked out of my mouth. My head grew heavy and a blinding light flashed before my eyes. I took in a gasping breath and stumbled forward and collapsed against a metal shelf inside of a dim and small room. I blinked my stinging eyes a few times and allowed them a moment to adjust to my new surroundings. I was in a small janitor's closet.

My head was still spinning and I started to feel nauseous.

"Ah, crap."

I quickly leaned over and threw up in one of the empty buckets sitting on the ground. After finally emptying my stomach, I coughed, spat, then slowly stood back up with a groan. The side effects of making a jump should pass within a few minutes.

I turned around and carefully opened the squeaky metal door, and saw large empty hallways with rows of red lockers; I was in a high school.

I stepped out and closed the closet door behind me before proceeding to pat down my white T-shirt and dark blue jeans. I adjusted the simple leather jacket on my shoulders and briskly made my way down the hallway and towards the large blue double doors leading outside.

The school bell then rang as I pushed open the double doors and hundreds of kids swarmed into the hallways, completely unaware that a soldier from the future just time traveled into their janitor's closet.

Everything seemed so different, but the same all at once. I couldn't help but be amazed. I just traveled back through time fifty-four years into a different time period and no one knew but me.

I then shook my head and brought my mind back into the mission. I pulled out a leather wallet containing two thousand, five hundred dollars in bills, a driver's license with my new name (John Doe), and the address to my target's house written on ripped lined paper.

I took out the small piece of paper and read it while slipping the wallet back into my pants pocket. The paper read *101 NE Crimson Dr.* I repeated the address over and over again in my head until I knew it by heart, then tore up the paper and threw it away in a trashcan I passed.

I crossed a few streets and headed towards the suburbs of identical houses, with grassy yards lined with white picket fences. It took me awhile, but I finally came to home 101. I stopped and stared over the white gate with a terrible feeling.

The house looked like all the others: white, clean, well-kept with flower pots on both sides of the front door; but this one had a little red fire truck lying in the front lawn. The husband was out, but the wife was still home; I saw Mrs. Smith's silhouette in the kitchen disappear. My eyes then drifted to the white front door standing a few feet in front of me at the end of the brick walkway.

"It's just a mission. Countless lives depend on you. Don't get cold feet now," I muttered.

With a breath, I opened the white gate and carefully walked towards the door. I then bent down, picked up one of the flower pots and chucked it down the walkway, causing the orange ceramic to shatter, and the dirt and red flowers to shoot across the clean brick. With my diversion in motion, I ran to the left side of the house and peered past the wall as the front door opened. Mrs. Smith, wearing light blue jeans, a loose white blouse, and flats, stepped outside. She was beautiful and wore her blonde hair short and curled.

She curiously walked over to the broken pot with her hands on her hips. "How strange." I heard her say.

With a breath, she headed back inside to get a broom and dustpan. I, myself, made my way to the back of their modest house and crept to the sliding glass door. I peeked inside and saw that Mrs. Smith was in the kitchen, which was separated from the living room by an island counter. She grabbed a broom and dustpan. She turned and walked into the living room where a little boy, about three years old, was sitting on the white carpeted floors playing with blocks, toy cars, and a train.

"Mommy will be right back, honey. You be good." Mrs. Smith bent down and kissed little Cesar on the forehead.

He babbled something and continued to play with the toy car in his hands while his mother left to go clean up the mess I made. Once the front door was shut, I slid open the glass door and stepped into the living room. Cesar peered up at me as I crept closer to him.

I only had a few minutes before Mrs. Smith would be coming back in; I needed to make this quick.

I stared down at the little blond, blue-eyed boy gazing up at me. His innocent eyes watched me slowly pull out my pistol and bring it forward. I aimed it down at Cesar's head; the black silencer leveling with the child's skull as he looked down the barrel. I had my finger on the trigger, but couldn't seem to pull it.

"Come on, you need to do this," I growled grimly, and got a stronger grip to steady my shaking hand.

Cesar then reached up with his tiny fingers for the barrel in fascination.

I shook my head. "No, Cesar don't — please don't touch that," I told him weakly as his fingers felt the metal. He smiled and giggled a little.

I bit down. "Please, don't."

And pulled the trigger.

Pew!

Cesar collapsed backwards and I opened my eyes. The child fell still, and blood began to stain the white carpeted floor from underneath his little head. Crimson seeped into a pool from where he laid while I reluctantly lowered the gun with my eyes still locked on the increasing red.

Mrs. Smith, who was hosing down her walkway, stopped when she heard the peculiar sound my gun made. The front door then opened.

"Cesar?" she stepped into the house. "Cesar, honey, did you drop something? Are you ok?"

I hastily fled out the open back door and down the side of the house. I made my escape past the half-cleaned walkway and casually through the white gate. My heart was pounding in my chest. I made it a few houses away when the sound of a blood curdling scream radiated from the Smith's house. My heart stopped. I winced, but kept walking.

And at that moment, I knew I just changed the future. Let's hope it was for the better.

My mission was over. I did what I came here to do. I can't go back, I can only go forward. So, now what?

I sat on a park bench a couple miles away from the suburb's

community. A few police cars came speeding down the road behind me as I kept my gaze forward. There were open grasslands laid out in front of me and a playground to the right. I could hear the children's laughter as they played.

I just changed the course of time. Saved countless lives and no one here will ever know, I thought grimly.

I leaned back and let out a long breath when a man sat on my bench a seat away from me.

I casually glanced at him. He looked about my age with his black hair buzzed under a baseball cap. He was wearing a dark grey shirt, black leather jacket, and dark bootcut jeans. The man sat back and stared forward.

I had a bad feeling about him.

"Nice day, don't you think?" the man asked, but didn't turn to me.

I glanced at him. "I suppose it is. You have a kid here?" I asked.

"No. You?"

"Not even married."

We both fell silent and that gnawing feeling in my gut worsened. I needed to get away from this man. Something was off about him. Something dangerous.

I began to get up.

"Sit back down," the man ordered.

I slowly sat back down and the atmosphere around us grew dense.

"Who are you and what do you want?" I asked firmly.

"*Zip it,*" he growled in response. "We're in a public space, so let's keep this civil. Understand?"

"Yes."

"Good. Now, you are Soldier Z, correct?" He glanced at me from under his hat

He's from the labs!

"No, my name is John Doe. I just moved here," I responded bluntly.

The man turned to me. "This isn't a joke. You're Soldier Z, correct?" he barked.

I looked at him. "First, who are you?"

"I'm asking the questions here."

"And you're not gonna get any answers until you answer *my* question. Your. *Name.*"

The man stared at me with hard, dark eyes.

"I'm Soldier Y," he answered.

"Soldier Y? There was never a Soldier Y— Wait. You … you're familiar. Soldier X? From the North Dakota labs? We went on missions together."

"I'm *aware,*" he interrupted roughly. "I know who you are. And because of your treason, I got promoted and was sent here. You're no longer one of us." His voice grew grim. "You're my target."

I looked down and saw that he was now holding a pistol close to his waist and pointing it at me. I didn't even notice him going for his gun.

"I guess you don't want to hear my explanation?"

Soldier Y scoffed. "What excuse could you *possibly* have for murdering a three-year-old child in his own home?" he asked harshly.

He wasn't going to make talking to him easy, and right now, I was under the gun. I needed to get away without complicating matters.

My gaze settled on Soldier Y's dark eyes. "I'll explain everything later—" *when I have the upper hand* "—I just need you to understand that *I had to do it*," I said roughly.

And without hesitation, I pushed Soldier Y's gun against the backrest of the bench and swiftly punched him in the temple on the side of his head. Soldier Y's body went limp and he collapsed backwards. I grabbed him and laid him back while taking the gun from his weak grip. I then adjusted him to make it look like he had just fallen asleep in the park.

Gradually, I glanced around; no one noticed. I let out a breath, pocketed Soldier Y's gun and casually walked away. After hailing a taxi, I arrived into the city and out of the family friendly neighborhood, leaving Soldier Y to wake up on a bench without his target or gun. I needed to find a place to stay; somewhere cheap and overlooked. It didn't take long to find a place like that. I discovered a cheap hotel and rented a one-bed room for the night.

Once I finished paying cash, I hiked up seven flights of concrete stairs where room 204 was waiting for me. With a Chinese take-out container in one hand, I unlocked the door and shouldered it open. The room was dark before I flicked on the dull lights, drowning everything in a subtle orange. I closed the door behind and walked over to the bed and nightstand. There was a large window at the end of the room opposite of the door and overlooking the city streets, tall buildings, and short apartment roofs.

I placed my Chinese food on the nightstand and sat down on the side of the bed with my back to the window. While resting my arms on my knees, I stared tiredly at the worn-out carpeted floors and listened to the sounds of honking cars and distant police sirens. The sound of a radio playing sports in the next room over. The sound of my gun going off in house 101. The sound of the three-year old's body hitting the ground. The sound of a mother's screams and cries as she looks down at her murdered baby boy.

I dropped my head into my hands and began to shake from the sheer realization of what I had just done a few hours ago. I struggled to catch a gasping breath as tears slipped from my eyes. The sight of blood pooling around Cesar's head stained my mind.

While squeezing my eyes shut, I let out a sob and shook my head. I then peered up at the chipping ceiling with a staggered breath and blinked away the tears. It took a while, but once I had finally gotten myself under control, I cleared my throat, stood up, and grabbed the takeout from off the nightstand. I shuffled over to the old armchair under the window. My food was drowned in soy sauce and, now, cold. I quietly ate my dinner and watched the sky slowly dip into darkness.

Somewhere out there, Soldier Y was looking for me.

By killing Cesar Smith, I had changed the future indefinitely. I don't know by how much or how little, but I changed it enough.

Soldier Y and I were two trained soldiers hunting each other down in a different era while also trying to keep the past intact. Only time can tell how this journey ends.

Morning came unforgivingly as I dragged myself out of bed and outside to try and start the day off early. With a banana nut muffin in one hand and newspaper in the other, I sat on a bench across the street of my hotel and waited for Soldier Y. He was more determined to find me then I was.

It was dark when I finally saw him. He was making his way into my hotel's front door. I threw away my newspaper and jogged across the street and cautiously peered inside the hotel door's window, where I saw Soldier Y disappearing through the stairwell door. I carefully followed in after him and up the concrete spiraling stairs to the seventh floor. I stalked down the red hallway and towards my now open room. I could hear Soldier Y ruffling through the things inside.

I stepped into the doorway. "I don't remember asking for room service," I stated.

Soldier Y spun around and stared at me. His dark eyes went hard and his hands formed into fists as I closed the door.

"We need to talk," I said calmly. "There's no need for this to get violent."

"You forfeited that option when you killed that little boy!" Soldier Y barked, and charged me while throwing a hard punch.

I caught his fist and punched him instead. He stumbled back and I grabbed the nightstand lamp and hurled it at him. It collided with the side of his face and he hollered in pain and fell to the ground alongside the shards of lamp. Blood dripped from the scratches on the right side of his pained face.

"It's gonna take a lot more than a lamp to make me talk."

He then jumped up and tackled me to the ground. I gasped as my back collided with the floor and Soldier Y landed on top of me. While straddling my waist, he gripped my neck with both hands and pushed down. I grabbed his wrists and tried to lift them up, but only managed to loosen them a bit.

Breathing grew difficult. He then reached into my jacket and pulled out the pistol I took from him. He released my neck and pointed the gun to my head., but I grabbed the barrel and pushed it to the side as he pulled the trigger. The gun went off, and I twisted it out of his hands and shoved him off of me.

I got to my feet, coughing, and pulled out my own gun. Soldier Y had already picked up his gun again and was pointing it at me while I took in rough breaths. I could feel the bruise around my throat spread, which was nothing compared to the blood dripping from Soldier Y's face and neck.

Then there was a pounding at the door.

"This is the police! We're responding to a gunshot! If you know what's good for you, you'll put your weapons down and stand in the middle of the room with your hands behind your head!" a police officer barked.

"*Shit*. Nice one, trigger fingers," I growled bitterly at Soldier Y.

"Shut up."

"Look, if you don't feel like screwing anything *else* up, I suggest you lower your weapon and help me get our assess out of here," I told him, and lowered my gun.

But he kept his up.

"We're coming in!" The locked door shuddered.

"*Fine*." Soldier Y growled. "But I'm keeping the gun."

I nodded. "Help me with the chair."

We both pushed the armchair until it was up against the door. We watched as the police officer managed to bust open the door, but was stopped by the piece of furniture in front of it.

"Let's go," Soldier Y said. We ran to the window.

After lifting it open, I jumped to a roof below and tuck rolled with Soldier Y doing the same behind me. We both got to our feet and glanced up at the window right as the police officers burst through the door.

"Run!" I ordered, and we ran across the roof.

We then jumped off the side and landed on a large closed garbage bin each, before tumbling off and hitting the hard ground. Groaning, we slowly stood up, bruised and scraped. The alleyway was dark and traced with much larger buildings then the one we jumped off of.

"We need to go," I told him.

And with a nod, we both ran further into the alleyway; the sounds of our feet hitting the pavement echoed off the walls. Once I was sure we weren't being followed, I picked up a piece of wood we sprinted by and turned to Soldier Y.

"I'm sorry."

He looked at me and I swung the piece of wood, hitting him hard on the side of his head. He collapsed heavily to the ground and came to a tumbling halt. I stopped and looked down at him and dropped the piece of wood.

Dark clouds began to harshly form above us and the wind picked up with the smell the rain. Droplets started to pour and soak our clothes and hair; drenching Soldier Y from where he laid. A few stragglers ran down the sidewalks to avoid getting wet, but they still had time. Everyone still had time.

Soldier Y slowly bobbed his head as he opened his eyes. He blinked and looked up at me. I was sitting on an overturned wooden fruit crate in front of him. He, on the other hand, had his hands tied behind him to a pipe, and was sitting on the wet concrete. We were further in the alleyway. I watched him look down at his tied hands curiously.

"What are my hands tied with?" he asked.

"Your shoe laces."

He scoffed and peered down at his black boots stripped of their laces.

"Ok, you got me. Now what?" he asked bitterly while looking at me.

"*Now*," I sat forward and rested my elbows on my knees, "you finally answer my questions."

He let out a rough laugh. "*Questions?* I've been trying to kill you all day and you're still hell-bent on me answering your *questions?*"

"Think of it as a dead man's final wish," I offered.

He stared at me for a few moments, then relaxed against the pipe and crisscrossed his legs with a shrug.

"Fine. Ask away."

"How is it that you can go back to your time, but I can't?"

"They gave me something, a prototype device called the Time Jumper. It was created by a man named Dr. Young."

I stiffened a little, but shook off the shiver that ran up my spine.

"Ok, so Dr. Young is the difference. That name isn't familiar."

"So, you're saying, because of what you did here, it somehow changed the science to the point that we can now *retrieve* people from the past. But how?" he asked skeptically.

"Maybe since Dr. Smith never entered the program, there was an opening and this Dr. Young filled it," I thought out loud.

And by completing my mission, the second I killed Cesar, it appeared to the others that I had just walked through the Eye with the intentions of killing an innocent child.

"Ok, but why kill me? Why not just take me back to our time and detain me for interrogation?"

"Because the Time Jump can only carry one living organism. Remember, it's a prototype. If we both were to go back, it was theorized that only parts of us would return or even worse, we'd mutate into one. We couldn't risk someone as dangerous as you running loose in the past. So, here I am."

I nodded and sat up, thinking of my next question when Soldier Y asked one of his own.

"Why did you do it? I've thought about it over and over and over again and I can't make sense of it. So *why?*" he asked harshly.

I looked down into his hard eyes. I tried to find the right words to explain *why* without sounding like a twisted excuse, but I couldn't. How do you explain to your assassin that you're innocent when all the right evidence is in a different timeline?

"I ... I was sent here on a mission to a kill a child by the name of Cesar Smith. The reason is because that child, who would've grown up into a respected scientist and help build the Eye, snaps. He rigs the Eye and goes between five to ten years into the future with a neutron bomb capable of committing one of the largest mass-genocides this world has ever seen. To prevent this, I needed to go to a time before I was born and before he could impact the future. That's why I'm here. That's why I killed Cesar Smith," I explained steadily.

Soldier Y stared at me. I couldn't tell if he believed me or not. His eyes held nothing.

"Do you believe me?" I asked.

"I don't know."

"Why?"

"I don't *know*," he barked.

"You don't know because you want it to be a lie. You want me to be making this all up because I'm your assignment and you don't want any doubts for killing one of your own ... but think about it, Soldier Y." He held my gaze. "Why would I risk *everything* just to go back in time and kill some random kid? You've worked with me. You *know* me and trusted me with your life at one point. You were like a brother to me — everyone in the lab was. So why? Why would I do it?" I asked.

He looked from me and to the ground in thought. I could see him search the wet cement for answers, before closing his eyes and dropping his head. I peered up at the dark sky and towering buildings surrounding us while a cold breeze blew through our bones.

"It was my mission," I said quietly.

Soldier Y looked up at me, but I kept my eyes to the dark cloud-stained sky.

"If I didn't do it, then someone else would have. I had to kill him, okay? And it will haunt me for the rest of my life. I have taken countless lives. I was a sniper in the Army before I was transferred. This meant that every time I pulled that trigger, someone was guaranteed to die and I saw it. But this." I looked down at him. "I never wanted this. I'll never be able to get that image out of my head … to not hear that gun whenever someone closes a car door or see his blood in every shade of red." My voice strained.

Soldier Y held my gaze. He looked torn.

I dropped my head. "My life is in your hands. I heard my answers and pleaded my case," I stated quietly, and stood up.

I stepped up to him, knelt down and cut the shoe laces binding his wrists with my knife, then slipped it away and stood up. He got to his feet while I took a few steps back.

"Well, Soldier Y, what will it be?" I asked, and pulled his gun from my jacket and tossed it to him.

He caught it and slipped the weaponry in his right hand and carefully lifted it up. I stared down his barrel once again with steady eyes.

I waited, but he was hesitant. His finger rested on the trigger as I watched him slowly squeeze it. I tensed up, thinking these were my final moments alive, until he lowered his gun.

"No," he said simply.

I stared at him. "No?"

"No, I can't kill you." He let his arm fall to his side.

He then walked up to me and grabbed the dog tags tucked inside my shirt and yanked them off.

"I believe you, and you're right; I do know you and I do trust you. You're a soldier just like me, and was told to do an impossible mission and is now getting punished for it. I'll take these dog tags back with me and you live here," he explained.

"You're letting me walk?"

He tucked my dog tags into his jacket pocket, along with the gun, and looked up at me.

"Yes. This way, I'm giving you a second chance to life," he said simply.

He was right. I didn't have many hands to play. This was my best bet.

"Thank you."

He smiled a little and reached inside his shirt and pulled out a long chain connected to a bulky box with a blue button illuminating in the center. He placed his thumb over the button and looked up at me.

He then raised his right hand to his forehead in a salute while standing at attention. I did the same.

"I hope you have a good and early retirement, sir," Soldier Y said.

I smiled a little. "Take care of the future for me. And who knows, we might meet again someday," I mused.

He nodded and lowered his hand, but I kept mine up. I watched him turn from me and press the button. A sudden circle of swirling blue light warped in front of him with the same glowing mass in the middle as the Eye. He glanced back at me and I smiled with my hand still to my forehead. "Thank you," I said again.

With a nod, he turned back to the portal and stepped through. After disappearing behind the blue and white mass, it shrunk and rippled the air around it before falling still, then I saluted.

I stood in that spot for what seemed like hours. But, nevertheless, I let out a breath, smiled, and turned towards my new beginning.

I *did* live my life in that era. I found myself a wife. Beautiful woman. She was a waitress in this big city at a little diner. She tripped when a kid ran out in front of her, and dropped a plate of pancakes all over the front of my shirt. I laughed it off and told her it was fine, but she insisted on repaying me somehow. I told her that if she went to dinner with me, it would work as a payment.

We went to dinner once, twice, four times, eight before it became serious. We dated for three years and I proposed to her in the same diner we first met; in the same booth. A few years later, we had a little boy who we named after my dad: Henry.

I feared the years following that. I didn't know what would happen to me once I hit the day I was born. Would I disappear? Create a paradox? Maybe nothing would happen to me.

I didn't know.

And as I watched the years tick by, I grew even more and more anxious and nervous. I started looking up theories and reading the limited books on time travel, but all that left me was with more questions. With years' worth of possible theories, I concluded that I would not disappear due to the fact that I'm still me of my first timeline and was just blasted back in time.

Unfortunately, my own timeline was now very fragile, due to the fact that there was most likely two of us living within the same period. I made a self-note to never meet anyone from my other life to avoid a possible paradox. I didn't even go to my home state.

When nothing bad happened on the day of my birth, I continued with life. I lived with my wife and son in the suburbs of New York. Henry grew up curious and smart, a lot smarter than his old man. He attended a top engineering college, and after eight long years of hard work and studying, he got his PhD and was accepted to work on a secret government project. He couldn't tell us anything, but I think I knew what it was.

Soldier Y stepped through the portal and stopped to look at the silent room of people staring at him. Then the room burst into a roaring applause and cheers at their success and the safe return of Soldier Y. He walked down the ramp and towards General Wilton, who was applauding with a wide grin on his worn face.

"I take it since you're back that the mission was a success?" General Wilton shook Soldier Y's hand with a strong grip.

"Yes, sir," Soldier Y said, then reached into his jacket pocket and pulled out Soldier Z's dog tags.

He handed them to the General, who took the pieces of metal and looked down in almost sadness.

"It's a shame, you know. What a fine soldier he was. I can't believe he could have done something like this. Did he say anything to you? Try to explain why he did it?" General Wilton asked curiously.

Soldier Y held the General's gaze. "No, sir," he said quietly.

General Wilton nodded. "Ok, soldier, you get yourself to the infirmary. We gotta make sure all of you came back."

Soldier Y nodded and headed straight to the empty infirmary cluttered with a few metal examination tables and other medical equipment. He sat down on a table and waited patiently for the doctor while slipping off his jacket and placing it next to him.

Then, there was a light knock at the door. Soldier Y looked up and saw a young scientist in the doorway. He was maybe in his mid-20's, with kind eyes and slightly messy brown hair.

"Hi, sorry to bother you, but are you Soldier Y?" the scientist asked.

"Yes, I am. And you are?"

The man walked towards Soldier Y with a friendly smile.

"I'm from the engineering department. My name's Dr. Young." He held out his hand and Soldier Y shook it.

"Then I guess you're the man of the hour. The Time Jumper worked, and I want to thank you for that." They let go.

"Thank you, but I'm actually here on personal matter, if that's alright," he said.

Soldier Y raised his eyebrows. "A personal matter? Regarding what?"

Dr. Young reached into his lab coat and pulled out a simple piece of folded paper. He handed it to Soldier Y, who curiously grabbed it.

"I'm not quite sure, but my father told me to give this to you right when I see you," Dr. Young explained.

The paper was folded three times and had "To Soldier Y" written in pen on the front.

"Do you know my father?"

Soldier Y shook his head. "No, I don't think so."

It went silent for a few moments while Soldier Y stared suspiciously at the folded paper.

"Well, I'm sorry, but I have to be going. I got a big briefing to look forward to in the conference room upstairs." Dr. Young grinned.

Soldier Y nodded. "It's fine. And thank you again, Dr. Young, for bringing me back home."

Dr. Young waved goodbye and left the infirmary. Now, it was just Soldier Y and this letter. He slowly unfolded the piece of paper and read the three words inside. A laugh escaped him and he shook his head.

> *Thank you.*
> — *Soldier Z*

Bianca Wemhoff

Kindred spirits meet while on vacation. But they aren't the spirits you'd guess, and the vacation is further afield than average.

WHEN HARRY MET BOB

James C. Glass

Harry met Bob on the Brin Mesa trail along red rock buttes and spires west of Sedona, Arizona. It was a winter day: clear blue sky, bright sunshine, a cool breeze, and the temperature near sixty. Harry had made the final climb up rock and slippery scree to a ridge which sloped down to a wooden bench and a panoramic view at the end of the trail. Just below the ridge, where he now sat on a flat rock, he had an even better view of the Verde valley, its monumental buttes and pinnacles of layered sandstone, limestone and basalt stained red by iron.

His breathing was heavy from the climb, a consequence of the high gravity, and he cooled himself in the shade of a shaggy Arizona Cyprus bordered by Manzanita and one hearty prickly pear cactus. *Pristine country*, he thought. *It has beauty, clean air and a delicious solitude. No wonder this is touted as the new-age capital of the country, maybe even the planet.*

A man was climbing up towards him, moving clumsily on the rock and bent over with effort. He wore jeans, a yellow chamois shirt and black, cowboy hat. His breathing was audible from twenty meters away, and his aura was deep blue from the effort. Suddenly he looked up and smiled. He had a pleasant old face, round and flushed.

"Almost to the ridge. You doing the loop?" asked Harry.

"Absolutely not," said the man. "This is far enough for me. I'll take another photo, and then I go down again." The man stuck out a hand. "I'm Bob. Only got here yesterday, and I'm one of those foreign flatlanders you hear about."

"Harry," said Harry, and he shook Bob's hand. "It's over five thousand feet here. At my age I take it easy the first few days. You wintering, or just here for a weekend?"

"A month this time. I got lucky and found a small house uptown."

"Been here before? You are lucky. The portal has filled up on me twice. I've been here a week, and two more to go. Some interesting geology here. I was a geologist at home. Don't see these kinds of formations there."

"You're retired?" asked Bob, brightening.

"Yep," said Harry. "The white hair gives me away every time. You?"

"Two years ago. I was an organic chip engineer for Telarts, mostly for these things." Bob took a palm-sized module from his shirt pocket and opened it. It was a Model 20 Jaziril Telecom, still state-of-the-art.

Harry felt like he'd found a kindred spirit. "I have an older model. It's sort of backwoods where I live."

Bob smiled. "Small universe," he said. "You here alone?"

"Never got married," said Harry. "Never had the time, or stayed around long enough."

They both laughed. "I had a wife, but she went elsewhere," said Bob. "Got tired of my little pranks, I guess. Look, if you don't mind company I could show you around. I don't know geology, but I've been studying the culture here; fascinating, and nothing like it at home."

"That's what I hear," said Harry. "Sure, it'd be good to see the most important things instead of just wandering. Takes me a few minutes to get into town. The only place I could find on short notice is in Oak Creek."

"No problem," said Bob, then, "Get yourself a Sedona newspaper. It comes out Wednesday and Friday and lists everything going on. Let me know what interests you. We could start tomorrow by hitting a few art galleries and some of the tourist shops. There's exceptional primitive art here, and interesting foods. It's a great place for indigestion."

"One of the delights of increasing age," said Harry, and they both laughed again.

They exchanged addresses and telephone numbers, and made a date for the following day.

Time went quickly for Harry and Bob. They were the perfect traveling companions, interests broad and complementary, both of them eager to explore new things.

They began with the more mundane shops: western clothing, Native American arts and crafts, fine jewelry in silver and gems. They admired pottery, carvings in sandstone and alabaster, flutes of cedar, but purchased nothing. Bob was tempted by an F-sharp flute. Eventually he assembled a substantial collection of books about the area: geology, early history, sacred sites, vortices, and the new-age culture in the town.

Harry made no purchases until they hit the new-age shops, and he spent hundreds of dollars at a single mineral and crystal store near the edge of town. There were phantom and rutilated crystals of quartz, a plethora of thumbnail specimens of rare crystals from around the planet, all of which he carefully packed away in a small bag. Harry traveled light. For amusement he also purchased a book on the meditative and medicinal value of crystals, many of them supposedly tuned to a specific musical note and Chakra, whatever that was. Bob explained it all to him later.

Bob seemed more interested in odors, buying a large selection of incense sticks and cones, a brass burner, several vials of essential oils and an aromatherapy lamp. Even Harry had to admit that after several days of using these products, Bob's odor was distinctly pleasant.

"To learn the geology, one has to hike and climb," said Harry.

"To learn the culture, one has to experience it," said Bob in return.

Bob had to experience as many alternative medical techniques as possible. There was ear coning, acupressure, emotional clearing, reflexology, reiki, myofascia, quantum touch, rolfing, shiatsu, celestial touch massage, cranial-sacral, aromatherapy, transformational navigation and, worst of all, lymph drainage therapy! He tried most of them while Harry waited outside closed curtains, inhaling delicious odors and studying geological survey maps.

They went on long hikes together and visited sites touted for their mysteries. Near the airport they made a short climb to a mesa and found a young couple in a standing embrace inside a small circle of stones. The woman's eyes twinkled as she smiled and hugged her partner. "Absorbing some energies," she said to them, and then the couple hurried away.

"Believers make the stone circles, and unbelievers kick them away. This is supposed to be an electric vortex site," said Bob.

The panoramic view was grand, stretching east to Bell Rock and far west to high buttes. "I read about it," said Harry. "The Schuman resonance is supposed to be at seven or eight cycles per second, the earth charging and discharging due to global atmospheric electrical activity. They haven't figured out the earth grid stuff, or why the area here is so accessible to us, but then I don't understand all of it either."

Bob smiled. "Yeah, well, the way they present it is good for the tourists. Bell Rock out there is another electric vortex site, they say, but Cathedral Rock is a magnetic type, and there's supposed to be an interdimensional window that aliens and angels come through."

"Oooo, angels," said Harry.

They hiked the trail into the sacred area of Boynton Canyon and took photographs of a knobby spire called Katchina Woman. The spire was said to occasionally sport a blue aura, but the color was wrong. "South of here are the Palatki Indian Ruins, and beyond them there's supposed to be a secret, buried military base, and UFO's flying around. People say they've seen humvees and men in black out there where there are no roads. Black helicopters, too," said Bob.

Harry shook his head. "This is what happens when people have an untrustworthy government and naughty tourists who don't obey the rules."

Bob slapped his shoulder. "Oh come on, Harry, lighten up. This is a place to have some fun."

So Harry lightened up and even allowed his own sense of humor to surface. Bob's infectious enthusiasm made it easier for him to stop thinking like a scientist all the time. Without being conscious of it, the two of them were becoming close friends for many years to come.

Late one day they made a nervous climb on steep, rough rock up a buttress sprouting delicate, multiple spires and shelves. In a slot framed by two massive columns towering high around them they scrambled their way up to a high saddle for photography. Others were coming behind them, for Cathedral Rock was a landmark of the area, and visited frequently. Harry got one of his best pictures of the trip there, and the view was breathtaking. Suddenly he held up his arms and twirled like a child. "Oh, oh, I'm magnetic," he said, and Bob laughed.

"Do you actually have to leave so soon?" asked Bob. "You're really having fun now."

"Well no, I don't. I'm retired, remember?"

"You traveling with Aurora, or Trans-Di?"

"Aurora."

"Me too. Why don't you extend your stay a week, and we can take the same slip back," said Bob.

Harry thought for only a few seconds, then, "I'll do it. What else do I have to do these days? I'm still learning how to be retired. When do you leave? I'll call my reservation in tonight."

"Never mind," said Bob. "You can do it from here." He took his Model 20 out of a camera bag, made contact. Harry punched in his reservation code and did the rest.

Bob took back his Jaziril 20 and nodded at the puffing climbers now nearing their position at the panoramic viewing site of Cathedral Rock. "You know," he said, eyes twinkling, "I think we can have some real fun with this place."

"Oh, oh," said Harry.

And so there was another week and a half of fun in the high country of northern Arizona. They ventured out a bit, drove to Flagstaff and artsy Jerome, and visited nearby Indian ruins. A long tour by jeep took them to more ruins and a huge sinkhole formed by the collapse of a limestone cavern ceiling. The driver on the tour refused to talk about black helicopters or UFOs in the area. Sworn to secrecy, he said.

A day before their departure they had an expensive dinner together in uptown Sedona and walked nearly two miles to the Spiritual Center to hear a special lecture on UFOs. A kindly, white-haired man talked about alien visitations and showed photographs of their saucer-shaped spacecraft. There was even a photo of such a craft sitting in the driveway of a man who claimed continual contact with the many alien societies living on planet earth.

Harry whispered to Bob, "Atmospheric entry had better be slow in that thing. And what are all the spherical balls around the hub?"

"That is where they store their alcohol," said Bob. His expression was serious, but his eyes said otherwise.

A matronly woman seated in front of them turned around with an admonishing glare, silencing them.

They walked back down the hill to town in the light of thousands of stars. "One hundred eight alien civilizations indeed," said Harry, staying in the mood. "The number can't be more than forty, tops"

"I've counted twenty three," said Bob.

"That's more like it. And that picture of the alien, the one with the long earlobes, I've been wondering about you. Why is it *you* don't have long earlobes?"

"I have them trimmed every Thursday," said Bob, and sniffed primly.

Bob smiled, and sighed audibly. "Seriously, Harry, I'm going to miss this place. I missed it after the last time I was here. It has been even more fun being here with someone I could share it with."

"So why don't we do it again next year?" said Harry.

"You serious?"

"Absolutely. Let's exchange addresses and keep in touch. Plan ahead. I haven't had a massage yet, and we'll both be ready for a good rolfing by next year."

They shook hands on it, went back to their cars in a happier mood, and then home to pack.

Departure the following morning was complicated by their choice of location for it. Bob came to the rescue, finding two young men who, for a fee, would return their cars to the uptown lodge lot for them. They picked the men up at the lodge at sunrise, drove 179 and Back o' Beyond road to the Cathedral Rock trailhead.

Both of their backpacks were stuffed full. The young men looked at them curiously, and then drove the cars away, leaving them alone at the trailhead.

"Now I wish I hadn't bought all these books," said Bob, looking up at steep rock.

"Give me some of them. We'll sort it out at the other end," said Harry.

They repacked the bags quickly and went up the short but steep trail over rocky knobs and loose scree to a gentler slope around a buttress to the Cathedral Rock high saddle viewpoint. Passing the lower viewpoint they'd seen two vans pulling into the trailhead lot below; other hikers would soon be joining them. Bob looked at Harry. "We could get our travel permits revoked for doing this."

"Not likely," said Harry. "People see things here all the time, and more often than not their reporting isn't accurate or taken seriously."

Bob and Harry grinned at each other like two naughty children, and hurried on.

When they reached the high viewpoint no other hikers were in sight. They took two final pictures of each other, with twin walls of red rock in the background. Bob took out his Model 20 Jaziril and tapped a key. Behind them the air seemed to shimmer, as if suddenly heated.

"Here they come," said Harry.

A group of four hikers had come around a buttress base and were ascending the faint trail over smooth rock twenty meters below them.

"Now," said Harry, grinning.

Bob tapped the Jaziril three times. There was an explosion of color, an iris of air opening wide and shimmering brilliantly in emerald green.

"Aurora would be very unhappy if they knew we were doing this," said Bob.

There was a shout from below.

"I know," said Harry, "but they won't hear about it from me." He gestured Bob forward to the bright vortex of green. "After you, angelic one."

"And you need to have your earlobes trimmed," said Bob.

They hoisted their packs, and stepped inside the bright glow.

There was another shout, and then a scream from nearby as the five-dimensional Branegate closed behind them.

When Harry Met Bob

OTHERWORLDS

ABOUT THE AUTHORS

Leona Ahles graduated from the University of Idaho in 2007 with a Bachelor's degree in creative writing with an emphasis on fiction and poetry, and has been a member of the Sigma Tau Delta English Honor Society since 2004. "The Angles of New York" is her first published short story.

instagram.com/leonasfernweh

Sonya Bramwell is a massage therapist and instructor by day, a birth photographer and doula by night, and a mother of two lively boys. She attends a local writing and critique group, coedits the Otherworlds anthology, and is the writer of many, many stories.

www.sonyabramwellbooks.com

C. M. Daniels is a deputy coroner and goldfish wrangler in addition to being a writer. With a BA in anthropology and classics from the University of Southern California and an MA in forensic anthropology from the University of Montana, Daniels greatly enjoys using the knowledge and experiences gleaned from those programs in daily life, from attending deaths at crime scenes to cultural world-building for fictional universes.

calicofishquilts.wordpress.com

Jay Dearien is a reformed Tokyoite, poetaster, social critic, board game inventor, certified massage therapist, Japanese permanent resident, science groupie, terpa conjurer, trekkie, wannabe pseudo-intellectual, world traveler, recovering ne'er-do-well, comic/manga artist, pretty kosher for a goy boy, freedom-liker, stand-up comedian, and a Carnegie Mellon/École Polytechnique Fédérale de Lausanne (BS-EE) and University of Idaho (MA-Linguistics) grad.

porcadis.com

William Engels holds a doctorate in English Literature from Saint Louis University and taught writing and literature for thirteen years in Mongolia, South Korea, and Bangladesh. He currently tutors part-time at Washington State University's Graduate Writing Center and is editing the manuscript of a travel book about his walk across Mongolia in 2002.

mongolengels@yahoo.com

James C. Glass won the Golden Pen award for Writers of the Future in 1991. Since then he has published ten novels and over seventy stories to magazines such as Aboriginal, Analog, and Talebones. He is a retired physics professor and dean, divides his time between Spokane and the California desert, and is also a scenic painter in oils, watercolors, and pastels.

www.author-jamesglass.com

Zoe Lavander is currently an electrical engineer major at the University of Idaho. She is the 2014 Voltage Inc. romance apps international story writing contest winner. She divides her time between her engineering career and her writing career.

https://archiveofourown.org/users/masqurade/profile

Antonia Overstreet lives in Moscow, Idaho with her highly opinionated rabbit, Harvey. She is an avid reader, writer, graphic designer, workaholic, and woman of many geeky hats.

twitter.com/NiaOverstreet

Terri Picone has been writing both short and long stories since graduating with an English degree. She's won writing contests for her fiction and been published in Live, IDAHO Magazine, Talking River Review, newsletters, and an anthology, Outside the Box.

TerriPicone.com

Mark Rounds' history includes time spent as an Air Force electronic warfare officer in B-52s, a consultant, a geek in a cube in a couple of .coms, and a folk singer. Currently, he is faculty at the U. of Idaho. He has written scholarly works on computer security and geographical information systems. Mark's hobbies include Civil War reenacting, folk guitar, and gourmet cooking.

www.amazon.com/Mark-Rounds/e/B015EN7XSY and startroop@hotmail.com

Bianca Wemhoff was born and raised in a military family. She attends WSU with a major in fine arts and a plan to get her masters degree in teaching to become an art teacher. An aspiring author, she has been writing for about two years and hopes to get her first book published sometime next year.

instagram.com/galaxypiggywiggy

Guy Worthey is an astrophysics professor at Washington State University. He writes fiction in his spare time, with the Ace Carroway noir-fantastic adventure series as centerpiece. He is assisted by his corgi Sir Galahad and his multitalented wife Diane.

guyworthey.net

www.ingramcontent.com/pod-product-compliance
Lightning Source LLC
Chambersburg PA
CBHW071718140626
46557CB00012B/954